Going Down

Slocum dropped to the ground and made his way toward an empty watering trough he intended to use for cover. Halfway to it, he felt wobbly in the knees. At first he thought he was simply sinking into the ankle-deep mud. Then he realized the ground was giving way beneath him.

He let out a startled cry as he plunged downward to smash hard into the bottom of the pit. He forced his eyes open to focus on the moving blurs fifteen feet above him, and then the effort was no longer possible.

Slocum blacked out.

DON'T MISS THESE
ALL-ACTION WESTERN SERIES
FROM THE BERKLEY PUBLISHING GROUP

THE GUNSMITH by J. R. Roberts
Clint Adams was a legend among lawmen, outlaws, and ladies. They called him . . . the Gunsmith.

LONGARM by Tabor Evans
The popular long-running series about Deputy U.S. Marshal Custis Long—his life, his loves, his fight for justice.

SLOCUM by Jake Logan
Today's longest-running action Western. John Slocum rides a deadly trail of hot blood and cold steel.

BUSHWHACKERS by B. J. Lanagan
An action-packed series by the creators of Longarm! The rousing adventures of the most brutal gang of cutthroats ever assembled—Quantrill's Raiders.

DIAMONDBACK by Guy Brewer
Dex Yancey is Diamondback, a Southern gentleman turned con man when his brother cheats him out of the family fortune. Ladies love him. Gamblers hate him. But nobody pulls one over on Dex . . .

WILDGUN by Jack Hanson
The blazing adventures of mountain man Will Barlow—from the creators of Longarm!

TEXAS TRACKER by Tom Calhoun
J.T. Law: the most relentless—and dangerous—manhunter in all Texas. Where sheriffs and posses fail, he's the best man to bring in the most vicious outlaws—for a price.

JAKE LOGAN

SLOCUM'S GREAT RACE

J

JOVE BOOKS, NEW YORK

THE BERKLEY PUBLISHING GROUP
Published by the Penguin Group
Penguin Group (USA) Inc.
375 Hudson Street, New York, New York 10014, USA
Penguin Group (Canada), 90 Eglinton Avenue East, Suite 700, Toronto, Ontario M4P 2Y3, Canada
(a division of Pearson Penguin Canada Inc.)
Penguin Books Ltd., 80 Strand, London WC2R 0RL, England
Penguin Group Ireland, 25 St. Stephen's Green, Dublin 2, Ireland (a division of Penguin Books Ltd.)
Penguin Group (Australia), 250 Camberwell Road, Camberwell, Victoria 3124, Australia
(a division of Pearson Australia Group Pty. Ltd.)
Penguin Books India Pvt. Ltd., 11 Community Centre, Panchsheel Park, New Delhi—110 017, India
Penguin Group (NZ), 67 Apollo Drive, Rosedale, North Shore 0632, New Zealand
(a division of Pearson New Zealand Ltd.)
Penguin Books (South Africa) (Pty.) Ltd., 24 Sturdee Avenue, Rosebank, Johannesburg 2196,
South Africa

Penguin Books Ltd., Registered Offices: 80 Strand, London WC2R 0RL, England

This is a work of fiction. Names, characters, places, and incidents either are the product of the author's imagination or are used fictitiously, and any resemblance to actual persons, living or dead, business establishments, events, or locales is entirely coincidental.

SLOCUM'S GREAT RACE

A Jove Book / published by arrangement with the author

PRINTING HISTORY
Jove edition / December 2009

Copyright © 2009 by Penguin Group (USA) Inc.
Cover illustration by Sergio Giovine.

ISBN: 978-0-515-14721-6

JOVE®
Jove Books are published by The Berkley Publishing Group,
a division of Penguin Group (USA) Inc.
375 Hudson Street, New York, New York 10014.
JOVE® is a registered trademark of Penguin Group (USA) Inc.
The "J" design is a trademark of Penguin Group (USA) Inc.

PRINTED IN THE UNITED STATES OF AMERICA

10 9 8 7 6 5 4 3 2 1

1

The reek of decaying fish mixed with even less savory odors inside the saloon, but John Slocum hardly noticed. He concentrated on the poker game to the exclusion of anything else, and rested his elbows on the nicked edge of the poker table to lean forward and better study his opponent across from him. The river man was so drunk he could hardly sit upright in his chair—or was this an act to make the cowboy think the man was unable to bet sensibly?

Slocum had been gambling in the saloons along the St. Louis docks for more than a week, and had seen every possible scam ever conjured up by the crookedest con men on either side of the Mississippi. The river men lived in their own private world aboard the steamboats working their way up and down the river, and thought it all carried over when they came ashore. He had seen more than one game of chance aboard riverboats, and knew better than to ever get involved there. The tinhorn gamblers fleeced all the other passengers with easy contempt using their experience, and if that failed, they relied on elaborate cheats far beyond dealing seconds or using a marked deck. Anyone calling

1

them on their double-dealing ways ended up with a lump on his head and getting tossed overboard.

This was no riverboat gambler he faced. Slocum figured the man had been ashore less than a day to have any money left in his pocket. The river man drank like there was no tomorrow, and his eyes crossed now and then. Or maybe they were permanently crossed, and the cheap rotgut served in the Floundering Fish Drinking Emporium merely corrected the problem.

"I'll bump that another ten dollars," Slocum said, pushing forward a stack of almost worthless scrip he had taken off another river man in an earlier game of dice. He pushed the whiskey-soaked bills into the pot, and kept his arms against the table to detect any unusual vibration. He had noticed several sailors who thought they could get away with sticking high cards under the table with a dab of tar, then pulling them loose when the need arose. It had taken him only a few seconds to realize that the sticky tar caused the table to shake as the cheater tugged on the hidden card.

He felt nothing through his forearms as the river man hiccuped and tried to look at his cards. One eye might have focused on the battered cards, but the other tried to run and hide.

"What'll it be? Call, raise, or fold," Slocum said.

"Don't rush me," the bleary-eyed sailor said. "I got to figger how to get the most outta you with sich a fine hand as this."

Slocum let the man talk out his strategy, take another drink, and finally belch as he came to a decision.

"All I got. Twelve more dollars." The river man pushed it in with a shaking hand.

"I'll see that and raise another five," Slocum said.

"I ain't got enough to call. You know that!"

Slocum had done a quick inventory on the man's poke and knew to a dime what he could meet and what he couldn't.

"If you can't call, you have to fold. Those are the rules."

The river man looked around, and Slocum prepared for trouble. The man was hunting for others from his crew to back him up. Before getting into the game, Slocum had considered this and decided the sailor was on his own, going from saloon to saloon until he was so drunk he had to be poured back onto whichever barge or steamboat he came from.

"I got a damn good hand," he said. "I ain't givin' up."

Slocum said nothing. The river man's hands remained in plain sight above the table, but Slocum slid his right hand around on the table so his fingers rested only inches from the butt of his Colt Navy in the cross-draw holster.

"Look, mister, you got the eye of a man willin' to gamble," the man said.

"That's why we're sitting here. To make money."

"I don't wanna do this, but I kin put up somethin' worth a thousand times whass in the pot."

"There's fifty dollars there," Slocum said. He inched a little closer to the ebony butt of his six-shooter. Too many times, drunks thought they had treasure maps or knew ways of getting money that never panned out. With this pot, and the rest he had won during the prior week after he had drifted down from Minnesota, Slocum could finally leave town. He was sick of the docks, the river men, the pervasive fish stench, and cutthroats, and all the rest that made St. Louis a booming river port. It was time to head West again, get across the Nebraska plains and into the mountains where he could get away from civilization.

"Th-this is worth fifty thousand," the river man said, and then belched again.

"Let's see it."

The man fumbled at his shirt. Slocum tensed and curled his fingers around the butt of his six-gun, not knowing what would come flopping out. The boatman drew up a greasy string tied around his neck, and finally revealed a small golden key. A furtive look around told Slocum the man was either a good actor or thought this was worth stealing. No one else in the Floundering Fish noticed.

"Here it is. The key to the lock."

"So?"

"The treasure box, man! The strongbox with fifty thousand dollars in it!"

Slocum said nothing. If the man could open a single lock and spill out that much money, he would have done so already and not been getting drunk in riverfront dives.

"You ain't heard?" The drunk leaned closer. Slocum watched carefully to be sure the man didn't hide a quick attempt to swap his punk hand for a royal flush. The man was too intent on hiding the key and letting only Slocum see it. It was cupped in his calloused, grimy hands, and he held it like some sacred relic to be cherished.

"This is the key to riches," he said. "Opens the lock on Colonel J. Patterson Turner's strongbox out in Frisco. Or somewhere. Not sure where, but thass the point."

"Or somewhere? You have a key to a colonel's strongbox and don't know where it is?"

"No, no, where you been? This is it, I tell you. This is the real key, the only one that'll open the box. You gotta join the race, solve the clues, and when you find the box— nobody knows where it is 'cept the colonel—you git it all."

Slocum flicked away a fly trying to land on his nose. The annoyed fly's buzz melted into the buzz from the saloon patrons getting increasingly drunk and rowdy.

"I might have heard about this," Slocum said. "He's started a transcontinental freight line, and he's letting anybody who wants join the race." Slocum had ignored the details since they struck him as a waste of time. This was the first he had heard of money involved.

"Why join if you ain't got the key?" asked the river man.

"This is the only key? Then why would anyone else join the race?"

The river man laughed harshly, then belched. "He handed out fifty keys, so there's fifty in the race, but only one key's good to open the strongbox."

"So fifty people will damn near kill each other getting to California, but only one of them will have the right key?" Slocum had never heard of such foolishness.

"Might not be Cali-forny," the boatman said. He took another drink. "Might be Oregon or Washington. Somewhere out thata way."

Slocum looked at the key and wondered if it was painted gold or made of actual gold. He reached for it, but the river man yanked it away and hid it in his palm.

"You ain't gonna win this pot," the man said. "I got the best hand."

On the chance the key might be real gold, Slocum nodded once.

"You'll let me use the key to call?"

"It might not be worth anything," said Slocum. "Truth is, you've only got one chance out of fifty having it fit the lock."

"This is the real one, the only one," the river man assured him. "I cain't go myself since my brothers 'n me own our own boat."

"You called," Slocum said. "Show your cards."

The river man laughed out loud as he turned over three aces.

"You ain't gonna beat that!" He reached for the pot, but Slocum pinned his hands down.

"Flush," Slocum said. "Spades, ten high." He half drew his six-gun when he saw the shocked expression on the other player's face.

"You cheated," the river man said. He looked around desperately for an ally to bolster his claim. Seeing no one, he reached for a knife sheathed at his belt, then stopped when Slocum slid his six-shooter the rest of the way from his holster and laid it on the table.

"You don't want to do that. You'd better leave."

"You sonuvabitch. You cheated me. I had aces. Nuthin' beats aces." The river man stood and kicked over his chair.

"Leave the key." Slocum might have been inclined to simply take the money in the pot if the boatman had been a good loser. Then again, a cardplayer ought to pay his debts. When he lifted the pistol and centered the muzzle on the man's chest, he got what he wanted.

"Take it and die," the sailor spat. He threw the gold key to the table. From the sound it made when it hit, Slocum knew it wasn't pure gold, but only base metal painted gold. It didn't matter. He had won it fair and square and it was his now.

Only after the river man disappeared out into the close, sultry night did Slocum relax. He holstered his six-shooter and raked in the money. Most of it was paper money drawn on St. Louis banks, but he might outfit himself with a decent horse and enough beans and oatmeal to get him all the way to the Rockies. After tucking the wad of bills into his coat pocket, he lifted the gold key and let it spin slowly, catching the light and showing him what he had already guessed.

A steel key had been gilded to appear as if it were pure gold. He laughed ruefully, but took out his watch and fastened the key to the gold chain as a reminder about drunks, losing poker hands, and gullibility. He should find out more about Colonel Turner's race. If the key was the admission ticket and only fifty existed, selling it would bring him a few more dollars.

Slocum leaned back and looked around the Floundering Fish to see if he might land another sucker. The Regulator clock above the bar ticked slowly and surprised him so much, he drew the watch from his pocket again and opened it.

"I'll be damned," he said, snapping the cover shut and returning it to his watch pocket. The gold key pressed between his chest and the watch as it rested in his vest. "It's almost dawn." Sudden tiredness overtook him. He stretched, yawned, and decided it was time to catch a little shut-eye before continuing about his business. He could almost see the purple-cloaked Front Range now. Rumors that Denver was undergoing a new boom enticed him since the rest of the country was hurting. He had heard it called a depression, but Slocum could ignore anything that happened to banks and railroads as long as he had a rifle, an open range, and deer to hunt. The Coinage Act had cut the legs out from under the Western silver boom, putting the entire country on the gold standard. It didn't much matter to Slocum whether his coins were gold or silver, but metal was always preferable to the stained, crumpled scrip that floated around the cities. The doings of government and business didn't bother him the way it did town dwellers if he had elbow room and a river of crystal-clear water to drink.

He took one last look at the hangers-on, and knew the barkeep would be the only one profiting from anyone inside the four sagging walls. Even the whores had gone to hang up their bloomers and rest before their next round of drunk sailors came into St. Louis with the morning.

Stepping out into the hot breeze was like swimming in a bucket of water. In spite of this, all drowsiness vanished and he felt up to licking his weight in wildcats. With some luck, he could find a decent horse and be on the trail by noon. The promise of leaving the crowded, smelly city invigorated him.

As he walked down the street, he heard the familiar sounds of a fist hitting flesh, followed by loud moans. Slocum knew better than to get involved in another man's fight, but an outcry stopped him in his tracks because he recognized the voice.

Cursing under his breath, he drew his Colt Navy and held it at his side as he went to the mouth of an alley alongside the Floundering Fish to see a pair of men whaling away at the river man who just had lost his poke in the poker game.

"Not on him. The damned key's not anywhere on him," complained one attacker.

"I ripped open all his pockets. You got a knife? If he swallowed it, I'll cut it out of his gizzard."

"He ain't got nuthin' else. He's cleaned out."

"I know he had the key on a string around his neck. I seen it!"

The robber ripped open the boatman's shirt and clawed at his chest, as if he could dig out a hidden key.

"I don't see it, Clausen. Nowhere. He musta lost it."

"He would die before he gave it up."

The conversation became a shouting match between the two robbers and their increasingly insensate victim as they continued to pummel him and demanded to know where the key had gotten off to.

Something alerted the thieves to Slocum's presence. One tugged at the other's sleeve and both turned to face him. They were shrouded by the deep shadows, and Slocum couldn't see their faces, but with the rising sun directly at his back, his own face was hidden in shadow, too.

"You go on now, mind yer own business!" said the man called Clausen.

"Reckon I will," Slocum said, lifting his six-shooter and aiming it at them. Both robbers lit out like their tails were on fire. Slocum cautiously approached the river man, and saw how he bled from a half dozen cuts. His face was a giant bruise already, but his breath came in ragged gasps. He might have a broken rib, but he wasn't spitting up pink froth, so a lung wasn't punctured.

Seeing that the man was going to live and wasn't too bad off from the beating, Slocum backed away, got to the street, and thrust his six-shooter into his holster. He had a bad curiosity, and it itched like poison ivy right about now.

It took him close to an hour to find a newspaper and read the headlines.

Colonel J. Patterson Turner's Transcontinental Race was about all there was on the front page. Slocum scanned through the flowery words and found what he needed to know. A special train car had been reserved for race contestants and would depart from St. Louis at precisely nine A.M. on September 15, 1873.

Those details mattered less to Slocum than the reported prize of fifty thousand dollars. This was a princely sum—in gold—to the contestant who figured out where the strongbox had been placed and had the proper key to open it. Slocum wasn't interested in this, but from the amount of publicity the colonel got, he reckoned a lot of people were since this was the morning the racers were to start on their cross-country stampede.

He traced the outline of the key on his watch chain. Who wouldn't pay him five hundred dollars for the gold key and a chance to win fifty thousand?

Slocum was betting there was at least one onlooker who yearned for the chance to join the race. He set off for the train depot, and reached it a few minutes after eight. The crowd that had gathered numbered in the hundreds, all pressing close, but being held back by a small army of uniformed guards sporting a Turner Haulage Company patch on their right shoulders. Slocum worked closer, and saw the sewn patches showed a locomotive, stagecoach, horse, and boat.

Seeing his interest, the guard tapped the patch and said, "The colonel's braggin' on movin' freight however's fastest. You got the look of a freighter. You interested in a job?"

"Can't say that I am," Slocum said. "How many drivers is the colonel hiring?"

"Couple hundred, I heard," the guard said. "I'm fixin' on signin' on when this circus is over. Pay's supposed to be good."

People behind Slocum jostled him and pushed him forward.

"Let us through. Let the racers through!"

The guard thrust out a brawny arm and pushed Slocum to one side to clear a path for a strutting banty rooster of a man wearing a white Panama hat with a fancy hatband. His white suit had already picked up soot and dirt splotches, but no one would notice that. Their eyes would be drawn to the insignia and half dozen medals bouncing on the man's left breast.

Slocum didn't have to be told that Colonel J. Patterson Turner had made his grand entrance. A ragtag bunch of men trailed him, some with hard looks to them and others wide-eyed with amazement at being the center of attention, if only for a moment. Any fame descending on them would be reflected off a brilliant Colonel Turner swaggering along to a stage erected near a train waiting on a siding, the steam engine huffing and puffing clouds of white smoke into the air.

"Welcome to the greatest spectacle of this century!" the small, white-suited man shouted. His voice was a little shrill, and was almost drowned out by the idling steam engine. "One of the lucky fifty holding the gold keys will win the prize of a lifetime in commemoration of Turner Haulage Company's inaugural shipment. We offer the fastest, most secure transport of cargo from . . ."

Slocum stopped listening, and started looking around the crowd for someone likely to offer him a few dollars for his key. He stopped looking and stared when he set eyes on a tall, willowy dark-haired woman dressed in rugged traveling clothes at the edge of the crowd. The guards had gravitated to her, and Slocum couldn't blame them. He had seen a passel of pretty fillies in his day, but not one this lovely. Her pale oval face was punctuated by a pert nose, bow-shaped ruby lips, and blue eyes rivaling the sky itself. She clutched a large carpetbag and hung on Colonel Turner's every word, as if anything he said mattered one whit.

Slocum moved closer, just to be sure he wasn't overestimating her beauty. When he got close enough to see every curve of her body and every facial plane, he knew he wasn't. Just looking at her caused a catch in his throat.

"The fifty contestants will ride this train and be given clues to the next stop along the various routes pioneered by Turner Haulage Company," the colonel went on.

"Are they paying anything to go West?" Slocum asked a guard. It took the man a second to understand that someone had spoken to him. When he did answer, he never took his eyes off the captivating woman's beauty.

"Naw, all the transportation's paid for."

Slocum considered this. He had a key and could ride along, pretending to hunt for the clues to the next message left, and not pay a dime to reach Denver. The only problem with that was that his gear was still back at his hotel, and it was only a few minutes before the train pulled out with the contestants aboard. He looked around for someone to buy his key before it was too late. The lure of a free trip was canceled out by the loss of his gear. More than this, he preferred to set his own pace and choose his own trail rather than being part of a herd.

He tried to study the crowd for a likely buyer, but kept getting distracted by the woman. She breathed more heavily now, displaying even more of her allure as her breasts rose and fell under the thick blouse and jacket she wore.

"Will those with keys board the Turner Haulage Company train and partake of their golden destiny!"

Dozens of men pushed through the circle of guards, each showing a key to be permitted through. Slocum had started to bellow out a call for a buyer for his key when he saw the woman hold out a key of her own and be ushered toward the train car.

Slocum wasn't sure he thought about it as he took out his key and followed.

Not only was the colonel offering a free ride West, traveling with the pretty woman was an added bonus that offset the loss of his gear.

Flashing his key, Slocum followed her up the narrow metal steps into the train car.

2

"Very good, suh," the conductor said, staring at the key dangling from Slocum's watch chain. "Go right on in and good luck to you."

Slocum nodded and slipped into the car, looking over the heads of most of the men already inside to catch a glimpse of the woman. She seemed to have vanished into thin air. Slocum began pushing his way toward the rear of the car, only to be jostled and then shoved back hard. He caught himself on a seat back to keep from falling.

"Watch where you're goin'," a burly man growled. Slocum knew he wasn't any fresh flower, not after spending much of the past week along the docks and in smoke-filled, stinking-of-puke saloons and not bathing, but this gent reeked of onions and dried blood.

"You a buffalo skinner?" Slocum asked.

"What's it to you?" The man squared off, his impressive shoulders blocking the aisle. He stood only a little over five feet, but what he lacked in height, he made up for in bulk. The buckskins he wore hadn't been properly cured, and had probably not been taken off in months. At his belt he car-

13

ried two knives, either of which was a dangerous enough weapon. That he had a pair riding one at each hip told Slocum not to get too close or he'd find his guts spilling onto the train floorboards.

"You're sorely in need of manners," said Slocum. "You got the look of a man who spends too much time murdering buffalo and not enough time bathing."

The man roared like a mountain lion, and tried to wrap his arms around Slocum's chest. He never got the chance. Rather than stepping away, which would have been deadly, the aisle being clogged with others crowding into the train, Slocum stepped forward and brought his knee up as hard as he could. The buffalo skinner gasped and turned red in the face. As he reached for his damaged privates, Slocum punched him in the throat and knocked his head back. Before the buffalo skinner could collapse, Slocum stepped up and again kneed him in the groin.

It had taken that much punishment to bring the burly man to his knees. Slocum used both hands on the man's greasy collar to pull him along. The other men behind stepped out of the way and let Slocum wrestle his weakly mewling victim to the door. The conductor looked from the buffalo skinner to Slocum and smiled, his white teeth shining against his black skin.

"You surely do go for the big 'uns, don't you?"

"Big and smelly," Slocum said. He heaved, got the skinner to his feet and then turned to let him fall away. The man smashed his face against the bottom step and slithered on down to the platform.

"Thank you, suh, for doin' your housecleanin' on the side of the train 'way from the reporters. They is a chatterin' bunch."

"You work for the colonel?"

"The railroad, suh, but the colonel is a major stockholder. He wouldn't like it none to have his railroad or his contest besmirched."

"You have any interest in finding the strongbox?"

"Why's that, suh?"

"I can get his key and let you have it."

The conductor laughed until he had to hold his sides. He wiped away tears and then composed himself.

"I got no call to do sich a thing. I got me a wife and four chilluns. They wouldn't like it none if I went traipsin' off."

"And?" Slocum pressed.

"And I reckon y'all will end up like that one, or worse. The root of evil and all that."

"And all that," Slocum said, grabbing a metal handrail to keep his balance as the train lurched forward. The steam whistle screeched and the train pulled out.

"Leastways, there's one less to fight you foah the gold." The conductor shook his head as he watched the buffalo skinner's unconscious form disappear as the train built speed and left the depot behind. He adjusted his cap, touched the brim, and went forward without another word.

Slocum dusted himself off and went back into the passenger car. The general hubbub became utter silence as he felt all eyes on him. The clacking wheels and the creaking of the car as it took the gradual turns in the rail yard were all he heard, until someone at the rear of the car said loudly enough to be heard, "Served the bastard right. Besides, he stunk. Better off without him aboard."

Someone answered that the speaker shouldn't talk about lack of sanitation, and then the conversation level rose to drown out the train noises. As Slocum made his way along the aisle, he looked for the woman, but didn't see her. He frowned. He had acted impulsively because of her. At the very least, he wanted to find out her name. Along with the memory of her beauty, that would keep him warm many a night along the lonesome trail across the prairie.

As he made his way down the aisle, he looked not only for the woman, but for anyone else who might cause him trouble. The majority of the men stared at him almost guiltily—or maybe it was with a touch of fear. A few were bolder and more dangerous from the look of the way they slung their iron at their hips. Slocum sorted the men into three groups. One would get through using their wits. The other group would fling lead everywhere. The third group hardly mattered since they weren't likely to last long, either being outwitted or shot and left for dead on the trail.

"You surely did take care of that troublesome fellow," said a man wearing a bowler with a dark maroon grosgrain ribbon around the crown. His clothing had been expensive at one time—a long time ago. Slocum figured he was down on his luck and looking to get back on top by winning the prize.

"Wasn't that much trouble," Slocum said, finally seeing the woman huddled at the back of the car, slumped down in the seat and trying to vanish. Slocum kept walking, not wanting to get involved with the man in the bowler when his goal was in sight.

He stopped and looked down at her. She shrank a bit more, and looked out the window as the countryside slipped by faster and faster. The engineer had put full steam to the boilers, and drove the train along at thirty miles an hour.

"He's in a hurry to get us somewhere," Slocum said. "Do you know where we're headed?"

She looked up, her bright blue eyes fixed on him for the first time. A tiny smile crept to the corners of her lips, then faded quickly.

"You don't know?" she asked. "You've got a key, don't you?"

Slocum pulled the gold key out and let it spin slowly. She shrugged and turned away. He considered leaving her alone, then simply sat beside her. This startled her. She sat straighter and looked outraged at how forward he was.

"This seat is taken, sir."

"Is now."

"I am saving it for my brother."

"He wasn't the buffalo skinner I threw off the train, was he?"

"What?" She actually laughed. The merriment danced in her eyes for a moment and then quickly died. "How absurd to think that horrid man was my brother Harry."

"I'm John Slocum."

She responded out of reflex. "Molly Ibbotson."

"Pleased to make your acquaintance." Slocum spoke to the back of her head. She had turned and was staring out at the Missouri land slipping past.

"I reckon this line goes to Kansas City," Slocum said. "Is that where we're supposed to find out where to head next?"

She turned back to face him. "You know these things. You have the key."

"But none of the details. I came by the key only a couple hours ago."

"Oh." She shied away from him.

"I won it in a poker game. I didn't kill anyone for it, though some of these gents look like that's how they came by theirs."

"I'm afraid you may be right, Mr. Slocum."

"Tell me what everyone else already knows."

"You wouldn't be here unless you knew about the strongbox and the gold inside," she said. Slocum didn't contradict her. "The Turner Haulage Company is a new business, and the colonel thought this was a good way to get a great deal of publicity. I had heard there were reporters along, though I have seen no one who looks as if he can sign his name other than with an X." A hand covered her lips; then she smiled wanly. "I didn't mean you, sir. I was referring to others."

Slocum followed her gaze. He knew who she was most

upset over, and with good reason. The man was an obvious gunman and had a half dozen men with him, all likely to have wanted posters following them across the West.

"Who is he?"

"I heard one of his sycophants call him Sid Calhoun. Do you know him?"

Slocum shook his head. There were too many desperadoes for anyone, even a federal deputy marshal, to keep track of. For that he was grateful since he had run from a wanted poster on his head for years. Slocum had never thought what he did was a crime, but the law didn't agree. When he had returned to Slocum's Stand in Georgia after the war, his parents were dead and his brother, Robert, had died during Pickett's Charge. Without consciously knowing he did so, he touched the watch in his vest pocket. The timepiece was his only legacy from a brother he had revered.

But he hadn't returned to farm land that had been in the Slocum family for almost a century. He had wanted to recuperate after getting gut-shot on orders of William Quantrill for protesting the Lawrence, Kansas, raid that ended with children as young as eight being shot down like dogs. As he healed, a carpetbagger judge had taken a fancy to the farm, and had trumped up unpaid tax liens as an excuse to seize it for himself. He and a gunman had ridden out to take possession. Slocum had given them more than they expected.

He had buried the two bodies near the springhouse, and then had ridden out, with charges of judge killing dogging his heels ever since.

Having a price on his head meant nothing, but Slocum had seen men like Sid Calhoun before. They were cold-blooded killers who thought nothing of leaving lead-filled bodies in their wake. These were the men Slocum expected to go after a fifty-thousand-dollar prize.

"Why are you on this wild-goose chase?" Slocum asked the woman.

"It's not a wild-goose chase! I—we—intend to win. That much gold will put us on easy street the rest of our lives."

"You're educated," Slocum said, taking her measure. "You could earn a good wage as a schoolmarm. What about your brother?"

"Harry?" She laughed ruefully, and that told Slocum everything he needed to know. The sister had assumed the role of a parent and had tried to do right by a ne'er-do-well brother. He might be a gambler or a drunk or enjoy the ladies too much, but whatever his vice, Molly thought a pile of gold coins would solve his problem. And hers.

"Where is your brother?"

She glanced over her shoulder toward the back of the train car. Slocum remembered a half dozen cars attached to the rear. The caboose didn't matter, but there were a few freight cars and a mail car.

"He's seeing to things," she said.

"How do we find the next place?"

"I shouldn't tell you, should I? If we are competitors, you might take advantage of me."

"Only if you want," Slocum said boldly. His green eyes locked with her blue ones, and silent communication passed between them. He felt her responding, relaxing in his presence. Wherever her brother was, he could stay there for the rest of the trip as far as Slocum was concerned.

"You're not what I thought when I first saw you," she said.

"What was that?"

"You're more pleasant than Calhoun and his henchmen, but you look as deadly."

"If folks leave me alone, I get along just fine."

"How alone?" It was her turn to be forward.

"Not too alone," he assured her.

"Where *is* Harry?"

"Leaving you alone with a car full of road agents is hardly a brotherly thing to do."

"I can take care of myself. Where is he?" She strained to look over Slocum's shoulder. Molly half stood, and had started to call out when the door at the rear opened. When she saw it wasn't her brother, she sank back down and glumly stared out the window again. The mood that had built between her and Slocum was gone.

Slocum watched the man who had come from the rear of the train sashay over to Sid Calhoun and bend over to whisper in the owlhoot's ear. Calhoun nodded and clapped the man on the shoulder. The rest of the Calhoun gang joined in congratulating the newcomer. Something about their hilarity put Slocum on edge.

"What's your brother look like?" Slocum asked.

"That wasn't him."

"What's he wearing?"

"Why? Are you going to look for him?" She turned back, and something of the mood that had been between them returned. "You'd do that for me?" When Molly saw that Slocum intended to, whether she described Harry or not, she quickly gave him what information she could. Without another word, Slocum slipped off the hard bench seat and went to the rear of the car.

He peered through the filthy door window and saw no one in the space between cars. Slocum opened the door and shouldered his way over into the next car. A mail clerk looked up, eyes wide with fear.

"Don't go doin' to me what they done to that other fella!"

"What are you talking about?" Slocum looked around, thinking there might have been a mail robbery. The safe door was secured, but that didn't mean this frightened little man hadn't willingly opened it. "What's in there?"

"We ain't got nuthin' worth stealin'. I wouldn't lie."

"Have you seen a man about so high?" Slocum held his hand about shoulder height. He was six foot even, and Molly had described her brother as being about six inches shorter. "He's wearing a brown jacket with patches on the sleeves. The knees to his pants are shiny and so is the butt." Slocum stopped the description there because the mail clerk had turned white as paste, and his hands shook uncontrollably as he mopped his forehead with a filthy rag.

"I don't want no part in this. I done what you said."

"You haven't done a damned thing I've said yet," Slocum snapped.

"Not you, mister, yer partner. He said I had to obey him and all his cronies."

Slocum described the henchman of Sid Calhoun he had seen coming from this car. He didn't need the clerk's bobbing head to know this was who the man meant.

Slocum held up a hand. "He's not my partner. I'm looking for Harry Ibbotson. His sister's worried about him." Slocum hoped this information would calm the clerk's nerves. It didn't.

"You won't find him!" The clerk blurted out the words, then clamped both hands over his mouth. From the way sweat poured off his face and caused his clothing to plaster to his body, he was one drop away from drying up and blowing away. He backed away from Slocum and cast a quick glance toward the open side door.

Slocum went to the door and looked out at the tracks racing by under the clattering steel wheels. He started to look back when he saw a bit of cloth caught on the door. Prying it loose, he held up the few threads and sucked in his breath. Brown. He had no idea if this matched the color and texture of the jacket Molly had said her brother was wearing, but Slocum knew he would never bet against that supposition.

He turned in time to see the frightened clerk charging

him like a bull. The man had his head down and ran full tilt straight at Slocum. A slight turn took Slocum out of his path. The clerk would have thrown himself off the train if Slocum hadn't grabbed him by the collar and yanked so hard, the man's shoes left the floor and he hung suspended for a moment. Slocum didn't have the strength to support him, so he swung him back and dropped him just at the edge of the open side door.

"What did you try a damn fool thing like that for?" Slocum asked.

"You and those sons of bitches with you ain't gonna kill me! Not like you did him!"

"Harry Ibbotson?"

"Don't know his name, don't want to know. The son of a bitch tossed him out of the train back miles and miles. Said he'd do the same to me if I said anythin' 'bout it. The man's a killer! You can read it in his eyes. They're all crazylike and he laughed. He laughed when he threw that poor fool out the door."

Slocum knew it was pointless, but looked out anyway. All he saw were a lot of empty miles of Missouri. If Ibbotson had been tossed out only a few minutes before Calhoun's henchman had reported to his boss, he was a good two miles back. Every minute the train rattled on meant Harry Ibbotson was that much farther from his sister.

"What's the next stop?"

"Columbia. We gotta stop for water there, the way the engineer's been stokin' that boiler."

"Then on to Kansas City," Slocum said, thinking out loud rather than asking. The search for the strongbox with the gold had to be forgotten if Molly ever wanted to see her brother again.

He turned to the clerk, and asked pointedly, "Was he dead when he went out?"

"The way he was kickin' and shoutin', he was anything but dead."

"That's something," Slocum said. He eyed the mail clerk coldly to keep him seated on the floor so he wouldn't try anything that might really get him killed, then went forward to tell Molly what had to be done. Somehow, he doubted she would cotton much to quitting the hunt for the gold jackpot.

3

Slocum dropped down beside Molly Ibbotson as the train took a curve, forcing him to slide into her. He felt the warmth of her thigh and her startled movement as she responded. He slid back and half turned to better look at her.

"Is this from your brother's jacket?" He held up the scrap of cloth he had pulled from the mail car door. She took it and ran her fingers over it and then looked up, frightened.

"What happened to him? How'd you get this?"

"Might be that he had an accident and fell off the train a few miles back," Slocum said. He looked forward to where Sid Calhoun and his men passed around a bottle of whiskey they had brought aboard. It would almost have been worth it to leave Molly Ibbotson and join the owlhoots if they'd offer him a pull on that bottle. Right now, Slocum's mouth felt like the innards of a cotton bale.

"Harry is an idiot at times, but he'd never do such a thing," she said. "He's quite careful."

"Might be he had some help falling off the train," Slocum said. He put his hand on her arm as Molly shot to her feet.

25

She stared hard at Calhoun. The intent was obvious. If she had a derringer hidden away in the clutch purse she held on to for dear life, Calhoun was in serious danger of getting ventilated. "The clerk won't fess up to what happened exactly, so it's hard to prove anything."

"Someone saw this and won't speak? I'll—"

"You'll do nothing," Slocum said. "The clerk's scared of his own shadow, and he's got seven of Calhoun's henchmen up front here, all working to convince him to keep his mouth shut. There's nothing you could do to loosen his tongue."

"I—"

"Absolutely nothing," Slocum said, wondering what Molly was going to suggest. How far she'd go to help her brother, or to find her brother's killer, was something he needed to know.

"I'll pay you, John," she said urgently. Her voice lowered to a whisper and she bent closer so he could hardly hear her over the noise of steel wheels racing along steel rail under their feet. "I'll give you five hundred dollars to find Harry."

"What if he's dead?"

She heaved a deep sigh, chewed on her lower lip as she thought about it, then said, "Even if that's so, he deserves a Christian burial."

"Columbia's the next stop," Slocum said. "If I got a horse, I could ride back and find him in a few hours."

"But the next clue is supposed to be in Kansas City," she said, obviously conflicted.

"You go on, get the clue, and Harry and me'll catch up with you."

"If he's alive," she said. Slocum had no answer for that. He started to ask if she wanted him to retrieve the body or bury it where it fell on the prairie, but there would be time for such details when they arrived at the Columbia rail yard.

He settled back and watched Molly out of the corner of

his eye, but mostly he kept an eagle eye on Sid Calhoun and his henchmen. They were a rowdy bunch, but Slocum had seen worse in his day. Before he knew it, the conductor came through to announce their arrival in Columbia.

"Pardon," Slocum said. "When's the next train west?"

"Other 'n this 'un?" The conductor looked at him sharply. "No more 'n a day. This is a well-traveled road." He paused, then asked, "You and the lady gettin' off?"

"I am," Slocum said. The conductor smiled sadly as if wishing Slocum well, and moved on to alert the rest of Turner's treasure hunters about the brief stay to take on water.

As the train ground to a halt, Slocum got to his feet. Molly pressed close behind.

"You getting out to stretch your legs?" Slocum asked.

"I'm coming with you. Harry is my brother, and I need to know what happened to him."

"It might not be too pretty. A man falling from a train can get cut up something fierce."

"I need to know," she said firmly.

"The conductor can get your luggage," Slocum said.

"It's all here," she said, pointing. Slocum wrestled a bag down from an overhead rack and she took it. "The other is Harry's," she added. "We ought to get it, too."

Slocum grunted when he pulled down a larger bag. Her brother traveled with more gear than Molly. Lugging it to the rear door, Slocum shouldered it open, went on the narrow metal platform, and jumped down. He helped Molly, and in minutes they were standing on the depot platform watching the train with the rest of the gold seekers pulling out.

"I should have tried to sell my key," Slocum said.

"Your key?" The way she spoke made Slocum come alert like a hunting dog on scent. "I had not thought of that, John. Not at all. Come now. Let's find horses and go after Harry."

He watched her bustle off, wondering what had struck a sour chord with him. Shaking his head, he followed her to a nearby livery stable and, after fifteen minutes of haggling, bought a pair of horses and tack for a hundred dollars each.

"That is coming out of your five hundred dollars," she said. "I never knew horses and saddles could be so expensive."

"If it's coming out of my money, then I'll sell yours back and you can stay in town. I won't be more 'n a day or two fetching your brother, one way or the other."

"Please, John, I spoke in haste. This is all so upsetting to me."

He helped her into the saddle, and was pleased to see that she knew how to ride. Vaulting into his own saddle, he headed back along the cinder-strewn tracks.

"How far before we find the spot?" she asked after they had ridden in silence for almost ten minutes.

"When we get there, we'll be there," he said. For some reason, he felt cantankerous and reluctant to tell Molly that he guessed they had no more than twelve or fifteen miles to go.

They rode in uneasy silence, Slocum keeping a sharp watch ahead for familiar landmarks. He wasn't sure where Harry had been thrown off the train, but he knew that the few features on the grasslands he had seen when he did look out the open mail car door could not be more than a mile or two away.

The sun hammered down on him, forcing several stops to rest. Slocum began to get uneasy because of the shimmering heat and the way it radiated upward into the sky. At this time of year, tornadoes were likely to form, and even if they didn't, thunderheads formed with startling quickness.

"Is that what's worrying you, John?" Molly pointed ahead at the leaden clouds building. The heat boiled upward, forcing turbulence and creating storms.

He nodded once.

"Did I offend you? Is that it? I said something that insulted you. I'm sorry if I did so."

"I should never have let you come along. We need to make better time."

"Slowing you down was never my intent. I want to find my brother as much as you—more."

"He's worth five hundred dollars to me," Slocum said, not sure why he'd put such a harsh edge to his voice.

"He's worth far more to me," Molly said, looking straight ahead. She stiffened in the saddle and rode along rigidly, every step of the horse jolting her hard all the way up her spine. She bore the torment without glancing in his direction to see if he had softened his opinion.

Slocum hadn't. He picked up the pace and worried more about the storm brewing. The day's heat had turned to a stifling, humid blanket that caused him to sweat profusely. Repeated swipes with his bandanna did nothing to stop the flood from his forehead and into his eyes. Pushing his hat back a mite, he stood in the stirrups and let out a tiny cry of annoyance.

"What's wrong, John?"

"This is close to where he went out of the train. I recognize that stone cairn yonder from when I looked out the side door. It must have been left by a survey crew."

"I don't see him. Where is he?" Molly turned frantic, looking every which way and not finding her brother.

Slocum rode along the tracks for a couple more miles until he found a scuffed spot in the cinders and rocks forming the rail bed. His keen eyes picked out another piece of Ibbotson's brown jacket. Dropping to the ground, he picked it up and ran his fingers over it a few times, remembering the feel of the other patch he had found. They were the same material.

"This is where he hit the ground." Slocum walked a few yards away, looking for footprints in the hard ground. He was more than twenty feet from the track when he found crushed, dried grass marking Ibbotson's trail. "Harry went this way." He pointed out across the prairie.

"Why wouldn't he just follow the tracks to Columbia? He should have known I'd look for him, and the first place would be along the tracks. He . . . he's not injured, is he? A blow to the head might have disoriented him."

Slocum paced alongside the tracks, then looked up at the lovely woman. Even after the grueling ride in the hot sun, she was a picture of beauty.

"He's not stumbling along. These aren't the steps of a man who's been injured. He lit out with a purpose. That way."

As he pointed across the prairie, a distant clap of thunder reached him. He turned in time to see a lightning bolt lance from one cloud to the next, turning the roiling darkness momentarily brighter than the sun.

"Storm's coming on us fast. We can't slow down until we find Harry," he warned. Slocum stepped up into the saddle and began riding, hoping that he wasn't going to have to follow a meandering course on the prairie. As long as Ibbotson walked in a straight line, they had a chance of finding him. If, as happened in the desert, he began angling, he would slowly circle to the right and Slocum might never find the trail.

"It's not dangerous out here in the rain, is it?"

Slocum looked at her, wondering what sort of hothouse flower Molly Ibbotson was. He silently pointed to the deep ravines cut in the grassland by flash floods. It didn't rain in this part of Missouri. It *rained*. The sky opened up and dropped several inches of rain an hour. Getting caught in such a downpour could be deadly.

He threw caution to the winds when a heavy raindrop spattered against the crown of his dusty black Stetson. Putting heels to his horse, he galloped forward. In country like this, he might see a mile or two. If he found a rise he could see three on a clear day. That ought to be good enough to locate Ibbotson if he had kept walking and wasn't doing something stupid like taking refuge under a tree to get out of the storm.

New legs of lightning walked among the clouds overhead. When a wind kicked up and the rain began to come down with more fury, Slocum drew rein.

"Where is he? I don't see him. Where is he?" she asked.

"The rain's turning the dirt to mud and erasing any footprints. The crushed grass is springing back, making it impossible to follow that way. Even if Harry left a trail by dropping pieces of his coat, I couldn't track him now."

Slocum wiped more moisture from his face. This time it came from rain and not sweat. Somehow, it wasn't cooling him off at all. He had been in steam baths that were more inviting than this Missouri prairie.

"What are we going to do?" she asked. "We can't leave him out here!"

Slocum looked at the woman and shook his head sadly. That was exactly what they had to do. Harry Ibbotson might be a greenhorn and in danger of losing his life in the building storm, but Slocum saw no reason to throw his life away blundering through the cascading sheets of rain. Not for $500, not for Molly Ibbotson.

Harry had to fend for himself, for better or for worse.

4

Zoe Murchison gripped the splintery edge of the window, and bent forward until she pressed her nose against the glass and spoke through the small window just below. The ticket agent peered at her with some skepticism.

"Lady, I ain't got a ticket for you. Look. There's nothing here." The man rocked back and swept his arms around like the blades of a windmill pumping water. He moved so fast, his glasses slid down his sweaty nose, forcing him to push them back up using his middle finger.

"There must be. There simply *must* be a ticket for me. Miss Zoe Murchison. Is there someone else who might have placed the ticket in another file, one you know nothing of?"

"Lady—Miss Murchison—I used to have a clerk until he got the gold fever and went up north to Deadwood. Last I heard, he caught a Sioux arrow in the back and died."

"How unfortunate," she said. She backed off when she saw no progress was being made by being truculent. Changing her tactics, the blonde licked her lips, smiled just a little, and pressed her unruly hair back under her wide-brimmed hat. Emerald eyes locked with the station agent's rheumy

33

brown ones as she said in a voice as seductive as she could make it, "Are you sure? You must—"

"Damn right, I'm sure. Morgan was a good man. To die like that on a fool's errand to get gold outta the ground just ain't right. He could have been my right-hand man and made a decent living one day. This here's the only route from St. Louis to K.C. A gold mine, but not that much of a one these days," he added hastily.

"I didn't mean your unfortunate Mr. Morgan. I wanted you to be certain my ticket didn't simply . . . blow away." She tried again to be sexy without being too forward.

"There's no ticket for you. Not from the colonel, not from any Zellnov—"

—"Zelnicoff," she corrected automatically. Zoe's frustration mounted and she wasn't sure what to do. "He's my editor at the *St. Louis Dispatch*, and he was quite positive that I should be on the train going to Kansas City."

"You're a reporter? I do declare, you're 'bout the purtiest reporter I ever did see," the station agent said. "The whole staff, what there is of them bastards—excuse the language, ma'am—here in Columbia are the ugliest spuds you ever did lay eyes on."

Zoe was uncomfortable with the way he stared at her now, but she knew she had to do something to get onto the train with the contestants in the Turner Haulage Company race. Without the ticket, she could not get the story, and Mr. Zelnicoff would be disappointed in her. She had worked diligently in menial jobs and argued eloquently to be assigned to report on Colonel J. Patterson Turner's Transcontinental Race when a male reporter had fallen ill with the gout and was unable to stand without intense pain.

"I can do things for you," she said coyly.

"Do tell."

"I can print a story about how you were the kindest, nicest station agent in all Missouri or . . ."

"Or?" The man turned a little distant and looked at her sharply.

"Or I can let you languish, unnamed and unknown, forever a cipher as far as your fellow citizens—and your bosses on the railroad—know." Zoe was startled to see how this threat affected the man so. It mattered more to him not to be forgotten than to be favorably written about.

"Now why would you go and, uh, do that?"

Zoe shrugged eloquently, hating herself for the way her breasts bobbed to emphasize her reluctance.

"If I don't get aboard the train, how can I possibly ever convince my editor to publish anything I write?"

The station agent scratched his chin, but never took his eyes off her trim figure. She turned a little to the side so he could see her silhouette against the bright blue Missouri sky. It bothered her to use her gender in such a blatant fashion like some soiled dove might, but the man's resolve weakened by the second.

"Reckon I can give you the ticket and send a bill to this here Zellycove."

"That would be acceptable," Zoe said. "The newspaper will honor your invoice."

She heard the train approaching. The grinding of wheels against the steel rails as it slowed and the huffing and chuffing steam engine sent her pulse racing. She was seconds away from the story of her lifetime. With a contested race among the colorful characters the colonel surely had recruited to publicize his freight company, she could send a riveting, engrossing article every single day, and carve out a reputation for getting to the heart of any story, no matter how complex or dangerous.

"You just affix your John Hancock on this here line, so's I can be sure I got things all squared away," the station agent said, shoving a sheet of paper toward her. She took it and held it up so she could read it. Zoe looked up from the contract obligating her—or Mr. Zelnicoff—to the cost of a railroad ticket, and saw the train inching into the station.

"Yes, here," she said, scrawling her name across the bottom. "The ticket!"

"Miss Murchison, you got handwriting that'd put a doctor to shame, but then one of the town's doctors don't read or write. Said he was self-taught, and danged if he's not better than the fool with a fancy diploma hiding cracks in the plaster of his office wall." The station agent took the signed sheet, used a blotter to keep the ink from smearing, and then hummed to himself as he found the proper ticket.

"Thanks," she said. "I need to get aboard."

"Train's not leaving the depot until it takes on water," the station agent called. He leaned forward and yelled, "You didn't ask my name. I'm Herman Bronson! Wait! That's Herman Bronson, Sr.!"

"Yes, thank you, you've been a darling," Zoe said, not quite understanding what the agent had yelled at her. She was too intent on boarding the train and beginning her interviews. Fifty racers would require a considerable amount of work on her part to buttonhole them and finally distill what they said about their hopes and aspirations to a publishable story. It would not only get her national notice if the stories were syndicated, but it would cement her job at the newspaper. No more working as little more than a copy girl!

"Pardon," the tall man said, bumping into her as she hurried to board and he exited at the same time.

Zoe stepped back and looked at him, wondering if he were one of the racers. He was tall, dark-haired, and had eyes as green as her own. Rangy, moving with sure, quick movements, he had the look of a gunfighter about him. The pistol slung low in a cross-draw holster on his left hip convinced her he was a dangerous man. The worn ebony butt of the Colt only added to the picture of a no-nonsense hombre.

Zoe started to get aboard, and was almost bowled over by a woman rushing after the man. Zoe stepped back and watched, trying not to eavesdrop but being too close not to. Something about being a reporter turned her into a snoop. The woman was paying the man a princely sum to find someone—Zoe couldn't figure out who, but the dangerous-looking man was reluctant.

"I'm coming along, John," the other woman said. She stamped her foot and tried to look determined. Zoe thought it only made the woman look petulant.

Unconsciously, Zoe patted more of her hair into place. She knew she looked a fright after the frantic race in the buggy to reach the train depot. Why she wanted to appear as perfect as the other woman was something of a mystery since she had a job to do and neither the woman in her fancy traveling clothes nor the tall gunman with her needed to be impressed.

Still, Zoe wanted the man to at least glance in her direction. When he didn't, she heaved a sigh. The gunman and the woman hurried off, arguing in low voices as they went down the steps at the far end of the platform. In spite of herself, Zoe wondered what their story might be and if it wouldn't be better than the fifty men hunting for Colonel Turner's fabulous treasure trove.

"You gettin' on board, miss?"

She looked up to see the conductor studying her. A quick glance over her shoulder reassured her that the station agent wasn't rushing out to snatch the hard-won ticket away. All it would take was a simple telegram from Mr. Zelnicoff saying the newspaper would not pay for her ticket to rob her of this chance to justify herself.

The station agent remained where she had first seen him, seated in his tiny office, peering through the dirty window overlooking the platform. Unworried, the agent had not contacted the newspaper. Zoe worried that the man might wire ahead and have her arrested in K.C., but if he did, she would have a great start on her series and could wheedle Mr. Zelnicoff to pay if he wanted more of her fabulous stories.

"I am," she answered the conductor. "I'm a reporter. Do you have any objection to me speaking with the gentlemen engaged in the race?"

"Don't know how you're gonna do that, miss," the conductor said.

"I can—"

"Not a gentleman in the lot, so you talkin' to a *gentleman's* gonna be mighty hard."

In spite of herself, Zoe had to laugh. "You are such a card, sir."

"Yes, miss, reckon it goes with the job. If I couldn't laugh, I'd start flingin' them off my train."

She looked at the car loaded with men with a combination of trepidation and eagerness. These were fodder for her mill. These were the men she needed to make a reputation for herself as reporter.

"Wait," she said, grabbing the conductor's sleeve before he could go forward to the other passenger car.

"Miss?"

"The woman who just got off. Was she a racer, too?"

"Can't rightly say, but I reckon that to be a fact. Her and the tall man with her, both of 'em was askin' questions and soundin' as if they was in the race to get the gold. Are you one of them?" The conductor tipped his head in the direction of the men in the car, now all looking at her as if she were dinner and they were hungry wolves.

"I don't care who wins," Zoe said, "as long as I can be with him." She covered her mouth when she realized how that sounded. The conductor snorted and turned away quickly. "That's not what I meant . . ." She spoke to a closed door. Heaving a deep sigh, she turned back to her work. There were more than twenty men in the car, all waiting to give her an interview. Zoe knew that by the way they crowded close and peppered her with questions.

"Wait, please," she cried, holding up a gloved hand. "I'm a reporter and will want to speak with each and every one of you—in turn." She tried to look stern, and knew she'd failed.

Two of the men got into a scuffle and then a fight over who would speak to her first. Before she could order them to stop such foolishness, a burly man reached down, grabbed each by the scruff of the neck, and lifted. Zoe's eyes went wide when he lifted them bodily until the toes of their boots barely touched the floor. With a tremendous heave, he slammed their heads together and let them fall back to the floor, knocked out cold.

"Now, ma'am, you kin start talkin' with me."

"I'd be delighted," she said, feeling the opposite. Among dangerous men, this one looked the most likely to take a life and never notice—or if he did, he would no more care for the life snuffed out than he would a stepped-on bug.

"These yahoos ain't got no couth," he said, pushing his way through the throng, dragging Zoe along behind him. His huge hand circled her slender wrist like a prison manacle, and trying to escape was futile. With great reluctance, she let him pull her to the rear of the car.

"I need to get my pencil and—"

"We kin go on into the mail car fer a proper interview."

The train lurched and unbalanced Zoe. She grabbed the back of a seat and looked out to see the tall, dark-haired man with the woman hurrying down the steps from the platform. They vanished in the distance as the train gathered speed and its whistle let out a baleful screech.

"I said, come on!"

"You're hurting me!" She tried to fight, but could not overcome the man's immense strength. Thinking fast, she fumbled in her purse and got out her pencil. She used it like a knife, stabbing down hard into the man's wrist with the sharp tip. He jerked, but did not release her.

Contemptuously, he plucked the pencil from her hand and tossed it aside.

"We got bizness, me and you." He almost yanked her arm from the socket as he pulled her through the tiny door at the rear of the car, across the metal platform, and through the door into the mail car.

The clerk looked up in fright.

"I ain't got nuthin', mister. I swear!"

"You got a big mouth." The man grabbed the clerk and bodily tossed him out the open side door.

Zoe let out a gasp and ran to the door, clutching the edge so she could lean out far enough to see if the clerk had been injured. He struggled to sit up beside the tracks as she was yanked back into the car and flung to land heavily atop a heap of mail sacks. The rough canvas under her made her breath come faster. She knew this was going to be the bed where she was raped. The man worked to unbutton his fly and reached inside to pull himself out.

She tried to scream, but nothing came from her mouth. Her throat had tensed as surely as if he strangled her. She tried to back away on the mountain of mailbags, but only succeeded in miring herself down amid them. She realized too late that there was no place to run. Either she fought here and now, or she would endure the disgrace the man was about to perpetrate on her body.

"You jist lie back and enjoy it. Hell, you can squeal and kick around a mite. I like that." He stepped closer. Zoe prepared to kick him in the balls, but he was too quick for her. Before she could rear back and lash out, he dropped down, pinning her legs down under his knees.

He moved closer, his hands fumbling under her skirts.

Zoe was never sure what happened next. The rapist's weight held her down, and then she was so light she might have floated away. The man was choking, gurgling, strangling. Then that ugly sound disappeared.

Focusing her eyes took a few seconds. She saw a whipcord-thin man going through the would-be rapist's pockets. He found something worth keeping and tucked it into his own vest pocket, then grabbed a handful of throat and dragged the man to the open side door. Without seeming to exert any effort, he tossed the man off the moving train.

"Sorry I was late to this party, ma'am," the man said, touching the brim of his hat. He hadn't even worked up a sweat dealing with the mountain of gristle and meanness who had tried to rape her. "My name's Thom Carson. Big Thom Carson, at your service." He doffed his hat and made a mocking bow in her direction.

"Big Thom?" It was all Zoe could think to say. The man was half the size of the rapist, yet he had handled him easily. Manhandled! "You don't look so big. I mean—"

Carson laughed easily. "I know what you mean. I hear it all the time. I'm not some huge bear of a man, so how come they call me Big Thom."

"Yes, that's it," she said.

"It's not the men who call me that. It's only the ladies."

"I see," she said weakly.

He laughed again.

"You just might, if you're lucky enough." He reached into the vest pocket where he had stashed whatever he had taken from the other man.

Zoe knew then what had provoked the petty theft. Big Thom Carson had taken the other man's gold key. If only one opened the lockbox at the end of the hunt, a man doubled his chances with two keys.

"Now," Carson said, securing the key in his pocket. "Shall we get down to it?" He hitched up his pants and looked expectant.

"D-down to it?" Zoe felt faint. She had traded one rapist for another.

"You're a reporter. So interview me." Big Thom Carson flopped on a convenient stack of mailbags and lounged back, fingers laced behind his head. "I never been interviewed before by a reporter, much less a lady reporter as pretty as you."

Zoe struggled to remember any of the clever questions she had formulated before she had boarded the train in Columbia.

5

"It's never going to stop raining," Molly Ibbotson said, pulling Slocum's slicker up even more to protect her head. She huddled, cold, wet, and miserable, next to a scrub oak trunk that afforded little protection from the wind and blowing raindrops.

Slocum was inclined to agree. He had seen frog stranglers in his day, but this rainstorm threatened to go on forever. It had come up just before sundown, and had continued throughout the night until the prairie was an ankle-deep mud pit. Traveling in such treacherous weather over dangerous ground was more than foolish. It approached suicidal. Not for the first time, Slocum cursed Harry Ibbotson and the way he had lit out across the prairie instead of following the railroad tracks like any sane man would.

What had he been thinking? The train tracks obviously led to Columbia and the chance that his sister would be waiting for him there. To head across country without supplies made it seem to Slocum that the man wanted to kill himself. Living off the land wasn't difficult, but all Ibbotson had with him in the way of supplies was whatever

43

he had stuffed in his pockets. He night have a penknife or a small pistol, but Slocum didn't remember seeing a three-pound six-shooter strapped to the man's hip. Truth was, Slocum had barely caught sight of him as he boarded the train. Harry had left his sister immediately and gone to the mail car for whatever reason.

"He's a gambler."

"What's that?" Slocum had pulled his Stetson down so low his ears were bent out of shape, and he didn't hear much more than the rain pattering hard on the broad brim.

"My brother is a gambler, and not a very good one. That's what you were wondering, wasn't it?"

"Reckon so."

"He'll gamble on the turn of a card or whether the next man to walk through a doorway is left-handed. I saw him gamble on which fly would leave a piece of rotting meat."

"Did he win?"

The look Molly shot him told the answer. Her brother wasn't a good gambler. That might explain why they had gotten tangled up in the ridiculous scheme Colonel Turner had concocted. At the thought of the freight tycoon, Slocum touched his vest pocket. His finger outlined the gold key hidden there and, just for a moment, he wondered what he would do if he won the $50,000 in gold. Then he shook himself to get some sense back into his head. The chances of winning the race were small. Having the proper key to open the strongbox with the treasure was even slimmer.

He recognized the fever in himself for what it was. It wasn't any different from the men who struck out to find their fortune in a goldfield, or others thinking they could get rich following any other route to sudden wealth. Slocum recognized the fever and knew he was a better man than to succumb.

Still, $50,000 in gold was a lot of money and would take a long time to spend. A real long time.

"Rain's letting up," he said. "Must be close to nine o'clock."

"Seems like sometime next year instead of just nine in the morning," said Molly. She shook out the slicker and sent water flying in all directions before pulling it back down over her head. Her once-lustrous dark hair lay plastered against her skull, and her clothing had lost all shape not provided by her lush body. Every time she stood and tried to take a step, she squished. Her shoes had never been intended for the rugged Missouri countryside.

"I see some sky poking through the clouds," Slocum said.

"It's about time. I was ready to grow gills and swim away."

Slocum insisted they wait a spell for the rain to stop. He divvied up with the woman what trail rations he had, wishing he had taken more time to buy proper provisions.

"What do we do now to find him?"

"I marked the direction of his trail before the rain started. There's nothing we can do other than ride in the same direction and hope we find him alive."

"What?" Molly looked at him sharply.

"The deep ravines are there because rain like this isn't unusual. If Harry got caught in an arroyo, he'd be a goner." Slocum wondered if he wanted this to be Ibbotson's fate. If it was, he and Molly could return to Columbia, find a hotel, and take their sweet time while their clothing dried. He was sure he could assuage her grief if her brother was dead.

Slocum glanced over at the woman. She looked more like a drowned rat than the sexy, confident woman he had met on the train. Thinking about slipping up next to her in bed, naked as a jaybird, and then doing what came natural might be as much a fantasy as winning the $50,000 prize.

"He wouldn't do anything *that* foolish," Molly said, but he heard the doubt in her voice.

"You want to wring out your clothes while I do a little scouting?"

She started to disagree, then nodded slowly. Water fell forward as she moved her head.

Slocum worked methodically to dry off the saddle, and the blanket was as dry as anything could be after such a storm. If he could tell, the horse was grateful to get saddled and have the blanket next to its hide. Swinging easily into the saddle, he rode away from their pitiful camp, fighting to keep from looking back to see if Molly had begun stripping off her soaking-wet clothes.

When he topped a rise, all thought of the woman vanished. Ahead, not more than a mile, he saw three men on horseback slowly circling a man on foot. Slocum didn't need his field glasses, left back in St. Louis with the rest of his gear, to know who the man on foot was. The riders, though, were another matter. They seemed to be bedeviling Harry Ibbotson rather than helping him from the way they trotted close and then galloped off, only to return. It was as if they were herding him like they would a stray refusing to be branded.

He had started to ride straight for the horsemen and Ibbotson when he realized that would be impossible. The rain had cut a deep and treacherously muddy ravine through the prairie. If he fell into it, getting out would be hard. His horse could easily break a leg, and that might be the least of his worries. The swiftly moving stream at the bottom of the ravine flowed fast enough to sweep a man off his feet. Crossing it required some scouting—and he didn't know if there was time for Harry Ibbotson.

The three riders looped ropes around Ibbotson's arms, pinning them to his sides. They trotted off, forcing Ibbotson to run to keep his footing. When he tired, they would drag him along through the mud. Slocum thought they might be nothing more than cowboys out to have some fun with a tenderfoot, but as he watched them disappear, he doubted that. There was too much determination in what they were doing, as if they had found their prey and now took it off to their nest for safekeeping.

Slocum glared at the river flowing twenty feet below the lip of the ravine, backed his horse from it, and hurried back to camp. Molly had her blouse and skirt draped over a low branch. Hearing him return so soon, she grabbed her clothes and held them up to hide herself.

"Show some decency, sir!"

"Three men just took your brother prisoner," he said. "You better get dressed. It won't matter much if it's dry or not. We've got to cross a new river."

"There must be a ford somewhere," Molly said, looking around wildly. She fixed her gaze on him and demanded, "It was my brother?"

"Couldn't be anyone else, not wearing that brown coat."

"Damn," she said, startling Slocum. He had not expected her to use such an unladylike word.

"Don't just gawk," she said. "Ready my horse while I dress. We can't let Harry remain a prisoner."

Slocum thought it was curious she didn't ask about the men taking her brother prisoner—or was it hostage? He touched the key on his watch chain again. Somehow, Harry Ibbotson getting himself roped like he had fitted in with Colonel Turner's race and the gold at the end of it.

It took less than five minutes to saddle the horses and settle the saddlebags on their hindquarters. By the time Slocum was ready to ride, Molly had dressed. Silently, he helped her into the saddle.

They rode out, each lost in his or her own thoughts. Slocum set a brisk pace, knowing how easy it would be to lose the riders on this sloppy ground. If the ground hardened soon, good tracks would be left, but right now it was like trying to track a fish through water.

"What's that ahead?" Molly pointed. It took Slocum a few seconds to figure out what she had seen since he was so engrossed in not losing the trail.

He rubbed his eyes, squinted, and finally said, "Looks to be a town. I'm no expert on Missouri towns, but I don't remember any in this direction."

"It might have sprung up suddenly."

"A boomtown," he said. The riders had been going in the general direction of the town, so Slocum turned his horse's face that way, too. "It could spring up fast, and die even faster."

"That's a ghost town?"

Slocum picked his way across a muddy stream and got his horse up the slippery bank before answering.

"I don't see any roads leading there."

"Maybe they come in from St. Louis," she said.

"Makes more sense if they got supplies from Columbia, since it's not only closer, but it is on the railroad line." He scratched his chin before finishing his thought. "The town died because the railroad bypassed it. Why it was built didn't much matter if the railroad didn't put a depot here."

"I see someone, John. There. Did you see him? That's Harry. It's got to be!"

Slocum couldn't make out any details, even the color of the distant rider's coat. What worried him more was that there was only one man in sight. What had happened to the other riders he had seen with Ibbotson? The way the rider sat and waited made Slocum wary of being lured into a trap.

"Hold your horses," he told Molly. "Something's not right."

"But it's Harry. It has to be!"

The sun cracked open a hole in the heavy clouds and dropped a solitary ray of light onto the town ahead, giving Slocum his first good look at it. He had been right about the condition of this town. From the decaying boards and lack of paint, it had been abandoned some time ago. He tried to remember when the railroad had come through. Maybe five years back. That was plenty of time for this town to fall apart, victim to the wind and rain and termites chewing away at the wood.

"You're sure you don't know of anybody who'd want to kidnap your brother?"

"Of course not. We haven't been out here long enough to make that kind of enemy."

"How did you come by your gold key?" Slocum asked. He realized he knew nothing about Colonel Turner's contest other than the snippets he had overheard.

"The same way everyone else did," Molly said, glaring at him. When he said nothing, she spat out, "Harry stole the key. A clerk at a yard goods store had been given it for drumming up a thousand dollars worth of business for the colonel's freight company."

"Most folks came by their keys doing favors for the colonel?"

"I have no idea. Harry switched the gold key for another one he had. He saw the clerk being turned away when the colonel's guards determined he didn't have an official key."

"That makes one enemy willing to kill your brother," Slocum said. "Still, this clerk would shoot Harry outright and take back what was rightfully his. Why get friends to kidnap him and take him to a ghost town?"

Slocum chewed on his lower lip as he tried to figure this out. The clerk back in St. Louis had reason to bushwhack Harry Ibbotson, but why not kill him outright? Something else accounted for Ibbotson being taken prisoner rather than left for the buzzards to pick clean out on the prairie.

"Are we going after him or are we going to sit out here and let them . . . do things to him?" she asked. A catch came to Molly's voice.

"If he knows something and isn't telling them, it'll take a spell before they force him to talk."

"Harry doesn't know a thing." The woman's tone was

bitter, scornful of her brother. Slocum was coming to share that opinion and he had never met the man.

"They know we're out here," Slocum said. "The sentry must have alerted his partners by now." Slocum hunted for any trace of the mounted man Molly had spotted, but he had ridden into the town and disappeared. "There's no reason for us to pussyfoot around." Slocum slid his Colt Navy from its holster and made sure all six chambers were loaded. He usually rode with the hammer resting on an empty chamber, but now he needed the extra firepower. He wished he had a half dozen other six-shooters, like he had used when he rode with William Quantrill. Festooned with pistols, the company would ride into a Yankee town, firing until a six-gun came up empty, then switch to the next and the next. Each man in the company commanded thirty or forty rounds. With as many as fifty men, more than fifteen hundred rounds could be loosed in the time it took to ride the length of the main street.

All he had now were the six rounds and he faced three men, armed and ready for him. Worse, they had a prisoner who might get shot at any time they thought they were in trouble.

"What do you want me to do?" Molly asked.

"Can you fire a rifle?"

"I suppose, if I have to."

Slocum pulled the old Henry rifle from the saddle sheath, and wished he wasn't rushing into the teeth of a trap this way. During the war, he had been a sniper and a good one. It might take all day for him to get off one deadly shot, but it usually robbed the Federals of a high-ranking officer and threw their attack plans into chaos. If he had such luxury of time, he could find a spot and wait for Ibbotson's kidnappers to show themselves, then pot them like rabbits.

"Find a spot a hundred yards outside town," he said. "In ten minutes, start shooting at anything that moves."

"What if they use Harry as a shield?"

"They won't," Slocum said. He didn't want to make her mad by pointing out that an inexperienced rifleman with such an old rifle had almost no chance of hitting a man-sized target at that range. All he wanted was for Molly to create a commotion while he circled and came at them from the other side of town. It wasn't much of a plan, but was the best he could come up with on the spur of the moment.

"Ten minutes?" She took the rifle and held it gingerly, as if it would turn into a snake and bite her.

"Keep the muzzle pointed toward town. You pull back on the trigger and—"

"I'm not an idiot," she snapped.

Slocum nodded in agreement, then rode at right angles to their original path, circling the dilapidated buildings to approach from a different direction. He saw there was no time to get to the far side before Molly opened fire, so he cut directly for the town and worked his way between two buildings that had toppled into each other, creating a splintery tunnel showing only a sliver of light at the far end that opened onto the main street.

He brought up his six-gun when a flash of brown crossed in front of him. He urged his balking horse forward, scraped the sides of the buildings, and finally came out into the light of day.

Slocum saw Harry Ibbotson come from a doorway, only to be yanked back inside.

"Come on out," Slocum called. "You let him go and there doesn't have to be any gunplay." He didn't expect the man's captors to give in that easily. And they didn't.

A rifle report echoed from Molly's direction. He didn't hear the slug hit anything solid. She might have fired into the air for all the effect it had. He had hoped, rather foolishly, that her gunfire would drive the men out into the street where he could cut them down.

Slocum dropped to the ground and made his way toward

an empty watering trough he intended to use for cover. Halfway to it, he felt wobbly in the knees. At first he thought he was simply sinking into the ankle-deep mud. Then he realized the ground was giving way beneath him.

He let out a startled cry as he plunged downward to smash hard into the bottom of a pit. He struggled to keep from passing out. He forced his eyes to focus on the moving blurs fifteen feet above him, and then the effort was no longer possible.

Slocum blacked out.

6

"We're in this together, ever'body gettin' an equal share?" The gunman squinted as he studied Sid Calhoun, who lounged back in the passenger car seat trying to get comfortable. The clanking journey of the train over the steel rails kept them all on edge, including Calhoun.

"Dammit, you stupid son of a bitch, I told you we was sharin', didn't I? You callin' me a liar?" Calhoun reached for his pistol tucked into the broad linen sash secured around his trim waist.

"No, no, Sid, you got me all wrong. I was just, uh, just gettin' all square in my head. You know I don't think so fast."

"Curly, you're a complete idiot," Calhoun said. He watched for any reaction. If his henchman made so much as a twitch, he was a dead man. Curly looked confused and not a little bit scared. That was good. Calhoun could handle scared—in others. It kept his gang in line.

"Don't go ragging on him, Sid," said another of the gang.

"You crossin' me, too, Abel?" This time Calhoun didn't

watch. He acted. His hand flashed to his pistol, he drew, and swung as hard as he could, catching Abel alongside the head with a crunching sound that drew attention from everyone else in the car. After a moment of stunned silence, mumbled conversations began again as Abel lay flat on his back in the aisle between the seats. One man lifted his boot to keep blood from the gash on Abel's temple from staining the leather. He lifted his boot, but said nothing, and pointedly looked out the window to show he wasn't going to call out Calhoun.

Calhoun stood and glared down at the unconscious man.

"Throw the son of a bitch off the train."

"But he's done good, Sid," protested Curly. "He's got more of the keys than any of the rest of us."

"Take him into the mail car." Calhoun looked around to see if he had to deal with any other threat from the rest of the racers. Only a couple dared to look in his direction, but they were scared. He liked that. The rest ignored him. Some of them might be dangerous, but he doubted it. He was the wolf in this flock of sheep, and intended to keep it that way.

"He's too heavy fer me to drag," Curly protested. His feet slipped on the railcar floor that was now slick with Abel's blood. The head wound gushed now.

"All of you," Calhoun said, motioning with his still-drawn six-shooter. "Help him out. We got to palaver in the mail car."

He stepped over the fallen Abel, who groaned now, and led the way. He didn't bother holding the door for the others struggling with Abel's limp form. When he stepped into the mail car, he smiled crookedly. A right pretty woman stood to one side, busily scribbling in a small notebook.

"What do we have here?"

"A private conversation," came the cold voice. Big Thom Carson levered himself off a pile of mailbags. The way he squared off, he knew how to use the iron hanging at his side. "Why don't you clear out and let us be?"

Calhoun stepped to one side as Curly and the others pulled Abel into the car. With a curt gesture, Calhoun indicated what they ought to do with the unconscious man. Curly grunted as he dragged Abel to the open side door.

"Hold on," Calhoun said. He knelt and rifled through the man's pockets until he found three gold keys. Keeping them out of sight from the man still ready to throw down on him, Calhoun tucked the keys into a coat pocket along with the key he already had. He backed off and nodded to Curly.

Abel's body bounced a couple times as it hit the ground and rolled down a small incline away from the track bed.

"Oh." Zoe Murchison stared at him with eyes wide in horror. They locked gazes for an instant; then the woman began scribbling in her notebook.

"What are you doing?"

"I'm recording this," she said. Calhoun crossed the car and grabbed for the notebook. "No, that's mine!" she cried.

"You ain't recordin' anything. Give me the book."

"She doesn't have to unless she wants to," Big Thom said. The man's fingers curled just enough to tell Calhoun that lead was going to fly if he pressed the matter.

"Get on out of here. Take her with you."

Zoe scampered past Calhoun, but the look she gave Big Thom was hardly one of gratitude. Calhoun wondered what had been going on before he barged in, because the woman was as frightened of Big Thom as she was of him.

He turned to the man, and saw the tenseness in his shoulders and the way his trigger finger nervously twitched now. Calhoun had seen his share of men ready to draw, and knew the signs. Big Thom Carson was close to throwing down.

"Sorry to have interrupted your tryst," he said.

"What's that?" Big Thom wasn't distracted. The tension remained.

"You and that cute little filly. I saw how she was lookin' at you. Might be when we get to K.C., you and her can find a hotel room and continue your tryst."

"That's something good?"

"It's when a man and woman get together." Calhoun made an obscene gesture that brought a slight smirk to the gunman's lips. Some of the tension eased.

"Don't cross me again," Big Thom said, backing away so he could keep his eyes on Calhoun.

This suited Calhoun just fine. He shook his head when Curly started for his six-shooter. If brains were dynamite, that man didn't have enough to blow his nose. Calhoun waited for the door to click shut before turning to Curly and the other four.

"You owlhoots need to keep it straight why we're here."

"Aw, Boss—"

"Shaddup," Calhoun said automatically. "I talk, you listen. That's the way it works. And what I'm sayin' is that we need to collect even more of the keys. Those men in the other cars, they're pansies. They ain't gonna stand up to any of us."

"Why not just get down to some serious killing?"

Calhoun glanced at the sun-darkened man who had spoken. Gerald "Skunk" Swain never said much, but when he did, Calhoun took note. The man had killed a half dozen men, most all getting shot in the back. The greasy dark hair was split smack down the middle of his head with a snow-white band that gave him his appellation. Tiny eyes peered out from under bony ridges, demanding an answer. Ignoring the gunman would be a big mistake, and Calhoun knew it. Of the remaining gang, Swain was the most dangerous, especially if Calhoun ever turned his back or tried to catch a nap.

"We collect the keys a few at a time," Calhoun explained. "Let the others find the clues and lead us to the strongbox. We don't have to solve all the clues—and Colonel Turner promised that they wouldn't be easy."

"So we're not smart enough to solve them on our own?"

"So we let the others do the work. Then we swoop down

and take what's rightly ours," Calhoun said. He'd appealed to Skunk Swain's baser instincts, and saw he had hit dead center. Swain nodded slowly, considering how many men he could gun down from behind. The number tallied high enough to please him, because he fell silent, crossed his arms, and perched against a crate, waiting for Calhoun to continue.

"Abel had a half dozen keys and we throwed him out!" Curly cried, rushing to the open door and peering out. Calhoun restrained himself from kicking the man out for mentioning Abel or the keys he had.

"He didn't have that many," Calhoun said. He had found only three in Abel's pocket, but worried that Curly might be right. Abel had been a deft pickpocket besides being dangerous. If he hadn't been taken care of, he would have been calling out Calhoun for leadership.

"But, Sid, he—"

"Shut up," Calhoun said. "It won't matter. We can get enough of the others' keys to open the damned box."

"We could just shoot off the lock," Curly said.

"You stupid cow," Calhoun said. "You think we can just waltz up to the strongbox when we find it and do something like that? Turner'll have guards there and enough press and politicians to outnumber us a hundred to one. He's doing this to draw attention to his damn Turner Haulage Company. He's not going to keep that box hidden. Everything he's doin' is to make more people notice him."

"So we need the key."

"I'll have most all of them, so the odds will be good one opens the box."

"If it doesn't?" Skunk Swain uncrossed his arms and gripped the edge of the crate, where he shifted his weight enough to go for his six-shooter if he didn't like the answer.

"Then we'll have to see how many of the bastards we can kill and how fast we can get away with the gold," Calhoun said, giving his gang the answer they wanted to hear.

Too many of them were like Swain, more interested in spilling blood than getting rich.

That suited Calhoun just fine. While they were blazing away, he'd be getting away—with all the gold. He might have to take care of Swain first, though, since the man presented as much of a danger to him as Abel had. Calhoun smirked. Curly had his uses, and getting rid of Skunk Swain was about the best of them.

"How many keys we got?" Curly asked, breaking into Calhoun's thoughts. He held down his ire.

"Enough."

"I got two," Curly allowed. He looked around at the others. "What about y'all?"

Calhoun was surprised to see that among them they had ten keys, Swain having two. Two of the others had one each. That made them 20 percent of the way toward opening the lockbox and running their hands through a stack of gold coins.

He was a fifth of the way toward being rich.

"What's the plan for gettin' the rest?"

"We work real slow," Calhoun said. "Take out the dumb-lookin' ones since they won't help us any by solvin' the clues. By the time we get to the strongbox, we ought to have most all the keys."

"Some might have been lost," Swain said. "That gent in the brown coat prob'ly had one, and he got tossed off the train."

"That's only one key, and he might not have had it when he hit the dirt," Calhoun said. "Who threw him out?" He looked around and saw no one knew. It didn't much matter as long as his gang hung together and watched each other's backs. Swain was especially good at that. Calhoun felt the hairs on the back of his neck rise at the thought. Getting rid of Skunk might be necessary soon, but not until he had served his purpose.

And it wouldn't do to overlook the two keys Swain had.

"Uh, Boss, kin I talk to you in private?" Curly inclined his head in the direction of the open side door. "I got a worry."

Calhoun shot a look at Swain, then shuffled across the floor to stand with his back to the outer wall so Curly couldn't simply shove him out if that was the man's intent.

"What is it? We got work to do and this ain't doin' it," Calhoun said.

"Uh, Boss, what if some of them got more keys than they fessed up to havin'?"

"What do you mean?"

"They might be playin' their own game. Skunk, he said he had two, but he's got more. I know he stole a couple. That might mean the others are lyin', too."

"So what do you think I should do about it?"

"Call him out. He ain't got yer speed. Take him out 'fore he gets your spine in his sights."

Calhoun considered the request for a moment, then burst out laughing until tears ran down his cheeks. Curly had tried to play his own game and remove a rival. That meant he intended to double-cross the rest of the gang, Calhoun included.

"I didn't think you had that in you, Curly."

"What's that?"

"Such loyalty to me. You're worried about my safety," Calhoun lied, enjoying Curly's confusion. This wasn't the reaction Curly had expected from the gang leader.

"Yeah, sure," Curly said, warming to the idea that he had fooled his boss. "That's it."

Skunk Swain swung around, his six-shooter slipping from its holster. He leveled his gun at the door leading from the mail car to the forward passenger car. Calhoun covered his henchman, then saw why Swain had reacted. A face peered through the dirty window in the door.

"It's the bitch," Swain said. "Something's wrong."

"Get over here," Calhoun said. He kept his own six-gun

aimed at Swain, just to be sure. The others in his gang came over. Swain followed more slowly, but when he was a yard away from Calhoun, the train lurched and then screeched to a halt, throwing him forward.

Swain, Curly, and Calhoun went down in a pile. The other two gunmen fell atop them and they all slid toward the open side door. Calhoun tried to grab hold of the edge and failed. The lot of them fell heavily off the train, hitting the ground so hard they lay stunned.

Calhoun forced himself to his knees in time to see the huge plumes of smoke rise from the engine funnel as the train built steam again and roared along. He tried to get to his feet, and only became more entangled with the others. They fought and kicked and swung, making it impossible to stand. Calhoun fell backward and sat down hard. The train built speed and was leaving them behind.

"Get back on. Don't let them strand us out here!"

Calhoun began shooting at the train to attract attention. The train only moved faster and sped away. Calhoun stumbled along, clicking an empty six-shooter in the direction of the receding train.

"You sons of bitches! You can't leave me out here!"

"They did it on purpose," Swain said, shoving his six-shooter into his holster. "They did it to eliminate some competition."

"Like hell they eliminated me," Sid Calhoun growled. He stuck his pistol back into the sash around his waist and began walking, each step making him angrier than the last. Swain was right. Somebody had set them up and marooned them.

Somebody was going to pay with his life. Sid Calhoun made that promise, and it wasn't one he intended to break.

7

Zoe Murchison picked herself up off the passenger car floor and tried to smooth out the wrinkles in her only good dress. She worried they had become permanent, along with the stains and dirty spots. If she didn't present a professional appearance when she spoke with men such as Big Thom Carson, she had little chance of getting the news she needed for her articles.

"What the bloody hell'd you pull the emergency stop for?" A man the size of a mountain towered over her.

"Help me up." She held out her hand, and was almost yanked through the roof with the powerful tug. She landed and had to catch herself on the back of a seat. "Thank you."

"Why'd you stop the train?"

"We're moving again," she said, wanting to look out the window to see if Big Thom's scheme had worked. Getting rid of Sid Calhoun and those dangerous men with him was worth a little indignity and a tear in her good dress. She tried to hide the rent, but the man grabbed her wrist and pulled it up high, stretching her until she groaned.

"You're hurting me!"

61

"I'll do more 'n that if you don't tell me what's goin' on." He thrust his bearded face within inches of hers. She flinched at the gust of bad breath from the rotting teeth in his mouth.

"I'll do more 'n you ever thought could be done to you if you don't let the lady go."

"Who's—" The huge man spun and found himself staring down the barrel of Big Thom's cocked six-shooter.

"I don't want to waste any ammo on a son of a bitch like you, but if you want to know the truth, it wouldn't take but a single word out of your foul mouth to make me expend a round. Wouldn't need more than that, I don't think, no, sir." Big Thom thrust the gun forward until the front sight disappeared into the man's gaping mouth.

The incoherent mumbling must have communicated to Big Thom because he pulled the pistol back.

"You didn't let her go."

Zoe gasped with pain when the man suddenly released her. She rubbed her injured wrist and glared at him.

"I need this hand to write with," she said. "You have hindered a member of the Fourth Estate in her pursuit of a story."

"What are you goin' on about, bitch?"

That was the last thing the man said. Big Thom swung his pistol in a short, vicious arc that ended on the top of the greasy head. The mountain of a man collapsed in an avalanche.

"He shouldn't have spoke like that to you," Big Thom said.

"Your plan worked." Zoe stepped over the fallen man and peered out one of the car's side windows. The train had continued to gain speed until it was well past where Calhoun and his men were stranded on the prairie.

"It did," said Big Thom. "Pains me to have so many keys left in their pockets, but sometimes you have to ignore setbacks."

He collapsed into a seat and hiked his boot to the back of the seat in front. With his leg canted up, he studied Zoe closely.

"You got a bug in your ear 'bout this race, don't you?"

"I intend to cover every story I can until the moment someone opens the treasure chest."

"The way the colonel's got it set up, it might not happen that way at all. What if the only key that opens the box is with Calhoun or one of his men and they give up?"

"I doubt they will quit. They seemed determined, all of them," Zoe said. She sank down in the seat across the aisle from Big Thom. She tried to ignore the moans coming from the man he had buffaloed. That was only a little easier than shutting out the whispers from the other racers along with their intent stares. She and Big Thom were the center of attention in the car.

"Reckon you might be right, but part of this run to get the gold is making damn sure the others are behind you every step of the way."

"You succeeded in that."

"Seems like this leg of the trip has eliminated several of the other racers," Big Thom said. He spun the cylinder in his six-gun as he watched the man he had slugged return to consciousness.

Zoe caught her breath when she realized what Big Thom intended.

"You can't just murder him," she said.

"Why not? Think of how you'd like reporting that. My name bold as brass in every headline across the country. I'd be famous."

"For murder!" She was outraged at this, then calmed a mite and wondered if he'd only intended to rile her. Some men enjoyed doing that, or so she had heard. Her experience did not extend that far.

"The idea of watching a man die excites you. I can tell by the way you're all flushed. You're breathing faster at the idea of seeing him die." Big Thom aimed the six-gun at the back of the man's shaggy head.

"Stop!" Zoe grabbed Big Thom's gun hand and forced the barrel up and away. When the six-shooter discharged and the bullet dug a splinter out of the ceiling, she cowered back, frightened. "You would have murdered him in cold blood!"

"Can't say it would be so cold. Might be he killed my brother in Abilene," Big Thom said.

"Did he?"

"Never been to Abilene. Don't have a brother," he admitted.

"What's goin' on back heah?" The conductor pushed through the front door in the car and moved between the bench seats, homing in on the man lying in the aisle, moaning and stirring from his injury, and the man and woman wrestling over a six-gun.

"Nothing to get upset over," Big Thom said, tucking his six-shooter away. "Thanks for coming back to help."

"Help?"

"This galoot wanted to get off. Me and the lady tried to stop him, but he was determined. His wishes ought to be honored. Ain't that the policy of the railroad?"

"He wanted to jump off?" The conductor stared wide-eyed at the man, now getting to his hands and knees. "Mister, did you—" That was all he got to say before Big Thom brought his boot crashing down onto the back of the big man's exposed neck. The big man crashed facedown on the floor again.

"See? He said so."

"Who pulled the emergency stop?" The conductor glared unafraid at Big Thom, but Thom shook his head and held out his hands.

"Not me. Must have been someone else needin' to take a leak."

"There's a hole in the floor in the back of the car," the

conductor said, before he realized this was far from the real reason the cord had been pulled.

"Come on, be a good guy and help me." Big Thom got his feet under him and heaved, bringing the bulky, limp body to its knees. As he held the big man upright, he looked at Zoe and said, "The key. He's got a key. Take it."

"But I—" She saw the cold determination in Big Thom's eyes and knew better than to cross him. She hastily searched through coat pockets, and finally found the gold key suspended by a piece of string around the big man's bull-thick neck. Before she could do anything with the key, Big Thom snatched it from her.

"You can't jist toss this fella off the train, not whilst we're movin'," the conductor said.

"Then you can do it." Big Thom had his six-shooter out and aimed again.

"I'll help," Zoe said, thinking Big Thom wouldn't shoot both her and the conductor. The man's expression told her how wrong she was. Anyone getting in Big Thom's path to the $50,000 was expendable.

Zoe and the conductor dragged the man forward and out onto the small platform between cars.

"Missy, this ain't right," the conductor said.

"I know, but what choice do we have?" She saw how Big Thom held the door open just a fraction of an inch, his gun barrel thrust through. If she didn't carry out the man's orders, he would plug her and the conductor, too.

With some grunting and not a little bit of straining, she worked the fallen man's body down the metal steps. His arm—she hoped it was his arm and not his head—caught on something and he was abruptly yanked away. Zoe didn't have the heart to look around the train to see how he had fared. She might have contributed to the man's demise.

She might have *caused* his death.

"We're gettin' close to the depot, missy," the conductor said. "I'll let the marshal know what happened."

"We're a day's travel from Kansas City," she said. Seeing his reaction, she asked, "What do you know?"

"Jubilee Junction's where the first message for the treasure hunters is."

"But I thought—" Zoe cut off her statement. She had no idea what the rules to this race were, and had learned how the contestants changed them to suit themselves. Big Thom Carson had no qualms about killing. She thought she had found a savior when he had come up with the idea of a sudden stop throwing Calhoun and his gang out the open door. Now she knew he would have gunned them down if there had been a ghost of a chance of walking away alive. All Big Thom had been concerned about was the loss of the keys, not the possible injuries sustained by Calhoun and the others as they hit the ground.

"Will the treasure hunters remain aboard the train?" she asked.

"Don't know. I'm jist a train conductor. That's all I want to be."

Zoe let the man go back into the car. She started to follow, then thought better of it. She might know something Big Thom didn't. How she could use this to her benefit was a mystery, but she was a reporter and had to take any chance to get her story.

She slipped back into the car. Big Thom had settled down in the front seat. The rest of the men had all migrated to the rear to get as far from him as possible. Their instincts were better than hers when it came to recognizing a dangerous hombre. She stood, fists on her hips, glaring at Big Thom, when she said, "Now what?"

"Reckon you can ask more questions. I like the idea of bein' famous because you're writin' about me. Just spell the name right." He spelled out his name for her as she sat and dutifully entered it into her notebook.

Zoe chewed a little on the pencil tip since the lead had broken and was harder to write with legibly. She cried out in surprise when Big Thom grabbed the pencil from her and used a thick-bladed knife to sharpen it. He handed he pencil back. She tried to keep her hand from shaking too much as she accepted it from him.

"Where do you hail from, Mr. Carson?"

"You can call me Big Thom. You know the proper spelling. I don't come from much of anywhere. The notion of being from somewhere slows me up too much, so I keep movin' around."

"Are you a wanted man?"

"Will be 'fore this race is over, thanks to your stories," he said.

Zoe looked hard at him, wondering if he was lying. Then she decided he'd meant it. He was dangerous, and getting more so with every passing mile, but probably wasn't running from the law. Not yet.

"What do you intend to spend the fifty thousand dollars on if you win?"

"When I win," he said, correcting her. Big Thom got a dreamy expression and then said, "Hadn't thought much on it. See? You're bein' real useful to me, keepin' me focused on the task at hand. Well, there's booze and whores, of course. That much money in gold will buy a powerful lot of pussy." He laughed harshly and stared at her. "That much money'd buy *your* pussy, wouldn't it?"

"Do not be crude, sir."

He laughed. She realized he had intended to annoy her, to provoke some emotion. She wrote this down as an insight into his personality.

"Show me what you wrote about me."

"No, I can't do that," Zoe said, still writing furiously. A shadow moved across her notebook and she twisted away, to find herself pinned down against the wall of the car. She drew the notebook in and held it tightly against her body to keep Big Thom from grabbing it.

"You're writin' something evil about me, aren't you?"

Her eyes went wide with surprise. He was completely self-centered and irrational.

"Of course I'm writing about you, sir," she said, pushing her elbow into his gut. It felt as if she'd tried to move an iron wall. "But it's not evil. However could you get that idea?"

"Show me!"

The train whistle sounded and the engine began to slow. The passenger car creaked and protested the change in speed, and Big Thom flopped back into the seat on the far side of the aisle. He glared at her with what she took to be pure insanity. The crazy light faded, and he laughed.

"You're a piece of work, Miss Reporter. Too bad this is the end of the line for you."

Zoe tried to speak, but her mouth had turned to cotton. Her heart hammered, and her brain refused to function. He was going to kill her!

"Jubilee Junction!" bellowed the conductor. "All those taking part in Colonel J. Patterson Turner's Transcontinental Race git off here. Find the clue that'll git you on to your next stop. End of the line for the colonel's racers!" The conductor gave Zoe a meaningful look that pinned her to her seat.

Big Thom Carson pushed past the conductor and vanished through the door before Zoe could say a word. She began gathering her things, such as they were.

"Help me, please," she called to the conductor. She was caught in the rush of racers getting off the train to find the first clue that would put them on the road to riches. "My baggage!"

"Missy, you don't want to go followin' these folks," the conductor said, his dark face caught in a frown.

"I appreciate your attempt to look after me, but I *must* go. It's my job."

"You must be daft, missy, after what that one made you—us—do," the conductor said, pointing to the seat where Big

Thom had been. "You get cross of him, and he'll kill you and never notice."

"Oh, he'd notice," Zoe said. "He'd complain about how much the bullet cost."

"Sounds like you known him purty good, missy." The conductor shook his head as he pulled down her lone bag and swung it around for her. "We will be leavin' Jubilee Junction in ten minutes. If you know what's good for you, you'll be sittin' right there where you are."

Zoe rummaged through her bag, then looked out at the station platform and muttered, "Oh, drat. There's no time!"

With that, she snapped the bag shut and ran to the door. She turned to wave good-bye to the conductor, but he had already gone back to the mail car. Heaving a sigh, she hopped down to the railroad platform and looked around for some clue to where the men had gone. The Jubilee Junction platform was virtually abandoned, and none of those from the train, including Big Thom Carson, was in sight.

She went to the station agent, a smallish man wearing spectacles but still squinting.

"Where'd they go?"

"They got horses waitin' fer 'em," he said, trying to get a better look at her. "Instructions in the saddlebags, from what I hear."

"Where are the horses?" Her mind raced. So many of the men had been tossed off the train, at least one horse had to be available—one for her.

"Around the other side of the station. You one of the racers?"

"I'm with Big Thom Carson," she said. The station agent looked blank. The name meant nothing to him. "The horses," she said. "Are they fully provisioned?"

"You mean, is there vittles in them saddlebags? I was paid to provide it, and by jiminy, I did. I—"

He spoke to thin air. Zoe jumped to the ground, not bothering with the four steps down from the platform, and ran to the far side of the station. Only one horse remained. The racers had taken more than one each, she suspected, to prevent others from following. She gentled the horse as it stood nervously, fastened her bag over the saddlebags, and then clumsily mounted. It had been some time since she had ridden, but the basics were universal.

She started the horse at a walk, and then moved its gait faster until it trotted along, used to having her astride. As she rode, Zoe quickly realized that the colonel had given different instructions to each racer. It seemed that no two went in the same direction.

Just when she despaired of figuring out which direction Big Thom had ridden in, and was trying to decide if she shouldn't just follow another rider, the report from a handgun came rolling across the prairie. If she had a brain in her head, she would have ridden in another direction, but then, if she had any sense, she would never have wanted to be a reporter.

Galloping ahead, she topped a rise and saw what she had expected. Big Thom had gunned down another racer, and was searching the body for another golden key.

He spotted her as she made her way down the hill, heading directly for him.

"Wait, Big Thom, don't!" she cried, but the man vaulted into the saddle and galloped away.

She wasn't as accomplished a rider as Big Thom Carson, but she found herself slowly overtaking him. Then he simply disappeared. Zoe drew rein and looked around, wondering where he had gotten off to on the flat plain.

The glint of sunlight off the front sight of a rifle poking up over the lip of a ravine was all the warning she had before a bullet came arrowing in her direction.

8

Slocum coughed, rolled onto his side, and then spat out a mouthful of dirt. He wiped at his eyes and got more dirt from his face. Every bone in his body aching, he sat up and tried to look around. Panic seized him when he saw nothing. Then he calmed as he realized he sat in a deep hole with the only light coming down through a narrow opening high above him. With his hand pressed against the dirt wall, he got to his feet and braced himself until the dizziness passed. He brushed off as much filth as he could from his clothing, then got around to seeing what had happened to him.

At first, he thought he had fallen into a trap, but it looked more as if he had broken through a thin layer of dirt over an underground chamber dug out by flowing water. When the water went away—where, he could not say—the underground river had probably dried up during the drought, leaving this cavity behind. The people in the town had moved on and nobody had tromped hard enough on the dirt trapdoor to fall through—until Slocum had blundered onto it.

It took only a few seconds to realize he could never

71

climb out of the hole. The sides of the shaft were muddy, and refused to take his weight when he dug his toes into them. He stepped back and looked up at the thin sliver of bright blue sky ten feet over his head. Jumping up would gain him nothing but exhaustion. Shouting for help would only attract unwanted attention and make him hoarse. The men who had taken Harry Ibbotson weren't likely to offer any help more than taking a few shots at him, just for the hell of it.

Slocum took off his hat and slapped it against his leg. Getting a bullet in the head might be better than dying in a ready-made grave like this.

"It was a river," he said, putting the hat back on. "It came from somewhere and went somewhere in the opposite direction."

This buoyed his spirits and gave him some hope. Not much, but enough to get him to explore the pit in directions other than straight up to the phantom promise of freedom offered by the sliver of Missouri sky.

He clawed at the sides of the pit, and when a section of wall fell to his feet in a minor mud slide, he found a dark tunnel stretching beyond his sight. Slocum lit a lucifer and studied in the momentary flare the only hope for his escape. A cold knot formed in his belly. The channel cut by the underground river was hardly larger than his shoulders, was muddy, and ran for who knows how long. For all Slocum could see, the underground river might never have surfaced anywhere as it cut under the prairie. He could crawl into the darkness and never find a way out.

A quick breath settled his nerves. Then he reached into the tunnel and began crawling. In the wet. In the dark. For what seemed an eternity. The slippery floor impeded his advance, and for all he knew, he had been struggling along like a human worm and getting nowhere. Panic rose, but Slocum forced it down. He was stronger than his own fear.

More than once, he had been in dire circumstances and had gotten out alive. He would this time.

From what might be his grave.

New fears arose. The mud had not dried, meaning water had flowed through the channel recently. The thunderstorm could have fed it, and if another raced across the prairie, new water might fill the tunnel and drown him. He wiggled along a little faster. The only way he could prevent that was to get free as fast as he could.

When chunks of the tunnel roof began falling down ahead of him, Slocum did cry out in fear. He was going to be buried alive. In the dark and wet, and die and—

A huge chunk collapsed in front of him and filled his nose and mouth with dirt. For a moment, he didn't realize what new element had been added to his plight. Then he spat mud and cried out in joy. He began clawing his way upward, a hot wind against his face. Slocum burst through the ground and exploded onto the prairie, coated with mud and laughing at his escape.

The underground river had run less than a foot beneath the dried dirt at this point, and his passage had disturbed the tenuous roof enough to free him.

He sat and shook for a moment, then laughed again and began scraping off the filth that caked him. When he stood and looked around, the cold fear that had seized him underground returned. He thought he had been struggling along for hours and had gone miles. But the edge of the ghost town lay less than a hundred feet away.

Slogging back with mud falling from him with every step, Slocum got to the nearest tumbledown building and cautiously looked around. Ibbotson's kidnappers had to be somewhere nearby. He kept a sharp eye out for Molly, too, but nothing moved in the town save a vagrant wind pushing dead weeds down the streets.

Exploring the town had to be done with one eye on the

ground. Slocum didn't want to tumble down into another sinkhole. Getting out a second time might be impossible. After a half hour of searching, Slocum had discovered something else that was impossible: finding another living soul.

Circling the town, he found hoofprints leading to the southwest. The muddy ground held the prints, but also obscured the number of horses heading from town. More than a single rider, but other than that, he could not tell.

He drew his Colt Navy, went into a crouch, and had his six-shooter aimed when he heard movement behind him. Slocum relaxed when his own horse snorted and shook its head.

"Come on over here," he said softly, holstering his six-shooter and holding out his hand to the horse. The animal nickered and shook its head again, but did not run off. Slocum took the reins and spent a few more minutes gentling the horse. Wherever it had run off to had saved it from being stolen by Ibbotson's kidnappers.

Slocum swung into the saddle, headed on the trail after the riders, and soon lost the spoor entirely. Stumped, he kept riding in the same direction, wondering why he bothered. He had a key in his pocket, but could trade it with another racer for a few dollars, maybe more. If the cutthroat situation he had seen aboard the train continued, only a few men would ever get to the finish line, and they would carry most of the keys. Some of the golden keys might be lost, but Slocum knew that wouldn't be a problem for men like those he had already faced. The colonel would have the choice of eating lead or handing over the gold. From Colonel Turner's standpoint, it hardly mattered if the key fit. All he wanted was publicity for his freight company.

How could any amount of publicity be worth men dying trying to claim the prize? The newspapers would never mention that, but it would rest heavy on the colonel's soul for all eternity. There were any number of men for whom such a burden would be light and almost meaningless. Colonel Turner might be one of them.

"Hell, probably is," Slocum muttered. "He thought up this damned cockfight."

He reached a double-rutted road long overgrown with weeds. This gave the first hint where the riders had gone. The crushed weeds still directed him toward the southwest. He had instinctively followed the kidnappers. As he rode, Slocum worked to clean his six-shooter. The Colt was a finely machined killing device and required maintenance that he had neglected. Wiping off the dirt and getting the grime out of the mechanism, he cocked it several times, listening to the action. Only when he was satisfied it operated with its usual smoothness did he return it to his holster and once more pay attention to the trail and the horizon where Ibbotson's kidnappers would likely be silhouetted.

Since he had not seen any trace of Molly, he guessed she had either been killed outright, or was also a prisoner of the gang that had snatched her brother. It didn't make a great deal of sense that any of the racers would kidnap another. Better to simply shoot Ibbotson and take his key.

There were too many things Slocum simply did not understand, and he was reaching the point where he didn't give two hoots and a holler. He felt obligated to find out what had happened to Molly and her brother, but more than that, he was tired, beaten up, and in no condition to continue with the race. He traced a finger over the key on his watch chain.

"A hundred dollars," he said. "I'll get a hundred for the damned key or to hell with it." Satisfied with this as a goal, Slocum rode on hunting for the other party on the prairie ahead of him. So intently was he looking for a tight knot of riders that he almost missed the man crouched in a ravine off to his left. The man's attention was directed away from Slocum as he sighted down the rifle barrel.

Slocum came to a halt and watched, wondering what was going on. A posse might be after an outlaw, who had finally been run to ground and had decided to make a stand. That was no concern of Slocum's.

The ambush suddenly became his concern when he saw the woman appear over a rise and then slowly ride directly into the sniper's rifle.

Slocum drew and aimed, not sure if he should fire. When the hidden gunman fired at the woman, Slocum got off three quick rounds. One hit the owlhoot smack in the back. He threw up his hands, bent at a crazy angle, and then flopped about for a few seconds before dying. Slocum's slug had busted his spine.

Slocum worked his horse down a steep incline into the ravine, and splashed through fetlock-deep water. The runoff had turned this ravine into a raging river, but the storm had passed and the water had quickly vanished, all but the few inches he sloshed through to reach the dead sniper.

Kicking free, he slid to the ground and went to the man. Slocum's eyes narrowed when a flash of gold caught his attention. He fumbled in the dead man's vest pocket and drew out a gold key.

"Another of the damned racers," he said to himself. Seeing that an outline of a key still poked against the wet vest, he ran his finger about and finally worried out a second key. He tucked both into his pocket to go with the one he already had just as the woman peered down from the lip of the ravine.

"Oh, no!" She covered her mouth with her hand and looked as if she might faint.

"He tried to kill you. I got him first. Why'd he want you dead?"

"He's—that's Big Thom Carson. I interviewed him."

"What?"

"I'm a reporter, and he was in Colonel Turner's race—it's all about—"

"Fifty thousand in gold. I know," Slocum said. "A woman paid me five hundred dollars to rescue her brother from kidnappers who took him because he had a gold key."

"I recognize you!" she blurted out.

"Reckon I'd remember you if we'd met," Slocum said. She wasn't as pretty as Molly Ibbotson, but she had a button nose and a fine-boned face. Her blond hair was in disarray, but this only made her all the prettier, giving her a wild look.

"We didn't meet. I saw you get off the train at the station."

"In Columbia," Slocum said.

"Yes, there, not at Jubilee Junction."

Slocum didn't understand what she was going on about. He grabbed a handful of the dead man's shirt and pulled him upright so he could lean against the muddy ravine wall.

"What are you doing?" she asked.

"Thinking on how to bury him without a shovel. You don't have a shovel with you, do you?"

"No, all I have is my bag and—" She bit off her sentence, took a deep breath, and started again. "I'm Zoe Murchison and I work for the *St. Louis Dispatch*, covering the colonel's race. That man, the dead one, is Big Thom Carson."

"Never heard of him," Slocum said, wondering how upset Miss Zoe Murchison would get if he stripped the body of everything useful. There wasn't a whole lot Big Thom was going to need, dead with a fractured spine and all.

"I met him on the train," she said. "When the racers got off in Jubilee Junction, I followed him, thinking he would make a good story."

"Don't know about Jubilee Junction."

"But you are one of them, the contestants."

"I was hired to rescue Molly Ibbotson's brother, who is one of them." He tried to keep the contempt he felt from his voice. From Zoe's expression, he knew he had failed. It didn't matter to him.

Not much did right now. He had barely escaped dying

back in the ghost town, and had no good feelings toward anyone. Slocum began stripping Big Thom of anything he might sell or use later. To his surprise, Zoe said nothing except, "His horse is tethered a few yards away. Should I fetch it?"

Slocum nodded, finished his plundering, and stepped back to study the matter. The rapidly flowing water had undercut the bank where he had propped Big Thom. He moved the man around so his body lay entirely hidden by the overhang.

He silently unfastened the lariat from the man's horse when Zoe led it over, got a decent loop, and then cast it upward to drop around a post oak on the bank, half its roots exposed by erosion.

"I see," Zoe said. "You're a very clever man, sir."

"John Slocum," he said, tying the other end of the rope to the saddle horn. He slapped the horse on the rump and got it tugging hard on the rope until the tree began to fall. When its roots popped free of the wet ground, it brought down a small avalanche of mud that buried Big Thom Carson completely.

"It's not much, but it's more than he deserved," she said. "I can't imagine why he wanted to shoot me. Yet he tried. That was a rifle bullet that came this close." Zoe held out her hands, indicating a distance of only a few inches.

"You get shot at enough to know the sound of a rifle bullet instead of a pistol round?"

"I'm not the hothouse flower you seem to think, Mr. Slocum."

"The sight of a dead man made you almost faint."

"It was the idea he had tried to kill me that I found . . . disconcerting. He had no cause!"

"Where's Jubilee Junction?"

"Back along a road, possibly ten miles or thereabouts," she said.

"We're going back. If there's a marshal in town, he can find Harry Ibbotson."

"Didn't you say his sister had paid you?"

Slocum pressed his fingers against the wad of greenbacks Molly Ibbotson had paid him, but the roll had been diminished by the purchase of the horse and gear. He might owe Molly what remained, but she could ask him for it. He wasn't going to get himself gunned down, not when every mother's son in Colonel J. Patterson Turner's Transcontinental Race was so intent on murdering their competition.

With two keys to sell, he might make as much as Molly had promised him and could pay her back. If she asked personally. Slocum wasn't feeling all that charitable at the moment.

"That the town?" Slocum pointed to a spiral of smoke rising, to be caught on a gentle breeze and smeared out across the sky. Another storm was building, but Slocum sniffed the air and didn't scent it. The smoke from the town made his nostrils flare slightly, and reminded him why it was good to return to civilization now and then. He caught more than a little hint of baking bread.

"Jubilee Junction," Zoe said.

They rode to the edge of a town still abuzz from having the colonel's race come through. Slocum saw a few familiar faces from the train and knew not everyone had gotten the clue to move on to the next station along the race course.

"Mister, hey mister, I'll give you a hundred dollars for your horse!" Slocum ignored the man. "Two hundred! I'm gonna win fifty thousand dollars, but I need a horse!"

"The ones off the train first must have stolen the others' horses," Zoe said. "I didn't realize how lucky I was finding this horse."

"It's one of the colonel's?"

She shrugged. Slocum hesitated, hoping she would repeat the gesture. She didn't.

"There must be a clue in the saddlebags," he said. "Did you look?"

"I was too intent on pursuing Big Thom, more's the pity.

He would have murdered me. Then I would never have been able to file my story."

"Why don't you go to the telegraph office and send your story?"

Zoe looked hard at him, then smiled a little. "You understand my need to succeed, don't you, Mr. Slocum?"

"We all hunt for gold in different ways."

They dismounted in front of the telegrapher's office. When Zoe went inside, Slocum searched through the saddlebags on her horse for the clue to finding the next stop along the course. The supplies were adequate for a week on the trail, but he was damned if he could find anything that even hinted at where to head next.

"I got it, mister," came a weak voice. "I got it."

Slocum turned slowly and saw a man hobbling along, his right leg splinted from ankle to thigh.

"I busted my damn fool leg and can't ride. Hell, I can hardly walk."

"Too bad," Slocum said, not really caring.

"I took it."

"What?"

"I took this," the man said, leaning heavily against the side of the telegraph office. He held up an envelope. "It's got the instructions on where to ride."

"You're telling me for a reason."

"Buy it from me. I can't ride. There's no way I can get to the treasure chest first, not with a busted-up leg. Doc says I ought to keep weight off it for a few weeks to let it heal. Otherwise, I'll seize up and be a gimp for the rest of my life."

"Show me your key," Slocum said suddenly. The demand took the man by surprise. He started to protest, then grinned.

"You're a smart one, I'll give you that. You want to be sure I didn't just scribble down something to sell."

"Something like that."

Slocum watched the man fish out a gold key and hold it out so it caught a vagrant ray of sunlight. The storm moved in again. This time, Slocum smelled the familiar tang of moisture in air.

"Yeah, rain on the way," the man confirmed. "If you want to catch up with the rest, you'll have to get on the trail before it rains again. Real drenching rain in these parts." The man held up both the key and the envelope. "Two hundred dollars."

"Too much."

"For both. Key and instructions. The key's not doing me any good. Who knows, it might be the one that opens the colonel's strongbox. You'd be rich."

"Too much," Slocum said. He played enough poker to know when a man was desperate enough to make mistakes.

"A hundred. It's worth more 'n that. You gotta admit that."

"Who'd buy it? Everyone else has left."

"The town's full of men willing to join the race here."

"The colonel knows who started the race. Only the ones on the train from St. Louis can win." Slocum had told a bald-faced lie to gauge the man's gullibility. Since he had joined the race on the spur of the moment after winning his key from a river man only hours before, he doubted the colonel knew who had boarded the train. For Colonel Turner's purpose, anyone winning gave him the publicity he needed for the Turner Haulage Company.

"I didn't know that." The man pursed his lips, then said, "Cut me in. I'll sell you the instructions and the key for fifty dollars and you give me two hundred—*five* hundred if you win."

"What's your name?"

"Morrisey. Ned Morrisey," the man said. "I'll go back to St. Louis and you can get the money to me there."

Slocum drew a soggy wad of greenbacks from his pocket and counted out fifty dollars. Seeing that Morrisey wasn't able to come to him, Slocum went to Morrisey and handed over the scrip. Morrisey licked his lips, counted the money, and with some reluctance handed Slocum both key and envelope.

"Good luck," he said. "You're in the race for both of us."

Slocum slipped the key into his pocket and fingered the envelope, remembering how he had intended to chuck it all and go on his way. For all he knew, his intended path might have been the same as that detailed in the instruction letter.

9

"There," Zoe Murchison said, folding a flimsy sheet of yellow paper as she emerged from the telegraph office. "My story is sent." She stopped and looked around, then frowned. "Where did you go, Mr. Slocum? Mr. Slocum!"

"You lookin' for the gent who was out here a few minutes ago?"

"I am, sir," Zoe said, eyeing the man with the splinted leg. "Did you see where he got off to?"

"Not to take a leak, that's for certain sure."

"Really, sir." She drew herself up and started away.

"He bought the instructions."

This stopped Zoe in her tracks. She stared straight ahead for a heartbeat, then turned slowly to face the man, who hobbled out and caught himself on a hitching post.

"Which instructions might those be?"

"You're that lady reporter covering the race. I saw you on the train and overheard some of what you said to that ugly galoot Carson."

"Big Thom Carson, yes, what about him?"

"Bad company to keep, ma'am, if you don't mind me sayin' so."

"I'm sure that will not be a problem in the future. What instructions?"

"Do all reporters have a one-track mind?" The man hobbled a bit more and perched against the rail. "You know that all the racers got instructions on where to go next. Except you since you took that horse."

"I did, and there were no instructions . . . you took them!"

"I certainly did, and I sold them to your friend, the one you're lookin' around for. What'd you call him? Slocum?"

"Where is he?"

"He bought the instructions I took from those very saddlebags and rode on out like his tail was on fire."

She tried not to grind her teeth in anger, and failed. How could she have trusted John Slocum, actually believed him when he said he wasn't interested in the reward at the end of the colonel's race? He was like all the others. Worse! He had stolen what was rightly hers since she had picked this horse from the colonel's remuda without knowing the new directions were missing.

"You stole them, he bought them. Where is he?" She didn't try to keep from snapping out the words so they cracked like a whip. Even her harsh tone didn't make the man cower. If anything, he laughed at her.

"For a few more dollars, I can tell you what the letter in that white envelope said."

"You read it, of course."

"I'm no simpleton. Of course I did. I resealed the envelope so it would look like it was all pure as the wind-driven snow when I found someone to buy it. Like your friend, Slocum."

"He is no friend. What's the letter say?"

"Fifty dollars might jog my memory."

Zoe stepped closer, put her hand on the man's shoulder, and then kicked him as hard as she could in his injured leg.

He let out a howl of pain and collapsed to the ground, where he writhed around in the mud.

"What'd you go and do a thing like that for?"

"I will pay you five dollars to tell me what I need to know. That's only fair."

"Go to hell!"

She kicked him again. This time she had her left foot securely planted, and delivered a painful kick just above the knee. He turned pale with pain.

"I'll get the damn marshal and have you arrested!"

"Go on. I'm a reporter. I'll promise the marshal a front page story that'll make him famous. Who's he likely to listen to, a no-account like you or a pretty lady reporter?" Zoe reached up to her neck and unfastened a button to show just a hint of her snowy white throat. A second button opened and more skin appeared. A third button made the view even more interesting.

"Stop, I understand. You wouldn't do that to me! Have me arrested?"

"Fifty dollars? Is that what Slocum paid you?" She smiled crookedly when he nodded. "I'll give you odds of ten to one against that sum that I *will* have you arrested and see you rotting in jail for the next five years."

"West. The instructions said to ride west until he came to a crossroads. There's a lightning-struck stump with new directions there."

"How far is this crossroads?"

"I don't know. Honest!" He slithered away in the mud as she moved toward him. "That's all it said. I don't know how far. Could be an hour or a day. Ask around town. Somebody here has to know about crossroads and stumps."

"Thank you," Zoe said primly. She slowly buttoned her blouse all the way up the neck, then took her horse's reins and led it away. She fumed at how Slocum had treated her. She needed him for her story, but if he had ridden away as he did, she would just find another racer and write his story.

That'd show John Slocum a thing or two. He had just passed up a chance to be famous.

She walked along the boardwalk, but after the rain there was hardly any difference between the wood planking and the middle of the sloppy street. She finally realized how difficult and time-consuming it was for her to walk along the boardwalk and move the reins from one hand to another to get around posts holding up dubious overhangs. Securing the reins at the corner of the dry goods store, she went inside, taking great care to use the boot scraper to get the mud from her shoes.

"Hello," said the woman behind the counter. She gave Zoe a quick once-over, starting at her shoes, moving up, and then returning to her shoes. "Thank you for taking the effort to remove the mud. It sticks so on our floor."

"I know," Zoe said, swinging into a story from her childhood about having to clean up mud from her mother's kitchen floor. By the time she had finished, the clerk had offered her some tea.

"Warms the body, it does," the woman said. "Since you're not from around here, you must have left the train with all those ruffians."

"I did," Zoe said. "It has been quite harrowing dealing with them, I must say."

They exchanged a few more words and then Zoe asked, "If I ride due west from Jubilee Junction, how far is it to the first crossroads?"

"Crossroads? My, you'd have to go ten miles or more," the woman said, sipping at her tea. "The road north goes to Benedict and south, why, it is a goodly thirty miles to Camp Larrup. That's the closest cavalry post to Jubilee Junction, so we rely on the telegraph and the train to bring any help we might need."

"Help against Indians? Are they a problem?"

"The Sioux are a constant thorn in our sides," the clerk said. "Time was, nobody was safe going out alone. My husband, rest his soul, was shot and scalped almost on this very doorstep."

"Recently?" Zoe wondered if she might get another story to go along with that of the colonel's race. Her hope faded when the woman answered.

"Seems like yesterday, but it was nigh on six years back. I've run this store all by myself since then."

"You're doing an admirable job of keeping yourself together," Zoe said, putting down the cup. "I appreciate your company, but I really must be on my way."

"Interest you in some gingham? No? A lady such as yourself would appreciate a yard of fine Irish lace."

Zoe chafed at the delay, but let the store owner show her some fine linen. She made appropriate compliments on the quality, and eventually worked her way out of the store. As she stepped into the street, she turned and hid her face from the tight knot of men slogging along through the mud. Only when they had passed did she stare after Sid Calhoun and his gang.

A crazy thought hit her that she might interview Calhoun or one of his men about their steadfast determination to continue with the transcontinental race. She stopped and swallowed hard when she saw how the men spread out. She overheard Calhoun as he choked a man who had come from the saloon and slammed him hard against a wall.

"I need to know where they went. The racers."

"Don't know," Calhoun's victim rasped out. "All gone, 'cept—"

"Except? Who's left?"

"Guy named Morrisey. Ned Morrisey. He busted up his leg and dropped out, but he had the directions. I swear he did!"

Calhoun dropped the man, who sank to the boardwalk as if his legs had turned to water.

"Boys! Find me an owlhoot named Morrisey. You'll recognize him. He was on the train with us."

Zoe stepped back and tried to become invisible as one of Calhoun's henchmen stomped by, spattering mud as he came. He barely glanced in her direction. Zoe wasn't sure if she ought to be offended or thankful. She was filthy from riding all over the muddy prairie and almost getting shot, and her hair must be a fright, but she wasn't in that sorry a condition that he wouldn't give her a second look.

Then she had to admit how much trouble would befall her if Calhoun did spot her. He might take it into his head that she knew where the instructions had sent the racers—and she did, because she had gotten the information from a man she assumed was this Ned Morrisey.

"Found him, Boss," bellowed a man not far from the telegraph station.

Zoe watched in horror as the gunman dragged Morrisey into the middle of the street and threw him facedown in the mud. The crippled man sputtered and tried to sit up, but a heavy boot to the back of his neck caused him to blow bubbles in the mud puddle. She almost rushed to his aid. He would drown in the mud if he wasn't allowed to breathe.

Zoe stopped beside her horse when she saw Calhoun and the rest of his gang converging. It was like ants to a picnic and they had found the chocolate cake.

"So you know where the rest of them have gone, eh? Where?"

"I got paid to—" That was all Morrisey got out before being forced back into the mud. Calhoun's intent was clear. Either Morrisey told him what he wanted to know or he would die in the middle of Jubilee Junction's main street.

Zoe looked around for a lawman, but saw no one. The foul weather and the promise of more rain had driven everyone indoors. Quietly, she led her horse away, and mounted only when she thought none of Calhoun's gang would see her. She walked the horse toward the western edge of town, stopping only when she saw the town marshal's office. A growing apprehension spread within her. She knew that

Morrisey would eventually tell Calhoun what he wanted to know—he might have already done so. It would be only a matter of time before the gang got horses, either by intimidation or outright theft, and rode west to the crossroads.

Where John Slocum would be.

Zoe was still irked at him for leaving her the way he did, but she had no wish to see him injured. He had, after all, saved her from being shot from ambush. It wasn't as if she owed him anything, because she hadn't asked to be saved, but he had done it at risk to his own life. Big Thom might have seen him and turned the rifle on him.

She owed him. But she wasn't going to write about him and make him famous. She still had some pride left.

Swinging her leg over the saddle, she dropped to the ground and sloshed to the door of the town marshal's office. She pounded on it until a sleepy-eyed man with thinning hair and a potbelly that drooped over his gun belt opened the door.

"What's wrong? The whole town ain't burnin', is it?"

"They're killing him. Poor Mr. Morrisey! They are killing him in the middle of the street." Zoe pointed so the still sleepy marshal wouldn't get too confused.

"Who the hell's Morrisey? Ain't nobody by that name lives here."

"He . . . he's a famous land speculator from St. Louis," she said, amazed at how easily the lie came to her lips. "He's going to offer everyone in town a huge amount of money for their property, but Sid Calhoun wants to steal it all. Oh, please, save Mr. Morrisey, Marshal. Hurry, before it's too late."

"Land speculator? Buy land? I got land outside of town that'd be worth a young fortune to the right buyer."

"Then you won't want to see him injured. He might change his mind if he's too badly beat up."

"Consarn it, nobody whales away on visitors from St. Louis, not in Marshal Caleb Wright's town!" He hitched up his gun belt and waddled away, so bowlegged Zoe got a good view of the ground between his knees.

She waited a few seconds to make sure the marshal wasn't going to reconsider, then mounted and rode from town as fast as she could go.

After a couple miles, her horse began to flag. Zoe slowed to a walk, knowing time was of the essence. Ten miles, the owner of the millinery shop had said. She had to reach the spot and figure where John Slocum had gone from there.

Then she drew rein and sat as still as a statue. Behind her, Sid Calhoun and his gang would be riding out anytime now. But ahead, she saw a dozen Sioux, all painted up for war and riding out of a ravine onto the road she followed. She was sandwiched between two bands of savages and had nowhere to run.

10

"Don't they ever stop arguing?" Harry Ibbotson huddled in on himself, wet and angry. "They're driving me crazy."

"As long as they argue, they aren't bothering us," Molly said. She strained against the ropes binding her hands behind her back, but the strands had gotten wet during the rain and were now drying and tightening on her wrists. She flexed her fingers to get circulation back, but this didn't work as well as she had hoped.

"You mean they haven't killed us yet because they want to kill each other more."

"That, too," Molly said. "How many keys do they have?"

"Ours," Harry said. "I think a couple others."

Molly looked around. The sun had set hours earlier, forcing the three men who had kidnapped her brother to huddle closer to the fire. They left their prisoners some distance away to shiver in the dark. For the moment, Molly was glad to do just that. Being closer to the fire meant being closer to the trio. She finally flopped onto her back, in spite of the way this tortured her hands and shoulders. The stars should

91

have told her the time and where they were, but she knew nothing about such things.

"That's the Big Dipper," her brother said. "When we left that abandoned town, we rode northwest."

"They're keeping us alive because we know something."

"They weren't on the train. I heard one say they were riding back from Jubilee Junction, intending to find people like me who got thrown off the train."

"That's not too bright," Molly said. "Anyone getting thrown off the train would have their keys stolen first."

"They aren't the sharpest knives in the drawer, Molly. Listen to them."

"They've got us all trussed up. So who're the stupid ones?" She wiggled about and found what she wanted poking into the small of her back. The sharp-edged rock buried in the ground proved exactly the tool needed to cut the ropes on her hands. It took a considerable amount of doing, and her shoulders felt as if they were ready to pop from their sockets, but the sudden pain in her hands told her that blood had rushed back.

Rolling onto her side, she let the circulation return. She didn't tell Harry right away she was free. He would blurt out something that would bring the kidnappers down on their heads, or try some fool stunt that would land them in even worse trouble. She knew. She had spent her life bailing Harry out of jails and paying off his debts to men who would kill him.

"We got three of the damn letters," one kidnapper complained. "They're all different. What do we do?"

"There's three of us. Split up," suggested the quiet one sitting on the far side of the fire. Molly watched him the closest since the other two had their backs to their prisoners. This was the one who might have an ounce of brains and was in the best position to see that she had escaped.

"We agreed when we teamed up. All or nothing," said the third.

"Afraid I might get the gold and not share it?"

"Damn straight! I don't trust either of you as far as I can throw you!"

"We don't have to trust each other, just get the gold and divvy it up."

"There's still the three different sets of instructions," pointed out the thoughtful one. "What do we do about that? We can't pick one, and all of us follow the directions."

"Why not?"

"There's a better chance one of the other two we didn't pick was right."

"Then we should pick one of them!"

The argument flared, but Molly caught the gist of it, and realized why she and Harry were still alive. The three owlhoots had learned that Jubilee Junction had the first set of directions, and had gone directly there and found the various instructions. Somehow, they thought she or Harry knew which set was right.

"They're gonna kill us, I know it, I know it," moaned Harry.

"Hush up. They need us, but we can fool them. You follow my lead and don't contradict anything I say."

"Molly, you can be such a bitch."

"Quiet!"

The three men came over, one lightly prodding Harry in the ribs with his toe.

"You awake? We got to know something."

"What?" Molly asked. "And why should we tell you anything? You've got us all tied up and kidnapped us."

"Wouldn't have taken you if you hadn't come along after him."

"Which of the three instructions is right?" demanded the thoughtful one. From the deep frown creasing his forehead, he was not happy with the other two men.

"Why do you think we know?" Molly asked.

"Not you, him." The man prodded Harry with his toe.

"We heard things 'fore we left St. Louis, and he matches the description."

"What description?" Harry asked.

"You was the only one on the train wearing a brown coat."

"There was another—" Harry grunted when Molly kicked him.

"What's he supposed to know?" she said loudly to drown out Harry's protests at her behavior.

"All three of these directions can't be right. The colonel didn't have that kind of preparation, so he set all but a third of the racers on the wrong trail. I think he doesn't want anyone to win. He wants everyone asking around the countryside and stirrin' up interest in his damned company. Might be he has a shill waiting to claim the prize when everyone is all lost and turned around and confused."

Molly bit her lip as she considered this. It made sense. Why would any businessman offer $50,000, no matter what publicity he got, when he could keep the money for himself by having a confederate claim it?

"How do you know there even is any gold?" she asked.

One man came to her and started to rear back and kick her, but the thoughtful one stopped him.

"Easy. We saw the money. The colonel loaded it on a train headed west a couple weeks ago. We tried to steal it, but he had it too well guarded, so we decided to win it fair and square."

"Only you don't know which trail to follow," Molly finished for him.

"Something like that."

"How'd you learn that Harry knows?"

"Molly!" Harry Ibbotson was outraged at her words.

"We overheard the colonel talkin' with somebody wearin' a brown coat. Didn't see him, but this one's got to be him."

"You'll have to tell them, Harry, so they'll let us go."

"No."

"Harry, remember what I said?" To their kidnappers she said, "Show him the three letters so he can be sure."

"Just tell us."

"I . . . I have to see them," Harry said, finally getting the idea. "Put them into my hands so I can feel them, read them, and choose which one's right."

The trio argued some more, then cut the ropes on Harry's wrists. Molly wanted to laugh in glee, but held back her triumph. The three men circled Harry, eyes on him alone as he held up the sheets of paper and read by starlight. From the way his lips moved, Molly knew he was actually reading the different instructions.

"Which is right? You know. The colonel told you."

Harry shook his head and fumbled with the papers some more, turning away from his sister. This gave Molly the chance she needed. Her quick fingers lifted the nearest kidnapper's six-shooter from its holster. The man was so intent on what Harry had to say about the three letters that he never noticed. Molly moved fast now, coming to her feet and reaching out just as the smart one turned. She shoved him hard, lunged, and got his six-gun from its holster before he could regain his balance.

She tossed one pistol to her brother and leveled the other.

"Move a muscle and I'll kill you," she said. Her tone of voice told the outlaw she was not joking.

"It's hard to shoot a man in cold blood," he said. "You up to it?"

The recoil from the .44 knocked Molly back a pace, but it killed her target. She spun, fired, and winged the still-armed third outlaw. He yelped like a stuck pig and scuttled off into the darkness. She fired three more times, holding back with the final round in case she needed it.

Harry still had the drop on the remaining outlaw.

"What do we do with him?"

"Look, mister, lady, this wasn't nuthin' personal," the

man babbled. "We just wanted the money. That's a power-ful lot of gold to tempt men as weak as us."

"Shoot him." The words hardly cleared her perfectly formed lips when Harry squeezed the trigger. The round caught the man in the heart. He let out a tiny grunt as he died, and then there was nothing. The only sound was a slight wind and the distant rumble of thunder as another storm threatened.

"What about the one that got away?"

"Let him go," Molly decided. She pawed through the pockets of the two dead kidnappers and found a pair of keys.

"He might have more," said Harry.

"I doubt it. The one I drilled was their leader. The others spent all their time blowing smoke, but this one had some deep thoughts." She searched him a second time and took a few dollars in greenbacks from him. Harry had already finished with the man he had gunned down, and had a palm heaped with silver coins.

"Not much," he said. "We should go after the other fel-low."

"No," Molly said. "We've got bigger fish to fry. Show me the letters."

Harry had dropped them. It took a minute to recover the three sets of instructions. He and Molly went to the fire to better see the contents.

"You watch for the one that lit out," Molly said, "while I study these."

Harry muttered something about being nothing more than a hired hand, then positioned himself where he could get off a shot if the survivor returned to take some venge-ance. After a few minutes, he asked his sister, "What do you think?"

"They might all be real," she said. "One says we ought to go to a crossroads and look for a tree that's been hit by lightning, but another sends the rider to an army fort."

"No!" Harry said forcefully. "I don't show my face there."

"You think the army cares about deserters?"

"I'm not taking the chance."

"No, no need for that," Molly said thoughtfully. "This one directs the reader to a town named Benedict. From what I remember, the town is placed about right to be reached by either of the other two locations. It might be the colonel wanted his racers scattered about on small side trips but always close to one spot."

"Benedict?"

"It looks like our best bet," Molly said. "If we ride hard, we can reach it by morning."

"You sure about that?"

"Here's a map they spread out and marked. If this is the ghost town where they caught me, then Benedict isn't more than a half dozen miles off."

"We can go to Jubilee Junction and see if there are other letters," Harry said.

"Benedict," Molly said firmly. "That's where we'll head. Right now."

11

Slocum looked around the crossroads, keeping his horse from crow-hopping on him as he twisted about. A signpost pointed south toward an army camp and north to a town named Benedict. Straight ahead, the road stretched as straight as an arrow until it vanished in the mist a couple miles away. He looked all around for a stump burned down by lightning, but saw nothing.

He fleetingly considered simply continuing west. The race was a foolish idea and too many had died already. Thoughts of Molly Ibbotson and her brother flashed through his brain, and he felt some qualms about simply leaving them to their fate, but he saw no way to track them across the Missouri plains. Once he had lost their tracks in the muddy ground, their kidnappers could have taken them most anywhere.

Leaving Zoe Murchison behind in Jubilee Junction also wore a bit on him, but not as much. She was in no danger, and would eventually give up on her notion of reporting on the race.

"Which way?" His horse turned about and then headed

99

south. Slocum didn't stop it because this was as good a direction as any. The army camp might provide some diversion since the post sutler always held a poker game for the soldiers. Slocum had yet to meet a private or corporal who knew odds. If he stayed out of games with sergeants and officers, he could add to the poke he had gained since leaving St. Louis.

He had ridden less than five minutes when he tugged on the reins and brought the horse to a halt. His sharp eyes fixed on the twisted tree a dozen yards off the road. Standing in his stirrups, he looked around to see if anyone else had discovered the lightning-struck tree and now galloped toward it.

No one.

Riding within a few yards, he dismounted and let the reins drag so the horse wouldn't run off. The tree had once stood tall and proud, but now lay in burned pieces. The trunk had exploded when the lightning bolt had struck, maybe a year back from what Slocum could tell of termites chewing at the wood, and had sent boiling sap in all directions. The grasses had long since grown back, but the slower-growing bushes were hardly ankle high, making it appear as if someone had scraped clean a large circle.

He went to the tree, and immediately saw a metal cylinder stuck into a crevice. It took some doing to yank it free and unscrew the cap. Inside was a single sheet of paper.

Stone cairn. To the north.

Slocum held the paper up so the sun shone through the page to be sure someone hadn't altered the message. This appeared to be the original message, although he held out the possibility that the original note had been replaced. A gut feeling told him that probably wasn't so.

He considered taking the note, but it appealed more to him to send anyone else finding this on a wild-goose chase. Carefully tearing the paper, he left it with the cryptic message:

Stone cairn.

He crumpled up the part he had torn free and stuffed it into his pocket before carefully replacing the remaining part of the note into the cylinder and putting the cylinder back in the crevice. A quick vault into the saddle, and he headed away from the army post and back to the cross-roads. From there, he trotted on, wary of someone lying in ambush. He finally realized how nervous he had become, and for what? If it had been Colonel Turner's intent to send out fifty men to kill one another, he had a ways to go before he succeeded. If he wanted them all jumping at shadows, he had succeeded with John Slocum.

"The cairn," he said with some satisfaction, finding it less than a mile north of the crossroads. Examining it, he found a duplicate metal cylinder, but the note inside simply read:

Benedict.

He was on the right road. He was sure of it. As he trotted along, the lure of $50,000 kept rising to torment him. It was just a little farther down the road. To the west. To the north. A couple more hours of riding. Beyond his reach.

Slocum looked all around, and decided he alone had found the messages and knew where to seek out the next set of instructions. If he got to Benedict first, he could scoop up all the letters and burn them. Or he might sit back, sell them to the racers as they trickled through, and chuck the entire race and still make a few dollars from it. There was plenty of time for him to decide since a signpost told him Benedict was close to fifteen more miles down the road. If he kept a steady pace, he could reach the town by sundown.

"John! John! Danger!"

He jerked around in the saddle, his keen eyes hunting for the source of the outcry. It took him a couple seconds to realize the warning didn't come from behind on the road but to the southeast. Sunlight glinted off a silver bracelet as the distant rider waved frantically.

He had seen that bracelet before. Around Zoe Murchison's wrist. She had followed him and now intended on tagging along.

He started to gallop off as if he hadn't heard her, but again she shouted, "Indians! Ahead of us!"

Slocum considered that she might lie to slow him, but a quaver in her voice warned him she wasn't acting. He turned his horse's face and rode toward her. They met five minutes later at the foot of a small hill.

"Never expected to see you again," he said.

"You rode off and left me," she said angrily. Then the anger faded, replaced by real fear. "I saw them. Sioux. They had on war paint and were riding in this direction. If we keep going, they'll find us for sure."

"Describe them," Slocum said, thinking she had made it up. After she finished a complete and surprisingly accurate description of a Sioux war party, he said, "Did you read that or did you see them? That's a powerful lot of detail to take in when a brave's waggling a coup stick about."

"I am trained to remember details. I don't know how many there were, but at least two dozen."

Slocum said nothing. That, too, was about right for a war party. The way they had painted their faces and their horses told him it wasn't a hunting party. Some chief had a bug up his ass and had gone on the warpath.

"There's a fort to the south," he said. "Ride there and let the commander know what you saw."

"You're going on, aren't you? To Benedict. Is that where the next clue is?"

"You want to get that pretty blond head of yours scalped? If you don't, ride south right now."

"I'm staying with you."

"Why?"

"You're my story. Indians go off the reservation all the time. People are bored with stories about atrocities, scalpings, and torture by the red heathens. The colonel's race is a front-page article."

"You've been out in the sun too long," Slocum said. "Or eating locoweed. No story's worth getting an arrow in your back."

"I don't intend to die out here, Mr. Slocum. I intend to file the story before anything like that happens."

"You called me John before."

This took Zoe aback. Her mouth opened and then snapped shut. Slocum had finally found something to turn off the flood of words that gushed from her like some artesian dictionary.

"We're safe enough here, but we'd be safer if we got to Benedict," he said. "The Indians won't attack an entire town with only twenty or so braves."

"I might have seen only a small fraction of them." Zoe looked over her shoulder, back in the direction of Jubilee Junction. "There's something else."

"Who's on your trail?"

"I rode out ahead of Calhoun and his gang. They have it in for you, and I wanted to warn you. Then I saw the Sioux."

Slocum felt as if he were caught in a vise with the Sioux on one side and Calhoun on the other. He wasn't sure which was worse. He touched the keys in his vest pocket and knew he had some leverage with Calhoun. The murdering swine would want the golden keys. The Indians wouldn't. That hardly mattered because Calhoun would kill him after he got the keys.

"Why's he after me?"

"He tried to kill a man with a splinted leg who said you knew where the next clue was." Zoe scowled, deep in thought. "I think he killed Mr. Morrisey, but I didn't examine the body to find out. A reporter is always precise. It wouldn't do writing that Sid Calhoun killed a man when he didn't."

"If Morrisey's not dead by Calhoun's hand, he might be the first to escape that fate," Slocum said. "I don't know him, but I suspect Calhoun has left a long trail of dead bodies behind him."

"What of you, John?" The question was so softly asked Slocum barely heard it over the thunder.

"I'm going to need to do some killing if I'm right."

"About what?"

Slocum silently pointed to several jackrabbits hightailing it from the north. The only thing that could spook so many was the war party. A single coyote or wolf would chase only one rabbit, leaving the rest to hide or go on their way. These were being driven.

He motioned to her to follow as he headed back toward the road. A rider there was exposed, but also had a better view of the terrain all around. Slocum needed to scout if he wanted to get to Benedict alive. Not for the first time since he had left Jubilee Junction, he considered chucking the hunt for the $50,000 and spending what money he had in his pocket in a nice, safe saloon. Denver was renowned for strong booze and willing women.

"We're in a world of trouble," he said softly.

Zoe didn't have to be told. She saw the Sioux scout stop, turn, and point directly at them. The brave shouted something that produced a thunder of hooves. It took several seconds for the rest of the war party to show themselves.

"They were riding in the ravines to keep from being seen," Slocum said.

"That's not good, is it? They're afraid of the cavalry."

"They're afraid somebody might spot them and report them to the cavalry," Slocum said. "That means there's a company out scouring the countryside. Otherwise, they'd be on our necks in a flash."

"What do you call that?" Zoe's voice rose to the point where it cracked with fear.

Slocum saw a dozen Sioux warriors galloping toward

them, their horses' hooves kicking up a curtain of mud from the road. The slop slowed the Indians' assault, but not enough.

"Let's see how determined they are," Slocum said, drawing his six-shooter and taking careful aim. He judged distances and windage and a dozen other factors before squeezing the trigger. Although a crack shot, he would have used up the luck of a lifetime to have actually hit one brave. As it was, his round zipped past the ear of a horse and caused it to veer sharply, throwing the rider into another rider so they went down in a noisy pile of hooves and flailing Indians.

He didn't bother telling Zoe to stick close as he veered away and rode for a ravine that had cut a deep gash through the road. Pulling up, he wheeled about to make a stand.

"Keep riding," he said. "I'll give you time to get away."

"You can't do that!"

"You don't want to stay and take notes for a story," Slocum said. Then he began methodically shooting. The Indians were forced to attack two abreast and had nowhere to run. Slocum aimed at their ponies and killed the lead rider's horse, causing another jumble.

"What are you going to do when you run out of bullets?" Zoe asked.

"Die."

Slocum's hammer landed with a dull click on an empty chamber.

12

"Son of a bitch," Sid Calhoun said, glaring at the instructions Slocum had altered. "We kill our butts finding the tree and then this. A cairn? What the hell's that?"

"A pile of rocks," Skunk Swain said.

"How'd you know a thing like that?" Curly asked.

Swain glared at Curly, then said, "I got me some book learning. More 'n I can say for you, you ignorant—"

"Shaddup," Calhoun said without rancor. "We got to find this pile of rocks. Any of you see anything like that?"

"Might be farther along this road," suggested another of his gang. "Toward the cavalry post."

This caused a silence to descend that Calhoun appreciated. None of them could show his face at any army camp or fort. The entire state was plastered with wanted posters accusing them of crimes they hadn't committed, and even a few they had. Sorting out the fiction from the fact wasn't something he wanted to leave to chance. More likely, the camp commander would simply string them all up.

"Whoever put this here was sneaky," Calhoun said. "He wants us to bounce around. Somebody got here before us

107

and ripped off half the sheet." He held up the message and let an eye-dazzling bolt of lightning on the far horizon illuminate the ragged edge. The rest had been cut cleanly. Only the bottom showed the way somebody had tried to dupe them.

"What's that mean?" Curly asked.

"We came south, so let's go north. Don't think we'd be sent due west yet. The colonel'd want to have some fun pokin' and proddin' the racers." He pressed his palm against his vest to be sure his gold keys were still where he had stashed them. He didn't trust Swain and Curly, but others might be holding out on him, too. This wasn't the time to shoot his henchmen and steal their keys. The road ahead was still dangerous and he needed a gang to take the bullets for him.

Then he could take their keys—and the $50,000.

"The signpost said a town called Benedict was to the north. Anybody know about it?" Calhoun looked around and saw nothing but blank expressions. "Then it's time we found out."

"What if the next message *is* down the road, at that Camp Larrup?" Skunk Swain spoke in an even voice that worried Calhoun. This was the man who would try to shoot him in the back and take over the gang, given the chance. It was going to be a chore sleeping with one eye open and not letting Swain ride behind him on the trail.

"Why don't you ride on a ways and see?" Calhoun suggested. "Me and the boys'll ride toward Benedict. Let us know if you run into any soldiers."

Calhoun saw Swain tense at the ridicule, then relax.

"Whatever you say, Boss." The sarcasm wasn't lost on Calhoun. He wondered if this was the right time to call Swain out and settle accounts once and for all. A clap of thunder rolled in from back in the direction of Jubilee Junction, warning him they were in for another gully washer.

"Yeah, whatever I say," Calhoun said. He rode past Swain,

the hairs on the back of his neck rising as he imagined the gunman going for his six-shooter and putting a round in the back of his head. The telltale hiss of metal scraping leather didn't come. Neither did the distinctive metallic click of a Colt cocking. Calhoun had survived a challenge to his leadership once more.

He kept a steady trot to the crossroad, then pressed on northward. He was so busy worrying about Swain getting off a shot at his back and the approaching storm that Curly had to shout at him to get his attention.

"Sid, lookee there. Ain't that the purtiest sight you ever did see?"

Calhoun looked back at the stone cairn on the west side of the road. A slow smile crept to his lips.

"Looks like I was right." He fixed his gaze on Swain, who wouldn't meet his eyes. "Why don't you go on over and see what the message says, Skunk, since you got all that book learnin'?"

Skunk Swain tensed and his hand twitched, but he didn't go for his iron. The shoot-out would come sooner rather than later, but Swain backed down again. Calhoun started thinking of ways of getting Curly or one of the others to cut Swain down and save him the effort.

"Here it is," Swain said, holding up another of the metal canisters.

"Well, don't keep us in the dark. What's in it?"

"How do we know this ain't been tampered with, too?" Swain worked off the cap and pulled out the paper. He stared at Calhoun and said, "Benedict. That's what it says."

"Then we keep riding," Calhoun said. "Get rid of the note. There's no reason to let anybody else know where the trail is."

"The golden trail," Curly said.

"Hush up," Calhoun ordered. "You hear that?"

"More thunder? You afraid of gettin' wet?" Swain made no effort to hide his antagonism.

"Gunshots," Curly said. "Comin' from up ahead. What are we gonna do, Sid?"

Common sense told Calhoun to have nothing to do with the fight. The shots came sporadically. If he was any judge, a pistol would fire and then be answered by several different rifles. A one-sided fight like that would be over quick.

"We'll take a look," Calhoun said.

"Why?" Skunk Swain thrust out his chin and looked ready for a fight.

"Who's likely to be up ahead but somebody who's already read this message, maybe tore up the one in the tree stump?" Calhoun didn't add that anyone preceding them along this road today was likely to have more of the keys riding in their pockets. Calhoun was willing to let others kill themselves, and then he could take on the winner since they were likely to be bloodied and out of ammo.

"I dunno, Boss," Curly said. "Might be dangerous."

Calhoun snorted in contempt and rode past his henchman. Again, he got the cold feeling of Swain watching him and evaluating when the time would be right to shoot his boss in the back. Once more, he survived. Swain was probably thinking that whoever was shooting it out ahead would do his work for him.

Rather than rush ahead blindly, Calhoun got off the road and followed the contours of the land, using the deep gullies to hide in as the sounds of gunfire came ever closer. When he reached the Y in an especially deep ravine, he saw a man and that damned woman reporter firing on an Indian decked out in war paint. He held up his hand, backed away, and joined his men down the branching ravine.

"Won't be long before the Injuns scalp them," he said.

He looked up when he saw Curly riding along the bank of the ravine, silhouetted against the lightning flashes. He almost took a shot at the fool, then froze when he heard what the man had to say.

"He's drivin' 'em back, Boss. One lone pistolero is drivin' back a whole band of Sioux."

"The hell you say."

"I seen him on the train. He's one of the racers. And the woman with him's that purty reporter, the one who—"

"I know who it is," he snapped. Calhoun came to a quick decision. The man couldn't have much ammunition left if he had succeeded in driving off the Sioux. The gunfire had died down, leaving an ominous silence punctuated only by the rising wind and occasional thunderclap.

"We ride, men," he decided. "We ride and make sure the Injuns don't kill 'em."

"So's we can find out if the second message was a lie?"

Calhoun looked at Curly with new approval. The man wasn't as stupid as he seemed.

"Don't worry a whole lot about keepin' the reporter and her beau alive too long," he said. "We just want to know if he substituted instructions at the pile of rocks."

"The cairn," Swain said loud enough to get Calhoun's goat.

"You got a problem, Skunk?"

"None at all, Boss."

Calhoun didn't like his tone, but knew they had only a few minutes to react before the reporter and the man with her hightailed it. He swung his horse around, motioned for Curly to remain on the ravine bank as lookout, and then galloped straight for the battlefield.

He didn't need Curly's warning to realize the size of the mistake he had just made. The Sioux hadn't given up. They had reformed and snuck up on either side of the ravine to shoot down into it. His attack startled them, but did nothing to force them to turn and run. Withering fire came in his direction, slugs ripping through the brim of his hat and into the men directly behind him. He saw one flop from his horse. Another groaned and bent forward, clutching his belly.

Calhoun didn't have to tell Swain to retreat. The man was already galloping away.

From above on the embankment, Curly shouted, "Cavalry's a-comin'! Whole damn troop of 'em. They got them redskins in a trap!"

Calhoun put his head down low until his cheek pressed into his horse's straining neck. Being caught by the cavalry was a damn sight worse than having an Indian shoot him down. Better to die with a bullet in the gut than a noose around his neck.

Sounds of a fierce fight behind faded as Calhoun and Swain found a way out of the ravine so they could join Curly. Calhoun fumed as he rode, having lost his chance to nab a key or two more.

"Where to, Boss?"

He didn't even know which of his remaining men spoke. He was too furious to figure it out.

"Benedict," he spat out. "It's all we can do."

To add insult to injury, it began to rain. Hard.

13

"We're going to die, aren't we, John? I don't want to die like this." Zoe Murchison sobbed, distracting Slocum for a moment. He glanced toward her, but bit back any sharp comment. She might be upset, but she wasn't running. He appreciated her courage in spite of her fear.

He emptied his six-gun and worked to reload.

"Th-they're running," she cried. "You scared them off."

"Don't count on it," he said. "They're regrouping, probably getting to high ground on the ravine banks." Slocum worried that the deep ravine would turn into their grave. The banks were more than five feet over his head even when he was mounted. The recent storm had done quite a job ripping through the prairie, probably chewing away at a gully left by earlier rains. It wouldn't take the Sioux much to start shooting down at them.

"What are we going to do? If you had another gun, I could shoot at them, too."

Slocum gripped his pistol and waited for an Indian to poke his head out over the edge of the ravine. He reacted instinctively, firing before he realized he even had a target,

113

and felt a moment of bitter satisfaction as his bullet hit the brave smack in the center of the forehead. The Indian tumbled to the bottom of the gully, but he was replaced in a flash by two more warriors.

"Find a way out of here. Not back down the ravine, but up the side. Go on, hunt for it!"

"But that'd put us up on the banks with them," Zoe said.

That was exactly what Slocum sought. If half the Sioux mounted their attack from each side, he would put a significant barrier between him and the half on the far side of the ravine. He heard Zoe ride off, hunting. Firing three times, he drove the Sioux back under cover, but felt them closing in on him.

"Hurry up!" he called.

"Here, John, I have a place."

He wheeled his horse around, and hesitated when he saw six men galloping toward him from down the ravine. Slocum worked his horse into the narrow gap Zoe had found and let the horse pick its way up to the top. As he struggled out onto level ground, he heard a bugle sounding commands.

"The cavalry," he called to Zoe. "They're attacking the Indians."

"We're saved!"

He wondered about that, but he said nothing as he pointed northward toward the town.

"John, who was that in the ravine? Not the Indians, the others?"

"I don't know." Slocum knew he lied. He had caught a glimpse of one rider and knew it had to be the Calhoun gang. The man with the white streak through the middle of his coal black hair had lost his hat as he galloped down on them. If the henchman had been there, Slocum reckoned the boss was also riding in the pack.

"It must be Calhoun. They left Jubilee Junction and were the reason I came to warn you."

"Could have been," he said. "Look out!"

Slocum got his feet secured in his stirrups, then launched himself. His arms circled the woman's trim body and carried her out of the saddle. He smashed belly down across her saddle, and then she slipped from his arms and crashed to the ground as her horse raced on. Slocum twisted hard to keep from being trampled.

He had reacted instinctively again—and it had saved Zoe's life. Arrows whistled through the air and a few rifle slugs ripped along with them. He and Zoe had blundered into another tight knot of Sioux.

Still on his belly, Slocum brought his six-shooter around and squeezed off a shot. Pain ripped through his body, but the recoil of the Colt Navy in his hand felt good. He knew he had hit his target. Another round also found an exposed chest. Then the fusillade died down, and the remaining Indians slipped away.

"You ran them off," Zoe said, getting to her feet. She took a few shaky steps, and then collapsed beside him. "I should stay down, shouldn't I? I wasn't thinking—not thinking."

"Come on," Slocum said, grabbing her by the wrist and jerking her back to her feet. "We've got to get out of here." He knew his accuracy hadn't frightened off the Indians. The sound of approaching soldiers had. Staying around to explain what had happened was the obvious thing to do, but Slocum had wanted to avoid the cavalry earlier because of wanted posters chasing him through the West. The soldiers who found him wouldn't know his face, but they might insist on taking him back to their post.

He had gotten himself out of a tight fix, and saw no reason to stick his neck in a noose when there wasn't any call to do so.

"The soldiers can protect us," Zoe said.

"And your story is in Benedict," Slocum replied, knowing that was the goad that would keep her moving away from the Indians, Calhoun, and the cavalry. A play of emotions crossed her face like a moving cyclorama, and then she nodded and smiled brightly.

"You're right, John. We ought to press on. There's a new clue in that town."

"Other racers might have gotten there already," he said.

"You don't believe that. I'm quite a good judge of character and what people mean when they speak. Why don't you think that anyone is ahead of us?"

"The colonel sent the racers in three separate directions, more to keep them apart than to confuse the situation," Slocum said. "He will have the racers come back together sooner or later. Otherwise, he would have scattered his messages all over the countryside. Granted, he might have done that, but this is more efficient."

"But the point is that you don't believe anyone is ahead of us."

"Calhoun and his boys are as close to being on the same trail as anyone. Do you think they'd leave any messages they found intact?"

"They'd destroy them," Zoe said, thinking on the matter. "Or they might counterfeit a new clue to send the poor wights coming after them on a wild goose chase."

Slocum nodded, letting her come to her own conclusions. He saw no reason to tell Zoe how he had played that game just a little. A noisy splat on the brim of his hat caused him to look up in time to catch another cold raindrop in the eye. He jerked, blinked, and worked to get the water clear so he could see again.

"Are you all right, John?"

"Neither of us will be if we don't get to town soon," he said. The rain fell harder. Within minutes, he knew they couldn't continue, but had to find a place to ride out the storm. Doing that would be hard on the prairie. He saw few trees, and there wasn't time to make a decent lean-to.

"There're trees," Zoe said. "I saw them ahead. Or I think

I did. The rain's coming down so hard now, it's difficult to say what I actually saw."

Slocum rode by instinct and found the trio of trees, flagged by the incessant winds and providing scant cover for them. Worse, in the storm, one of the trees might be struck by lightning. Being under it would fry them both good.

"I can lash down my slicker," he said, "and get us a little cover."

"Why bother? Just pull it up over you. The wind's not going to take kindly to anyone putting up what amounts to a sailcloth."

Slocum saw the truth in the woman's words. The wind whipped along the ground and then urged upward. If he tied down his slicker to a pair of tree limbs, this crazy wind would rip away the yellow raincoat and carry it away.

"It'll be hard enough for the horse," he said.

"We'd better get down," Zoe said with growing nervousness. She looked up at the heavy clouds filled with lightning bolts. So far, the lightning had arced from one cloud to the other in the sky, but the ferocity of the building storm promised to bring the electricity down to the ground.

Slocum dismounted and led the horses to a spot where they were partially protected from the wind but not the rain. They protested, but he was too wet and exhausted to much care. By the time he got the saddles off and made sure the horses were properly hobbled, Zoe had built a small mound on the lee side of the largest tree.

"It's not much," she said when she saw his frown, "but it'll keep the water from puddling around us."

Slocum scratched a deep trough at the base of her small hill and nodded.

"Wouldn't have thought of that," he said about the mound.

"I suppose you would have cowered under the raincoat and endured the elements."

"Something like that," Slocum said. He wiped rain from his forehead and swung around, sat, and held out the slicker for her. It was going to be a mighty wet night.

She crowded close, pulled the slicker around both their shoulders, leaving the edges flapping freely on either side.

"That lets in the wind. You're going to get cold," Slocum said.

She looked at him. Her eyes sparkled and a tiny smile curled the corners of her lips as she said, "Not if we stay close. Very, very close." Her hand slipped to his thigh and then worked tantalizingly to his crotch. Gentle squeezing got him hard. Looking at her with clothing plastered to her trim body by the rain had put ideas into his head, but he had never thought anything would come of them.

Now he wasn't so sure.

"I want to thank you, John." She moved closer, so he felt her hot breath against his cheek. She kissed him tentatively.

"What do you have to thank me for?"

"You saved my life back there. Indians. Calhoun. I would have been shot and raped or scalped or who knows what."

"If you hadn't ridden out to warn me about the Indians and Calhoun and his gang, you wouldn't have been in any danger." As the words left his lips, he knew that criticizing her behavior wasn't the right thing to do, but he realized then nothing could break the mood short of them being hit by lightning. Zoe pressed closer and nibbled on his ear.

Then she whispered, "Then we owe each other. And I'm collecting."

Her hand became more insistent, and she pressed so close to him he felt her breast mashing against his chest. As they kissed more passionately, the nipple hardened and threatened to poke a hole through him. Slocum couldn't think of a better way of dying.

She fumbled to open his fly. The brass buttons were slippery, and she worked at it to free his erection. He turned his own attention to opening her blouse. The pearl buttons popped free of the lace frogs holding them until he exposed her breasts. He caught his breath at the sight. Perfectly formed, apple-sized, they were firm and quivering from the cold, wet wind blowing across their naked beauty. Or was there something more causing the ripples of gooseflesh and the hard pink buttons of her nipples? He thought so.

He gasped as she finally got his hardness free and clutched it fiercely.

"You like that?" Her tongue snaked into his ear and then circled the rim, sending tingles throughout his body.

"As much as I'm sure you'll like this." He bent and buried his face between those firm mounds and began kissing and licking. He worked up one slope, tended the hard nubbin there, then spiraled down and around and up the other to similarly tease. He caught the hard button between his teeth and pulled gently, then sucked and licked and tongued.

He groaned as she gripped down even harder on him. Slocum felt as if he had been thrust into a closing vise.

"Not so hard," he said from his position at her chest. He sighed as she released her death grip, allowing him to move lower. It took some skilled work with his lips and tongue to further unfasten her clothing. Her skirt came free. She lifted up and tried to work out of it, but it clung with damp tenacity to her legs until Slocum helped.

Slowly, ever so slowly, he pulled her skirt down and peeled the cloth from her flesh to expose her bloomers. The undergarment was similarly plastered to every contour of Zoe's body.

Slocum licked and kissed and worked his way up the inside of her thigh. She groaned constantly now as he came closer to the dark triangle between her legs that was barely visible through the cloth. New dampness was added to that of the storm, this coming from within.

He stroked over her hidden nether lips and began massaging in the same tempo she used on his hardness. Soon enough, they were both moaning with pleasure, but Slocum stopped to reposition his body.

"More," he said. "I want more."

"Oh, John, yes! I do also!" Zoe lay back and supported herself on her elbows in the mud. The mound of dirt she had built up was being packed down by their bodies and the rain was washing away the perimeter. Neither noticed.

She lifted her knees and spread them to wantonly invite him to continue. Slocum tugged a little at her bloomers, and finally tore a hole where it would do the most good. She started to protest; then no words came from her mouth. She leaned back, cried out in joy, and lifted her knees even higher as he slipped into her.

He bent and returned to kissing and suckling at her breasts as he slipped back and forth with slow, deliberate movement. The way she tightened around his hidden length began to sap his stamina. He found himself thrusting harder, deeper, moving faster, until he duplicated the motion of the pistons on a steam locomotive. He clung to her as he continued to move with greater speed and urgency. Her fingernails raked his back and spurred him on. Every thrust lifted her off the ground and allowed her to grind down into him. Locked together, striving together, they found the proper frequency and cried out, their animal desires rivaling the howling wind.

He sank down atop her. She relaxed, her legs going to either side of his body. In his ear, she whispered, "It wasn't like I thought it would be."

"What?" He forced himself up on stiff arms to stare at her. The sweet smile and bright eyes told him she was toying with him.

"It was better," she said, confirming what he suspected. "It was the best."

"Out in the rain, in the dirt?"

"Those don't matter. You do." She laughed and grabbed for his limp organ and stroked over it. "That did!"

He had to laugh with her. He wanted to lie atop her for the rest of the night, but knew that wouldn't be comfortable for either of them. He scooted around, reshaped the small hill to insure some small amount of drainage, then pulled the slicker around both of them. Zoe's arms circled his body and held him close, her cheek pressed against his chest.

"Your heart's running away with itself," she said.

"I'll calm down," he assured her.

"I hope not. At least, not too soon." She began stroking over him again. It rained most of the night amid vicious lightning, but they were oblivious to it, lost in their own world, until the dawn thrust pink fingers through the heavy clouds and promised a better, drier day.

14

"I want to go live in the desert," Harry Ibbotson said. "It's dry there. I'm soaked through and through." To illustrate his point, he shook himself like a dog and sent water sailing in all directions.

"Stop that," Molly snapped. "You're acting like a child. Again."

"I'm wet and cold and there's no way in hell we can know this here town's the one we want."

"There's no point getting back on the train. We could never catch it, and it's probably all the way to Denver by now. Jubilee Junction is exhausted as a source of information. What else do you suggest, if you're suddenly an all-fired genius?" She put her hands on her hips and glared at him. She was as wet and cold as he was, but she didn't see fit to complain. All she wanted was a place to dry her clothes, a restaurant for a hot meal, and a bed to sleep the entire night.

And the next clue in the race. She had gold keys burning a hole in her pocket and wanted to find the treasure chest. The money loomed larger with every step her horse had

123

taken. There had to be some good reason to inflict such misery on herself, and if it wasn't a pile of gold coins, she'd know the reason.

"This looks like a jerkwater town," Harry said. "Or it would be if there was a train that came through. It's off the main line, and they didn't even see fit to run a spur line out here."

"From Jubilee Junction, there were only three possible destinations. I see no reason to trouble the officers and soldiers at Camp Larrup. Continuing due west avails us little since we are so far from that road."

"The ghost town," Harry muttered. "We coulda stayed there. It would have been drier than riding through the damned rain." He shook himself again, once more spraying water everywhere. This time, a passing cowboy stopped and glared at him.

"You're gettin' me wet, partner," the cowboy said.

Molly saw what her brother didn't. The cowboy rested his hand on the side of his holster, ready to draw his smoke wagon and let it roll.

"Go f—"

"Go find a drink on us for your trouble," Molly cut in. She fumbled in her purse for a silver dollar. She handed it to the cowboy in such a way that he had to take his hand away from his six-shooter. He glared at Harry, took the silver cartwheel from Molly, and then touched the brim of his hat before walking away.

"Why'd you give him hard coin like that?" Harry started after the cowboy, but Molly grabbed his arm and swung him around so hard he crashed into the wall of a pharmacy.

"You listen up," she said, gritting her teeth and trying not to lose her temper. "We don't want trouble. We don't go out of our way to get into fights we can't win."

"I coulda taken him. He looked like a pansy!"

"He would have chewed you up, spat you out, and then

pissed on the pieces," she said. Harry's eyes went wide at such language.

"You're turning coarse, sister," he said. "Your language isn't what it used to be."

"I want the colonel's gold, and I'm going to get it, with or without your help."

"You tryin' to cut me out?"

"If I wanted to do that, I'd've let the kidnappers keep you."

"You paid that gunman five hundred dollars to rescue me. Fat lot of good that was. You let him steal the money."

"You're free of those road agents," she said, fighting down her rising ire. The thought crossed her mind that her dear brother was becoming more of a hindrance than an asset. If he stood between her and the gold, he might become her dear late, lamented brother.

"If I hadn't got tossed off the train, I'd never have been caught by them."

"Your gambling is—" Molly stopped when she realized the crowd they were attracting with their bickering. She smiled, but it was sour. It turned even more sour when a man with a bulging belly and a six-pointed star pinned on his vest waddled over.

"Ma'am, any trouble here?"

"Oh, no, Marshal," she said, turning sweet. "My brother and I were trying to figure out what to do next."

"Take your argument off the street's a good idea," he said, glancing toward Harry, sizing him up for the amount of trouble he was likely to cause. Molly didn't like the way the lawman dismissed Harry with that single glance. He was too good a judge of character, knowing who to address and who to ignore.

"We're part of Colonel Turner's race," she said.

"That damn thing," the lawman grumbled. "More trouble than it's worth."

"There is supposed to be a message for the racers so we can hurry on to another location." Molly put it as straight as she could so the marshal would tell her what she needed to know and get them out of his town fast. The man's expression showed she had struck the right chord.

"The damn freight agent's over in his office."

"Agent for the Turner Haulage Company?"

"None other than. They's supposed to begin shipments any time now, but I ain't seen evidence they did anything more 'n open an office and have a layabout poke his head out now and then and leer at the womenfolk."

"Is that the only spot where such a message might be?"

"Don't know and don't much care," the marshal said, his attention drifting from her to a fight that spilled out of a saloon down the street. Two men grappled and tried to hit each other, but both were too drunk to do much more than roll about in the mud like pigs in a wallow.

The lawman left without another word. Molly heaved a sigh of relief that they had avoided a run-in with the badge-toting meddler.

"Let's get over to the freight office," she said. "Might be the colonel wants the racers to take one of his wagons to the next stop."

"Where'd that be?"

Molly heaved a sigh, then said, "I don't know. We'll have to study a map to see, won't we?"

Harry groused the entire way to the freight office. Molly saw what the marshal had meant about the agent being a layabout. He had pulled two chairs together behind the counter, sat in one and propped his feet up in the other, and was taking a nap.

"It's nine in the goddamn morning," bellowed Harry. "You shouldn't be asleep at this time of day!"

The agent stirred, scratched himself, and only then did he force up one droopy eyelid. He looked more like a hound dog than a human, and Molly expected his tongue to loll out at any instant. Instead, he dropped heavy feet to the floor, grunted as he stood, and leaned against the counter.

"You two wantin' to put somethin' on a freight wagon? Won't be here for another couple weeks, not one from St. Louis."

"What of one leaving here for points west?" Molly asked.

"You two ain't with the race, are you? Well, I'll be damned," he said when Harry nodded glumly. "You're the first ones. How about that?"

"Yes, how about that? Is there a message for us and the other racers?"

"Well, of course, dearie, there surely is." The man dived behind the counter and pulled out a stack of envelopes. He licked his thumb, peeled off the top one, and pushed it across the counter to Molly. She made no effort to pick it up.

"What about him? He's a racer, too." She eyed the remaining stack of envelopes.

"Can't the two of you share? I was told to be frugal passing these out."

"Frugal?" Harry started to grab for the man's throat, but Molly caught her brother's wrist and forced it down to the envelope on the counter.

"That one's yours," she said forcefully. She fished about and found a gold key and held it up. To the clerk, she said, "This is what you needed to see to deliver the message, isn't it? We each have our own key."

"I reckon so. I kinda forgot what they told me." The agent licked his thumb and peeled off a second envelope and passed it to Molly. She took it, graced him with a smile, and backed away.

"Wait a second," the agent said. "I seen your key. Where's his?"

"Go on back to sleep, why don't you?" Molly said. She had all their keys and wasn't about to hand one to her brother unless it was necessary.

"Others will be a-comin' soon, won't they?"

Molly eyed the remaining envelopes, and wondered if it was worth the effort to shoot the agent and take them. As the idea built, a shadow passed across the floor and fell on the counter between her and the freight agent. A quick glance confirmed that the marshal had followed them and stood outside in the morning sun, watching them like hawks.

"We can only hope no one else will find your lovely town," Molly said. She looped her arm in Harry's and pulled him away and into the morning. She bowed slightly in the marshal's direction, smiled, and walked on, head high as if nothing in the world was wrong.

They came to a restaurant, and she remembered how hungry she was. She steered Harry inside.

"We got to keep moving, sis. You saw the way that lawman eyed us. He's thinkin' up charges. I know it."

"Of course he is, but the same argument works with him that did with the freighter."

"Huh? What argument?"

"The less trouble they cause us, the faster we're out of their hair."

"Don't know about that," Harry said. "The marshal didn't have much more than a fringe above his ears. Bald as an egg's my guess."

She ordered for both of them and sent the waiter scurrying away to fetch some coffee. Holding the envelope up to the light pouring through the single plate glass window in the front of the café, she tried to read the message inside. The paper was too heavy to allow that.

"Just get on and open it. There's no need to be all sneaky, sis."

"If I can read what's inside without opening the envelope, we can see if all the messages still in the agent's hands are identical."

"Oh."

She opened the envelope, and quickly scanned the few terse lines.

"The stagecoach goes to a town named Clarkesville over in Kansas. The directions say to go there."

Harry fumbled and tore the end off his envelope, blew into it, and drew out the folded sheet.

"I'll be damned," he said, shaking his head. "This is completely different. Says to get on the train at Moberly and go to Brunswick. What are we going to do?"

Molly considered how many other possibilities there were in a big stack of envelopes. All might be different or they could have the only two messages.

"We are going to eat our breakfast," she said, her mind working on the problem of multiple messages. "Afterward, we shall see to the matter of differing clues."

Harry chattered on about this and that, but Molly ignored him. Occasionally, she looked out into the street and craned her neck a bit to see what foot traffic went into the Turner Haulage Company office. There was such a small amount that she realized the clerk could sleep most of the day and never be disturbed.

"Finish your eggs," she told Harry. She pushed her plate away, dabbed at her lips with her napkin, and finally decided on their course of action. "We've got work to do."

"Which way are we going?"

"That depends on what's in the remainder of the envelopes."

"We're gonna steal them?"

"We are. Go to the general store and buy a dozen envelopes of this kind." She drew the edge of the envelope from her purse and showed him, then quickly stuffed it back. Molly stood and said, "Pay the waiter. When you get the envelopes, join me down the street."

Harry sputtered at being ordered around, but then he always did. She considered taking their keys and pressing on herself, but seeing two different destinations in the instructions worried her. It might not matter in the long run, if the colonel brought all the racers together at a single point some distance away from the strongbox with the gold, but she dared not take that risk. Too much money rode on getting to the finish line first—with as many of the keys as possible.

She walked slowly down the street, eyeing the livery stable and the corral behind it. Harry would be a few minutes, giving her time to ask questions.

"Good morning," she said to the stable boy. He was fresh from work and covered with muck from the stalls. Her nose twitched at the stench, but she smiled sweetly and tried not to look at him in a fashion showing any distaste at all.

"Ma'am, you want the owner? He's inside. I kin fetch him for you."

"Oh, that's fine," she said. "I wanted to know about those horses in your corral. I'm in the market, but am embarrassed to make an offer since I have so little money. Are any of the horses for sale?"

"None of them, ma'am. What all we had for sale was sold this past week."

"Draft horses?"

"All the stock from the new freight office. Said they wanted stronger horses, but the ones they had was plenty big enough to haul a good-sized wagon."

"The Turner Haulage Company? That freighter?"

"Them's the ones. Hardly got started and they sold their animals. Only a couple wagon loads was brung in from St. Louis. Nuthin' I know was sent on to Clarkesville, but that don't matter."

"Why not?"

"The stagecoach runs often 'nuff. Can't send freight on the stage, but most other things get sent that way."

"The stage leaves regularly?"

"Every single day at noon," he said. "Look, I don't know

anybody with horses to sell, but my boss does. He knows 'bout ever'thing."

"Thanks, I'll pursue other routes." She left the stable boy chewing his lip, wondering what she'd meant by that. He finally gave up the hard work of thinking, and went back to moving a wheelbarrow load of muck from the stable to a pile beyond the corral.

"There you are. I looked everywhere for you," Harry said, running over to her. "This was the best I could do matching the envelopes. They sold them to the agent from the colonel's company, but had only a half dozen left."

"Seal them."

"What do I put inside?" Harry frowned.

"Nothing." She took the stack of envelopes, made certain they were sealed properly, then handed them back. "I'll cause a ruckus outside the freight office. You know where the clerk put the others. Take them all and put these in their place."

"There aren't as many. Maybe I ought to leave a couple to make it look right."

"Maybe we can use the fifty thousand dollars to buy you some common sense," she said. "It won't matter. The clerk's not paying much attention. Let the next ones along find the empty envelopes."

"You want I should destroy them?"

"Not until we've read the contents," Molly said, heaving a deep sigh. Harry was getting stupider by the day. She studied his furrowed face and waited until understanding bloomed. Without another word, she walked down the center of the muddy street, looking for a decent diversion that would draw people out, including the freight agent.

She found her mark, made certain Harry had moved around behind the freight office, and then went to a man who was cursing as he dealt with a broken belly strap on his saddle. His horse shied away, and he finally swung the saddle off and around. Molly's timing was perfect. She collided with the man and crashed into him, knocking him backward with his saddle between them.

As he fell, she kicked up her legs and sent her skirt flying to expose legs and more. The harder the man struggled to get up, the harder she fought to keep him down. Then she began shouting.

"How dare you! Take advantage of a woman, will you!" She slapped him, then shoved and sent him tumbling back.

"Lady, you bumped into me. I didn't do anything."

"How dare you make a suggestion like that?" She lit into him, clawing and hitting like a wildcat. Molly let him grab one wrist and hold her at bay so a crowd would gather.

"You finally got yourself a filly, Curtis. Now you gotta break her!" shouted someone in the crowd. Other catcalls flustered the man. Molly kept fighting. When she didn't see the agent come out to join in, she played her trump card.

Nimble fingers pulled Curtis's six-shooter from his holster. She fired a round through the freight company's glass window. The instant the pistol discharged, she dropped it, backed away, and cried loudly at being so victimized.

The agent boiled out and looked around in time to see Curtis picking up his six-gun. Molly pointed, then backed off and let the two of them create an even bigger ruckus. Harry slipped out the door, his hand over his coat pocket to let her know he had finished stealing the race instructions and substituting the empty envelopes.

She cursed him under her breath. He ought to have retreated out back the way he had entered to keep anyone from seeing him.

By the time the Benedict marshal showed up, Molly and Harry had torn open the stolen instructions and read them.

"What do we do now, sis?"

"You take the horses and ride for a railhead and go on to Denver. I'll go to Clarkesville on the stage and follow the new message there." Again, she wished she could get the gold key from her brother, but they had to cover their bets. He might find his way to the gold and need the key.

"See you when we get the gold," Harry Ibbotson said.

Molly kissed her brother on the cheek and went to purchase a stagecoach ticket.

15

"We can both ride, John. You don't have to walk," Zoe said.

Slocum plodded along resolutely, not bothering to answer. His horse had pulled up lame a mile back, and he had to watch it carefully as it picked its way along the muddy track they followed, to be sure it didn't hurt its leg further.

His luck had gone like this for the past few days. Being caught in the rain with Zoe had been the pinnacle, and it had all been downhill after that. They had ridden into Benedict in their quest for the next set of instructions on where to go. The colonel's envelopes had been emptied somehow, and Slocum wasn't sure the freight agent hadn't had a hand in doing that.

"Stupidity," he muttered.

"What's that?" Zoe bent over and reached out a hand to brush his shoulder. "You're not stupid, John. Or did you mean me for wanting to keep going?"

"The agent back in Benedict," he said. "Never think a man is a crook if there's a chance he's only stupid."

"He didn't seem too clever a fellow," Zoe said.

"He let them steal the instructions from under his nose."

135

"From the sound of the furor Molly Ibbotson created out in the street, how can you blame him for rushing out? She shot out the window and exposed herself and got the men fighting. By the time the marshal broke up the fight, a herd of buffalo could have run through the freight office and not been seen."

Slocum walked along glumly. Everything she said was true.

"We're not stupid, though," said Zoe. "We figured out where she is headed."

"That wasn't hard," Slocum said. He had asked after Molly and been told by a half dozen men that she had bought a ticket on the stagecoach to Clarkesville, Kansas. What happened to Harry was a complete mystery, but the men all agreed her brother had not been on the stage with her. If he had, those men would have been envying him.

"Why'd they separate? The waiter at the restaurant said she treated her brother like a small child, and that he resented it."

"The waiter said he would have resented being treated like that. Harry Ibbotson might not have noticed."

"True, but Harry disappeared from town. She must have sent him off, because he wouldn't have gone on his own."

"Two sets of instructions," Slocum said. "That's the only answer. He took their horses and rode somewhere else while she followed a second set of directions."

"What if there had been three?"

"Only Molly would know that," Slocum said. He shook his head as he thought on it. "There were only two, or if there were more, she chose the most likely destinations. The colonel is splitting up the racers, but I think the clues will all funnel back to a single location before the final run for the gold."

"That seems sensible," Zoe said.

"She'll beat us to Clarkesville by a day or more," he said. The bitterness he felt boiled up. If he swapped places with Zoe, he could be in the town not long after Molly and find out what she already knew—where to look for the next instructions. He took a deep breath and tried to settle his chaotic thoughts. Letting Molly get to him like this was foolish. The colonel had planned every turn of this race to garner the most publicity.

"I see smoke rising ahead," Zoe said from her vantage point astride her horse.

Slocum saw the smoke gently curling upward not long after. From the number of smokestacks spewing out smoke above the town, it was smaller than even Benedict.

"How's he going to make a dollar bringing his freight to a nothing of a town like this?" Slocum asked.

"The colonel? I don't know," Zoe admitted. "The financial situation is hardly optimal for beginning a business of such magnitude. Going off the silver standard, which Congress made law earlier this year, has caused more than one business to go belly up."

"Gold is better," Slocum said. "I'd rather have a twenty-dollar gold piece in my pocket than twenty cartwheels."

"It caused all manner of financial woe," Zoe said. "I spoke with an editor on Mr. Zelnicoff's staff who said the whole country was going to be in serious trouble soon."

Slocum hardly listened. He didn't need more than a rifle and a countryside filled with game to survive. Let the banks crash and the railroads go bankrupt. None of that mattered if he could bag a deer now and then, or lose himself in the high mountains where he could live well for years. Financial shenanigans only mattered to those who trusted banks.

None of that would matter if he had $50,000 in gold weighing down his saddlebags.

"How much money do you have left?" she asked.

The question took him by surprise.

"Not that much," he admitted.

"I'm scraping the bottom of the barrel, too," Zoe said. "I need to send a telegram to my editor and get an advance on my travel fees. When I receive it, then we can continue after your Miss Ibbotson."

"She's not *my* Miss Ibbotson," Slocum said, more forcefully than he intended. It rankled that Molly had left him to die in that hole back in the ghost town. She might have been kidnapped along with her brother but at some point they had escaped and picked up the scent of Colonel Turner's gold again, leaving him to his own fate.

"You know what I mean," said Zoe. "She employed you to rescue her brother."

"That money's long gone. I spent a fair amount back in Benedict, not that I had much to begin with."

"I wasn't criticizing," she said. "I merely pointed out the facts."

"To what end?"

"I—nothing." Zoe seemed to fold in on herself. At least, she shut up and stopped her incessant chattering. Slocum had heard magpies that were quieter.

As they entered Clarkesville, Slocum leading his limping horse and Zoe riding, they drew a considerable amount of attention.

"They know we're racers," Zoe said. "There's no other reason for such interest."

"I'll see to my horse," Slocum said. "It needs liniment and wrapping for its leg."

"I'll find the telegraph office and let Mr. Zelnicoff know of our plight. I'll also file my story."

"You have enough money to send that long a 'gram?"

"Well, no, but I am sure I do have enough to contact my editor, who can vouch for me so I can send the article."

Slocum wished he had such unbridled optimism. Zoe rode off in search of the telegraph office, leaving Slocum to get his horse to a livery stable.

"Pulled up lame or step in a prairie dog hole?" asked the stable man.

"Lame. The mare's been put to the limit these past few days."

"Muddy trails, slippery as all get out, rocks floating up," the stable man said, nodding in agreement. He leaned against the horse's shoulder, grabbed the right front leg, and heaved to get a better look. He ran his hand gently over the length of the horse's leg, and finally released it. "Not so bad. She'll be right as rain in a day or two."

"All I've got is two dollars," Slocum said, fishing around in his pocket. He had spent most of his money in Benedict for provisions, but he was loath to swap the trail grub for treatment. He was getting riled up over Colonel J. Patterson Turner's Transcontinental Race—or the people taking part. How many had been killed already? And Molly had abandoned him.

That rankled more than anything else. He had been shot at and struggled through inclement weather, and still trailed behind Molly Ibbotson and her brother after they had stolen the instructions. Winning the race was taking on more of a challenge because of the way everything so far had stung his pride.

"Five," the stable man said. "You can work off the other three. You got the look of a man who can ride any bronco."

"You have one to break?"

"A couple, but there's one sunfishin' son of a bitch that nobody here can ride."

Slocum rubbed his butt. So much walking had worked muscles more accustomed to sitting in a saddle and riding all day.

"I break this horse and we're square?"

"Something like that."

"Deal," Slocum said, shaking on it.

When he saw the bandit in the corral, he almost reneged on his promise. The squinty eyes, the powerful chest, the very attitude all told of a gargantuan battle to be fought between man and horse. Slocum would have every bone in his body jolted and twisted every which way before he put a saddle on this one.

"John!"

He glanced over his shoulder, and only quick reflexes kept him from being killed. The horse lashed out with its deadly front hooves and knocked the top rail of the corral in his direction. Slocum ducked, threw up his arm, and deflected the rail so that it didn't smash him in the head. He rubbed his forearm where the flying wood had skinned off a few inches, leaving a bloody swath behind.

"Are you all right?" Zoe hurried over and tried to look at his arm. He pulled away.

"I'm all right. What's got you so het up?"

"I have a job!"

He looked at her, wondering what she meant.

"I'm running low on available cash, you see, and getting in touch with Mr. Zelnicoff requires more than I have, so I inquired of the local paper and the editor hired me. He advanced enough so that I could contact my editor—my St. Louis editor—and transmit my story. He asked for the story to run here since Clarkesville is the center of the race, or so it seems to the residents."

"Who else has come through?"

"Other than Molly Ibbotson? We're the next ones, but I am sure others will follow." Zoe looked sheepish, then grinned. "That's what I told him so he'd give me the job. After all, we *could* be the vanguard of dozens of racers."

"What's the colonel's interest in Clarkesville?"

Zoe shook her head and said, "I can't tell. There was supposed to be an office established here, followed soon by a depot and a half dozen employees, but so far nothing has happened."

Slocum looked back at the rearing bronco and wondered if it was worth his life to break the animal. Zoe had a job and they could live off that for a few days until his own horse was healed enough to ride. He felt nothing but foreboding when he thought about trying to stay on this monster's back.

Even as the idea crossed his mind, he pushed it away. He had promised and there was no way he would leech off a woman's earnings.

"I've got to ride that," he said. "You might get a good story out of it for your new paper."

"Why?"

"I suspect this outlaw is a legend in these parts." He heard the stable owner chuckling when he overheard Slocum's appraisal. That confirmed everything Slocum had guessed. Nobody had come close to breaking the horse, and whoever did would be a legend in Clarkesville, for whatever that was worth.

"It might be a good story at that," Zoe said, eyeing the horse. "When are you to attempt the feat?"

"No time like the present."

"John, do you have to? Your arm's all bunged up, and a doctor ought to look at it."

Slocum flexed his right hand. The forearm gave him the twinges, but no bones were broken. He had strength in his hands and knew there would be no disgrace using both to hang on to break this horse.

"Give me a hand, will you?"

"Mister, I was funnin' you. You don't have to ride ole Eagle."

"Eagle? That's what you call him?"

"'Cuz he spends more time in the air than he does on the ground."

"Hold him so I can mount."

"You're crazy, but I gotta see this," the man said. He put his fingers in his mouth and let loose with a loud whistle that brought men and boys running from all directions. "If you're gonna try, I want folks to see you're doin' it of your own free will."

Slocum said nothing as he took the horse's measure. The coal black horse had a white face, reminding him of another disagreeable cuss he had come across recently. One of Sid Calhoun's henchmen had a white streak through the middle of his black hair. Skunk they had called him. He was a bad one, too.

"Eagle, Skunk, it doesn't matter," Slocum said to himself, getting his mind wrapped around the chore ahead. Four men moved Eagle to the side of the corral and pinned the horse against the rails, giving Slocum a chance to get on. It took three men to get the saddle on. Slocum made sure it was cinched up as tight as possible, then climbed up and swung his leg over.

He saw Zoe come over. Thinking she was going to beg him to stop, he started to tell her he was going to do this, no matter what, but she surprised him.

"What's it feel like with such a powerful animal beneath you?" She held her pencil poised over her notebook.

"Feels like I've roped a lightning bolt," he said, nodding to the men to release the horse.

Slocum was a good rider, a damned good one. Eagle hadn't taken four steps before spinning and bucking high into the air. Slocum went even higher, dislodged by the first stunt the horse pulled.

He landed hard, got up, and motioned for the men to get the horse ready for a second try.

He lasted almost five seconds this time before Eagle found a way to twist, turn, and buck to unseat him. The third time, Slocum refused to be thrown off. The horse turned frantic under him, finding ways to move no other horse ever had. Resolutely, Slocum clung to the reins and pommel for dear life. He was violently tossed about and more than once almost lost his seat, but this time the horse was weakening.

Slocum was dizzy and wobbling in the saddle by the time Eagle stopped soaring and started pawing angrily at the ground. Slocum tried a few movements, left and right, then put his heels to the horse's flanks to give it the idea to move ahead. Eagle began bucking again, but this time Slocum was ready. After ten minutes of fury, Eagle abated.

Slocum jumped to the rail and clambered over. He hit the ground outside the corral, and his legs gave way under him. He wasn't too proud to let Zoe support him long enough to get his strength back.

"Riding a horse like that takes it out of a man," he said.

"You did so well," Zoe said softly, "that maybe you might like to try riding and putting it into a . . . woman."

Before he could answer, men crowded around, slapping him on the shoulder and offering to buy him drinks. He was the man who had ridden the horse that no one else could, and he basked in momentary fame.

"Go on, John," she said. "I have a story to write."

After a dozen rounds of drinks, most of the aches and pains had vanished in Slocum's body. Strangely, he thought more clearly after so much tarantula juice. After downing that much liquor so fast, he was usually knee-walking drunk. But not now.

Zoe and her words kept coming back to him. She wanted to break him to saddle just as he had done with Eagle. If he hadn't been so bunged up from the ride, he would have let her slip in the bridle and lead him to the corral. She was a fine woman, pretty and smart and determined.

A woman like that always had plans for her man, and Slocum preferred to ride his own trail.

He went to the stable and checked his horse. The liniment stunk up the stall, but he saw that the horse was standing easy on the hoof. He gently probed and found no hint of soreness. The sprain hadn't been as severe as he had feared.

"You kin ride the mare, if you've a mind," the stable owner said.

Slocum looked up.

"I'd consider you a damn fool to leave behind a filly like

you rode into town with, but then I'd have thought you were a crazy goddamn fool for climbin' onto Eagle the way you did."

"What do I owe you for the liniment and bandages?"

"Here," the man said, fishing in his vest pocket and hading Slocum a twenty-dollar gold piece. "Eagle's worth a couple hundred broke. I'm coming out ahead on the deal."

Slocum tucked the coin in the same vest pocket with the gold keys.

"The only stage outta town headin' west goes to Denver. The other racer, that woman that came up from Benedict on the stagecoach, stayed on it for the big city."

"No messages," Slocum said, thinking about the unopened Turner Haulage Company office. "That means everyone in the race ought to keep on going."

"Don't know, but it seems likely," the man said.

Slocum saddled his mare and led her from the stall, wary of any hint of limp. The horse pranced along, looking in fine fettle.

"Still think you're a fool leavin' behind the reporter lady, but then I caught sight of the one on the stage. You have a way of surroundin' yerself with lovely women."

"That might be my problem," Slocum said, swinging into the saddle. He winced as pain hit him from all directions. The livery owner silently handed him the bottle of liniment. He'd need it more than the mare.

Slocum rode out of Clarkesville, following the stagecoach route westward. Leaving Zoe Murchison behind was hard, but it was something he had to do. Otherwise, he might find himself settled down in Clarkesville ten years from now.

The prairie wind against his face energized him and made it easier to put the town—and Zoe—behind him.

16

Sid Calhoun sat close to the guttering fire and spread the keys in front of him on the ground. The fan-shaped array glinted pleasingly golden as he touched each key in turn. Eight of them. He ran his finger along the notched edge of the closest and closed his eyes, imagining how he would insert the key into a lock, turn it, and open a chest to $50,000 in gold. Would it be in gold coin or dust? Maybe Colonel Turner had it all in a single bar. He tried to estimate what the bar would weigh. Over and over, he painstakingly did the numbers in his head, and let out a low whistle when he finally came up with an answer.

"Two hundred goddamn pounds of gold," he said softly. "I'll need a pack mule to carry that off."

Sudden anger filled him as he thought that Turner might try to give him a stack of greenbacks rather than the actual gold. What good was a piece of paper only a few banks would honor? Even if the colonel gave him bank notes drawn on a U.S. federal bank, it wasn't the same. He wanted gold. He wanted to run his hands through the dust or the coins or bust a gut trying to lift all two hundred pounds in bars.

"I'm gonna be rich."

He picked up a key and pressed his calloused thumb into the notched edge. He picked up the next key and compared them, thinking they might be identical. Holding them out so the embers lit the keys from behind, he saw that the notches were different. He carefully studied each of the eight keys, and came to the conclusion the gossip had been right. Fifty keys, but only one opened the treasure chest. That meant he might cross the finish line first and still not win the gold.

Returning the keys to his pocket, he drew his six-shooter and knew that he would collect. The colonel couldn't deny him the gold if his life hung in the balance. There wouldn't be any question that Calhoun would kill the tycoon— Calhoun knew he could look menacing, especially sighting down the barrel of a six-gun. Turner was a rich man who owned a huge freight company challenging Wells Fargo and any number of others for supremacy moving freight from the Mississippi ports across the country. From what Calhoun could tell, the colonel intended to deliver freight to towns not on the rail lines, though he had heard Turner was part owner of at least one railroad.

He could collect from everyone that way. Profits from the railroad would fill his pocket; then the freight company would take the goods to smaller towns bypassed when the railroad went through.

"Hell, the man's a saint," Calhoun decided. "He'll keep some of those worthless towns alive doing this. He'll think payin' me fifty thousand dollars will be cheap advertisin'." Calhoun snorted and spun the cylinder in his pistol. "It'll be a cheap price to stay alive."

He tucked his six-shooter into his holster and warmed his hands on the dying fire as he lamented that the keys weren't identical. If they had been, he could have given Curly and Swain keys and sent them to different West Coast cities. Calhoun thought the prize lay in San Francisco, but it could be in Seattle or San Diego since those were other towns on the colonel's freight routes. Calhoun knew. He had found a brochure advertising rates to those cities.

With the keys being unique, he wasn't going to let them out of his sight. Better to keep Curly and that back-shooter Skunk Swain with him since they could be useful doing scouting he was reluctant to take on. When he finally found the final instructions, their usefulness would be at an end.

"Hey, Sid," called Curly, riding up and dismounting. He approached the fire as if it might burn him. "Got bad news."

"What?"

"I poked around in that town like you asked. Clarkesville, they call it. But nobody knows anything about messages or anything left by Colonel Turner or his men."

"You're not lyin' to me, are you, Curly?"

"Hell, Sid, I wouldn't do that!" Sweat gleamed like beads of silver on his upper lip. He was about ready to piss his pants.

"No, you wouldn't do a thing like that," Calhoun said. "You asked around?"

"I asked plumb near ever'body I saw. They told me the Turner Haulage Company was supposed to open an office but never did. Ain't even seen hide nor hair of any of the colonel's men. They did know about the race, though."

"If there's not an office and no message, how's that?"

"They said a woman on a stage from Benedict asked around and got folks real curious. She rode on west, headin' out for Denver on the stagecoach."

"Just one woman?"

"They said there was a fellow with a real purty filly what came immediately after. The cowboy busted a bronco that nobody else could, and the woman got a job at the local newspaper."

Calhoun sat up. "You find out what she looked like?"

"Nobody I found knew since she only just came to town, but they're all talkin' about her. She sounds real purty."

"A lady reporter," Calhoun said. "What are the chances

it's somebody other than the one what rode on the train out of Columbia?"

"I was thinkin' the same thing, Boss."

Calhoun heard the lie. Curly never thought much on anything, but once the truth was pointed out, it was obvious to him.

"They're still in town?"

"The man ain't. The stable owner tole me he left right after bustin' the bronco."

"He left the reporter behind?"

"Reckon so."

Calhoun frowned, stared into the coals, and tried to sort it all out. That didn't make a whole lot of sense unless the cowboy double-crossed the reporter and wanted the prize gold all for himself. Or maybe he was in cahoots with the woman who rode the stage for Denver. Calhoun was sure the reporter had had something to do with the sudden stop that had thrown him and his gang out of the mail car before Jubilee Junction.

"Get back in the saddle. We're all goin' to town." Calhoun kicked dirt onto the nearly dead fire, and watched the smoke rise fitfully and then vanish. He had the feeling he was chasing a puff of smoke in the cowboy who had broken a horse and gotten folks in town talking about it. He saddled his horse and trotted after Curly, wondering if he ought to wait for Swain to return from his scouting. This might be the time to cut him loose.

Calhoun and Curly hadn't ridden a mile toward Clarkesville when Skunk Swain overtook them.

"What's going on?" Swain demanded.

"Curly here's got a lead on three of them, but nobody in town knows squat about a new message."

"The race ends here?"

"You gotta be kiddin'," Calhoun said, looking at Swain. The sun would rise in a few minutes, but it looked as if the white streak through Swain's coal black hair glowed with a light all its own. When he had been a kid, Calhoun had enjoyed shooting at skunks. He'd lure them into houses of people he didn't like; then he'd take a few shots at them and get their stink working hard. When he was sure they couldn't get any meaner or smellier, he'd kill them. The people he hated had to remove the skunk and carried their mark—Sid Calhoun's mark—for days.

Killing Swain wouldn't likely leave that kind of stench, but it might. He'd have to find out.

"Why are we always a couple days behind? We ought to be a couple days ahead if we want to win the gold."

"You're right, Swain," Calhoun said. "We oughta be in the lead. Why are you screwin' everything up so bad that we're not?"

"It ain't me!"

Curly rode a little faster to put distance between the two men, but Calhoun wasn't going to have any part of it. He wanted Curly to learn a lesson. Nobody crossed Sid Calhoun.

"I think you're anglin' to keep the gold for yourself," Calhoun said. "You know more than you're tellin'."

"No, honest, Sid, I don't!"

The argument went on with Swain finally lapsing into sullen silence. Calhoun felt a sense of triumph at putting the back-shooting son of a bitch on the defensive. He settled down and rode, eyes fixed on Swain's back until they reached the edge of town. Then Calhoun began looking around for any sign that Curly had failed, but no sign bannered over the street advertising Colonel J. Patterson Turner's Transcontinental Race as it had in Jubilee Junction. There had been a more muted presence in Benedict—and nothing here.

The sunlight on Calhoun's back made him sit a little straighter as he rode through the town. Clarkesville was larger than he expected, but nowhere did he find evidence of the race.

"There it is, Sid. There," Curly said, pointing to an empty

building. Gold letters on the plate-glass window revealed this was the Turner Haulage Company office, but a cursory look inside showed it had never opened.

"Where's the stage depot?"

"Over yonder," Swain said. He sounded ornery, putting Calhoun on guard.

"Thanks," Calhoun said. "Let's me and you ride on over there, Swain, while Curly finds out more about the cowboy who broke that bronco." He tipped his head in the direction of the livery until Curly got the idea. Curly grunted and hurried off to find out what he could.

"Why do you put up with him?" Swain asked.

Calhoun saw it was time to smooth some ruffled feathers.

"He'll be useful until we get close to the gold. You got any problem with just me and you splittin' the prize?"

Swain looked sharply at him, started to speak, then simply shook his head.

"Good. Curly can scout and do simple things, but he isn't too swift on the uptake, not like you, Skunk."

"You want me to kill him?"

"No, nothing of the sort." Calhoun saw the disappointment, and knew then how to keep Swain loyal—to a point. "Not yet," he said more softly. "Then you can do it."

Swain nodded once, and looked happier than he had in a week.

They dismounted at the side of the depot, and Calhoun motioned for Swain to remain with the horses. What he learned inside might determine when he took a different trail from his two henchmen.

"Morning," the stage agent said in greeting. He was a young man, hardly out of his teens, but he wore small rectangular glasses and squinted a little at Calhoun. "You wantin' a ticket outta Clarkesville? We got a stage leaving for Benedict tomorrow."

"What's to the west?"

"Denver."

"Do tell," Calhoun said. "How many stops along the way before Denver?"

The young man pursed his lips, then began counting. Calhoun watched the process as the agent ticked off each stop, and knew the answer before the man spoke.

"Eight."

The thought flashed through Calhoun's mind that this was the number of keys he had in his vest pocket.

"Show me on the map," he asked, seeing a large map of the United States and its territories on the back wall.

"Well, sir, the stage goes from here to here and then . . ." The agent dragged his finger along, leaving a tiny black trail as the ink smeared.

"The last stop's called Dry Water," Calhoun said. "If they split, they'd want to get back together before going into Denver."

"Who you mean?" The agent peered at Calhoun. "You the law?"

"Something like that. The woman on the stagecoach," Calhoun prodded.

"Oh, she was a looker. Seldom seen a woman that lovely, and certainly not here in Clarkesville. Made me want to buy a ticket and go wherever she was headed. Real polite, too. The sort of lady you want to do things for. She smelled nice, too, considerin' how she musta been out on the trail."

"The man with her? What do you remember about him?"

"Didn't see much of him. Weaselly-looking fella. Couldn't see why she was travelin' with him. Not that he went on the stage with her, mind you."

"Oh?"

"He rode off with their horses."

Calhoun swung around when the door was flung open and Curly burst inside.

"His name's John Slocum, and he lit out yesterday."

"Slocum? No, I heard her call him Harry. Never caught the last name," the agent said.

"We're talkin' 'bout different folks," Calhoun said.

"The one what rode into town with him's still workin' at the newspaper," Curly said. "He left her behind."

"Heard tell we had a new female reporter. Who'd have thought a thing like that," the agent said, shaking his head. "Next thing you know, women'll be doin' all kinds of jobs and puttin' us out of work."

Calhoun took one last look at the map and fixed the terrain in his head.

"Come on, Curly. Let's get Swain. We're ridin' for Dry Water."

17

Slocum rode slowly to be certain his horse's leg had healed properly. The going was easier because he followed the tracks left by the stagecoach and the mud was turning to firmer soil, giving better footing. From the way the weeds grew over the twin ruts, only one or two stages rattled along this road every week. He couldn't tell which direction they ran, but he guessed it was west for the first part of the week and back to Clarkesville from Denver at the end.

He appreciated the lonesome territory stretching as far as he could see. More than once, he considered veering off the trail and heading north—or south—or any way other than following the golden lure offered by Colonel Turner and his race. The keys in his pocket were an incentive, but he'd felt strangely uneasy at how he left Zoe Murchison back in town. He should have told her he was moving on.

Then he knew there was no point. She had found herself a job and one that suited her better than trying to send telegraphed stories back to some St. Louis newspaper. She could cover the important goings-on in a town like Clarkesville

153

and become an outstanding citizen before she knew it. There was scant chance her big-city editor would do anything more than steal her stories. Slocum had never asked if she had seen her byline on a published article, or if she knew for certain that the editor wasn't putting his own name on the series she was risking her neck to write.

Zoe was better off in Clarkesville.

Slocum still felt a pang of guilt about not telling her he was riding on, though. The race meant more to her than it did to him, as witnessed by the times he'd considered chucking it all and finding his way elsewhere. The lure of so much gold made his heart pound a little faster, but then the same could be said about Zoe also.

"Better to leave her behind," he said. Slocum laughed without humor. "Zoe would only get in the way when I track down Molly." The notion of two lovely women sharing his bed did more than make his heart beat faster. Riding became downright uncomfortable, but his thoughts turned to other things and soon he rode more comfortably.

He crested a hill and scanned the prairie ahead of him. He fancied he could see the Front Range in the distance, but that came from his imagination. He was several days' ride away from even a hint of the towering peaks, some of which never lost their snowy caps even on the hottest summer days. Before he saw them ahead, he would be in Dry Water.

He kept a steady pace, but began to worry a mite when his mare missed a step now and then. He was in a hurry to find Molly Ibbotson and get what he could from her, which wasn't likely to be more than a golden key or two. He was worried that her brother had ridden away in a different direction, as if they had information Slocum wasn't privy to. Slocum decided, for the hundredth time, that it didn't matter what messages they had gotten in Benedict as long as he followed Molly. She would not quit the race. Finding her would keep him on the course better than any cryptic instructions the colonel might have left for the racers.

"But it's pretty devious to steal the instructions and leave nothing but empty envelopes," he said as he dismounted and patted his mare's neck. The horse moved easily, but Slocum still was worried.

Did he worry as much about the mare's leg as he did about Zoe Murchison?

"Time to camp. We've got an hour or so until sundown. The rabbits ought to be leaving their burrows. You munch some of that grass while I hunt."

The horse whinnied, and let Slocum go about his hunting without further protest.

It was sometime after finishing his meal that he grew increasingly edgy. His horse swayed back and forth, asleep. If a wolf or coyote approached, the mare would have come awake instantly. Someone was doing his best to sneak closer. Thoughts of the Sioux flashed through Slocum's mind as he drew his six-shooter and rolled away, moving as silently as a cloud floating across the sky.

He had camped in a hollow protected from the wind and the sight of any traveler along the road by moderately sized hills. Moving into a shallow ravine, he made his way toward the road and looked around. He caught his breath when he saw a horse tethered to a low bush. He couldn't make out the details without going closer, but thought the rifle was missing from the saddle scabbard. Six-gun gripped firmly in his hand, he found the spot where the rider had chosen to attack.

Within ten yards, Slocum saw a figure huddled near a stunted tree. From there, it was an easy shot at anyone in the camp. He didn't see a rifle in the hands moving about fitfully, almost nervously, but he didn't have to. Slocum cocked his six-shooter and aimed it at the middle of the darkness.

"Move a muscle and you're a dead man!" Slocum almost squeezed off a shot when the figure suddenly exploded upward, half turned as if to fire, then tumbled backward down the hill toward his camp. He followed fast, not wanting to let the man get away.

"I said to freeze!"

"John!"

Slocum jerked his pistol off line so he wouldn't accidentally shoot Zoe.

"What are you doing here? I could have killed you."

"Why?"

"I thought you were getting a bead on me from up on the hill," he said.

"No, not that. Why'd you leave me in Clarkesville the way you did? You could have at least said good-bye. I deserved that much."

"I didn't see any point in making a long good-bye out of it," Slocum said. He shoved his six-gun back into his cross-draw holster and slid down the hill to stand beside Zoe. She had gotten up, and futilely worked to brush off the stickers and other debris that clung tenaciously to her skirt. She stamped her foot in anger, and then broke out in tears.

Slocum found himself with an armful of quaking woman. She buried her face in his shoulder and sobbed until he felt his shirt turning damp from her tears.

"I didn't do anything to make you treat me that way, John. I thought we were a team, you and I. We could have stayed in Clarkesville for a week or two, gotten money, and then gone on together to win the gold. I mean, you could have gotten the gold and I would have had my story. Not that I wouldn't have liked the gold, but that wouldn't be professional since I'm a reporter and Mr. Zelnicoff would never have let me keep the money and—"

"Hush up," Slocum said. "You're half hysterical."

She shoved him away. The tears were replaced by anger.

"Why'd you go like that? You thought you'd go on by yourself and keep the prize? Was that it?"

"You were as happy as a pig in a wallow getting the job as reporter," Slocum started.

"A pig? You think I'm nothing more than a pig! How dare you!"

"I didn't mean that—"

He found himself with an armful of clawing, struggling woman.

As suddenly as she had begun fighting him, she yielded. Zoe turned her tear-stained face up to him and her lips parted slightly. For a moment, Slocum did nothing. Then she said in a voice hardly audible, "Kiss me."

He did. Her response was immediate. She clung to him fiercely and her lips crushed hard against his until he thought she would bruise them. Her body began rubbing against his like a cat rubbing up against a piece of furniture, and then she was frantically skinning him out of his coat and vest, worrying at the buttons and then, fumbling so much, moving down to the buttons on his fly. She had better luck there.

He sprang out as soon as the last button was released. She dropped to her knees in front of him and took him into her mouth. Slocum's knees went a little weak in reaction. He stroked through her hair, and then laced his fingers through the strands to guide her in a motion that did the impossible— it excited him even more.

The feel of her mouth against his hardness sent tiny earthquakes throughout his body. He jerked harder in the warmth of her mouth as she used her tongue and lightly scored the sides of his manhood with her teeth.

"Enough," he said. "I want more than your mouth."

"What more do you want?" Zoe's eyes burned like coals as she looked up at him.

He answered through action. His hands stroked her cheeks, moved down her throat, and then insinuated themselves under her lacy collar. As he forced his hands lower, the buttons on her blouse popped open one by more. Soon enough, her blouse gaped open and both of his hands cupped her breasts. He felt the warmth and the vitality there as her heart hammered wildly. He caught one rubbery nip and tweaked it. Zoe closed her eyes and moaned softly. The moan came louder when he duplicated the effort on her other breast. She lifted her hands and pressed his into her soft flesh.

"More, John. Don't tease me. Give me what we both want."

He dropped to his knees and kissed her lips. His mouth moved lower to the hollow of her throat, and then to the deep valley between her luscious breasts. She sank backward to the ground, and he followed. His hands lifted her skirt and found warm, willing flesh underneath. Pushing up the useless cloth took only a moment until he had exposed her privates.

"You're not wearing your bloomers," he said.

"I don't need a fashion lecture," she said in a rasping voice. Her eyes were closed and a look of desire was etched on her features.

He wasn't going to give her a lecture. He moved into the vee of her legs, his thickness probing outward until he found her nether lips. Juices leaked out, and made his entry easier. Slick, quick, and deep, he sank into her heated interior. The entry took both their breaths away.

Zoe began thrashing about and lifting herself off the ground to drive her groin down into his with insistent need. She clutched at his upper arms and half sat up.

"Take me, John. Hard. Fast. That's the way I want it."

That was the way he gave it to her. He pulled back, hesitated, and then rammed down hard until he once more felt the woman's intimate flesh surrounding him completely. This time he did not pause, but withdrew as quickly as he had entered. Faster and faster he moved, until he felt like a piston on a steam locomotive. Every thrust drove him deeper into her until it felt as if he might split her in two all the way to her throat. But she clenched down tightly on his hidden length before that happened, and threatened to mash him flat.

Slocum kept moving but their fates were sealed. They both gasped in unison, and then he felt the hot rush until he was spent. Zoe continued moving beneath him for a few seconds more, and then she, too, sank down to the ground.

Slocum stared at her in wonder. It was as good as it had ever been for him, and he wondered why she had left Clarkesville to follow him. She'd had a life back in town that she could never have with him out on the trail.

"They're following," she said.

"What? Who?" His brain was muzzy, and it took him a few seconds to concentrate enough on what she was saying to understand. "Calhoun?"

"Him and two of his thugs," she said. "They came into town about sunrise and asked after you." She took a deep breath, which caused her breasts to jiggle about delightfully. Seeing how distracted Slocum was, she pulled her blouse over her chest, but made no move to button up. "They were inquiring about me, too, but were less interested in me than in Molly Ibbotson."

Zoe's eyes left Slocum's and stared out into the darkness. "They think she somehow stole the instructions that were supposed to be in Clarkesville and pressed on."

"So they're after her."

"And after you. Sid Calhoun was also interested in you."

"He'd probably shoot me out of hand if he finds me before I see him."

"You'd kill him?"

"I'd cut him down like a rabid dog," Slocum said.

Zoe laughed nervously. "You're such a kidder, John."

He didn't correct her. He'd meant it. Too many men like Calhoun roamed the West. Killing them before they could kill anyone else was a public service. Not only would Slocum be protecting his own life, but also the lives of countless others that Sid Calhoun might gun down for the hell of it.

Slocum went rigid as he balanced above the woman. With his pants down, he was vulnerable. She went on about things he had no interest in any longer, because he had heard his horse whinny. His and Zoe's amorous activities had awakened the horse, but it had not made any noise until now.

He rolled free, kicked and got his jeans pulled up, and hastily fastened them. Then he reached for his six-gun and got to his feet.

"What's wrong?"

"Be quiet. Somebody's out there."

"Oh, silly, you're having one of those odd moments where you think you know what's going to happen. I forget what the French call it."

Slocum didn't care what the French called anything unless it told him what was going on. He turned slowly until he located the spot where someone moved about out in the darkness.

"It's Calhoun, isn't it?"

Slocum put his finger to his lips to silence her. She worked to button her blouse and got it crooked, cursed in a very unladylike manner, then started over.

"Stay over there, in the shadow of the tree," he said, pointing to a spot dark with the night. He didn't wait to see if she obeyed. He moved away, making more noise than he would have liked, but he was still shaky from the lovemaking.

After going a few yards into the undergrowth, Slocum stopped and got his nerves settled. The familiar calm that had served him so well in the past descended on him. During the war, he had been a sniper—one of the best. Sitting all day in the limbs of a tree waiting for the glint of sunlight off a Union officer's braid took its toll on a man's nerves. Slocum had learned to relax, wait for the shot, take it, and then leave quickly before the Federals homed in on him. More than one battle had been won because Slocum had killed the enemy commander. That experience stood him in good stead now.

He began moving more quietly through the brush and became one with the wind, floating along until he saw the silhouette of a man moving ahead. Slocum veered away to get some distance between him and the man, who seemed intent on working toward the campsite. If that was Sid Calhoun, he had others with him. Zoe had mentioned two others in the gang with Calhoun, but Slocum needed to know if she had calculated properly how many there were. All he needed to do to die with a bullet in the back was to forget about just one of the sneaking owlhoots riding with Calhoun.

Slocum found two horses left not far from where Zoe had tethered hers. Try as he might, Slocum couldn't find any others.

"Two men," he muttered. Something about the two horses bothered him, but he didn't have time to examine them closely enough to satisfy his curiosity. He moved rapidly back toward his camp, the man he had seen skulking about ahead of him.

Slocum felt a pang of guilt because he had used Zoe as bait. She was hidden in the shadows, but not enough to hide from anyone intent on finding her. He moved faster when he heard the man nearing the camp cry out. The man had stumbled and hurt his leg.

"Drop your iron," Slocum called.

His answer was a stream of curses and a bullet zinging through the air. Slocum ducked, although the shot had gone wide. He was momentarily dazzled by the muzzle flash, but he had a better idea where Calhoun was than the outlaw did about him. Slocum aimed and fired. His reward was a loud cry of pain.

"Drop your gun or I'll ventilate you," Slocum warned.

He threw himself facedown on the ground as four more wildly fired shots filled the air above him. Working forward like a snake, he watched for his chance. It came fast. For a brief instant, the man was outlined against the starlit sky. Slocum took aim and got off two quick shots.

He saw the man buckle and drop to his knees. In the dark, he couldn't be sure he had even hit the man, but the way the shadowy arms reached around and clutched his belly strongly hinted that Slocum's bullets had found their target.

"You son of a bitch," came the pain-wracked words. A final shot sang into the night, but Slocum saw that the six-shooter was pointed toward the sky. An instant later, the man toppled backward and rolled down the hill, almost exactly where Zoe had fallen earlier. Slocum followed, but this time there wouldn't be any delightful end to the tumble.

The man sprawled on the ground near the fire.

"Get away from him," Slocum called. He worked to reload. Two horses, two men. Another was out in the night and might be drawing a bead on Zoe even as he called out his warning.

"John, it's the woman's brother, I think. He looks like you described him."

"Harry Ibbotson?"

"Yes, him."

Slocum slid down the hill and peered at the dead man. Zoe was right.

A thousand thoughts jumbled, and finally Slocum pieced everything together. Two horses meant Ibbotson had taken his sister's horse to make better time while she took the stagecoach to Denver.

"Oh, John."

Zoe clung to him again, but this time it was for solace rather than sex. That was fine with Slocum. He felt drained at the sudden gunfight that had ended in a man's death. He disentangled from Zoe, knelt, and searched the dead man's pockets.

He stopped looking when he found a gold key. It disappeared into his pocket to join the others he already had. Slocum stood and said, "I'd better bury him or the coyotes will gather before morning."

Zoe said something he didn't understand. Then he got to work burying the man he had been paid to rescue from kidnappers.

18

Molly Ibbotson opened an eye and looked sideways at the two men riding in the stagecoach with her. Both of them were either asleep—doubtful due to the rough road and sudden lurches they had endured for miles—or simply wanted to keep the dust kicked up by the wheels out of their eyes. She reached into her purse and took out a pint bottle. A quick move pulled the cork and brought the bottle to her lips. The rye whiskey burned like fire all the way down to her stomach, where it settled and spread warmth throughout her body. Within a few minutes, the aches and pains from her long travel faded into a dim memory.

She recorked the bottle and returned it to her purse. She didn't care about the men thinking she was a drunk, but she didn't want to have to share with them. Still, she considered taking another quick pull. But the view out the window through the dust cloud stopped her from wetting her whistle again. Denver was only a few minutes away.

Molly settled back and closed her eyes, letting the dust settle on her face like some strange facial powder. She knew she looked like her two traveling companions with a caked-brown complexion. A long, hot bath would go a long way toward restoring her vigor and sharpness.

She had misjudged the distance to town, but the stage did pull into the depot an hour later. The two men jumped up, rudely pushed past her, and dived out the door when the driver opened it. Before her foot touched the ground, both men had disappeared.

"Them fellas was sure in a hurry," the driver said, scratching himself. "Didn't think the ride was that bad. Seen some folks get sick from the rolling motion, but not you, eh, ma'am?"

"Not me," Molly said primly. She looked around, thinking Harry would be here to meet her. "Where is the waiting room?"

"You mean the ticket office? Inside. Ain't much of a place to wait. You're better off findin' a hotel. There's one not a quarter mile down the street, if you're thinkin' on waitin' fer another stage. We got a route over the mountains through Mosquito Pass. Trip takes a goodly week, but other than horseback and the railroad, you're not gettin' westward any other way."

"I'm not looking forward to such transportation any time soon."

"Well, you kin always count on us to git you where you want to go."

"Where is the Turner Haulage Company office?"

"They don't carry passengers, just freight. Or so I been told."

"You aren't familiar with the company?" Molly turned and stared at the driver in disbelief.

"We heard tell they was comin' into town but I never heard when. Don't affect us none. Like I said, they're supposed to move freight. We transport passengers."

"What do you know of the race?"

"Race? Well, heard tell there's a mighty fine racetrack

across the mountains, over in Leadville. High-stakes races, if that's what you mean."

"Colonel J. Patterson Turner's Transcontinental Race," she said, and saw not a flicker of recognition in the man's rheumy eyes.

"You got me. Never heard of that race. Might be something they do down south around Pueblo. They do danged stupid things there. Something in the smoke from the smelters affects their brains maybe."

Molly took a deep breath and saw that the man's vision wasn't so impaired that he didn't notice the rise and fall of her breasts. She spun about and went inside the depot, still thinking she would find her brother waiting. The room was empty.

"Help you, miss?" The agent looked up from a counter where he sorted through letters destined for the post office.

"I'm looking for my brother." Molly described Harry and finished with: "He might be a little the worse for travel."

"Didn't ride in on our stage then," the agent said sagely. "Nope, ain't seen anybody like that in the past few days. If you want, leave a place where you can be reached and I'll see that he gets the note if he shows up."

"That's all right. I'm sure we can find one another when the time comes." She interrogated the agent about the colonel's race, and got the same response that she'd had from the driver. There was no hint of guile or trying to sweep all mention of a commercial rival under the rug. He genuinely had not heard of the race.

Molly stepped outside the depot and looked up and down the busy street. Denver was a bustling town where a man could get lost quickly. For all that, news of a race starting in St. Louis and ending somewhere on the West Coast ought to mean something. She began walking, taking in everything she could. After asking a dozen people, she found the Turner Haulage Company office a dozen blocks from Larimer Square.

No banners proclaimed the fabulous prize or the status of the race. Molly looked around, wondering if she had somehow beaten all the others to the office. No one took more than a passing interest in her, and those men were not looking at her as a rival but as a conquest. She went into the office.

"I'm a racer and need the next set of instructions," she said without preamble. She was in no mood to bandy words.

"Racer? Oh, heard something about that. We're still gettin' set up."

"The instructions," she said. "You do have them? This is a stop along the race path?"

"All I've heard was that there'd be a telegram telling what to do. I don't have anything else to give you, 'less you want to ship some freight."

"What are your rates? What's your schedule?"

The agent's expression told Molly all she needed. The freight office was open but not for business. As had been the case in Clarkesville, the colonel hadn't done much to set up his way station along the very routes he advertised with his race. She chewed her lower lip, worrying about reaching the finish line and not finding any prize.

"Send a telegram to St. Louis and ask," she told him. "I'm the first?"

"You are, ma'am," the agent said. He looked uneasy. "There's a problem about that. I don't have money enough to send a telegram."

"Here," Molly said, fishing out a few tattered greenbacks and handing them to the agent. "You will tell no one else what instructions you get back. Is that clear?"

From his reaction, he needed a drink and was considering spending the money on booze. Molly took out the bottle she had sipped from on the road to Denver and silently added it to the scrip. The lure of the half-filled whiskey bottle along with the money settled the matter. He snatched up the bottle and took the money.

"I'll be right back," he said, coming around the counter and leaving the office. Molly saw him take a pull from the bottle as he hurried to the telegraph office.

Molly went behind the counter and satisfied herself that the man wasn't holding back. She found nothing about the race, and especially no stack of envelopes with different instructions. She rifled through documents on the man's desk, and found the Turner Haulage Company routes drawn onto a map. Her guess had been right about Denver being the point where race instructions would be dispensed. No matter where the routes began, they funneled through Denver coming in from both directions. Along the Mississippi and the Pacific Ocean were several terminus points. In the middle of the country, only Denver handled freight going to and from all the points.

Molly sat in the agent's desk chair and thought hard about this. She saw a newspaper to one side and pulled it in front of her so she could spread it flat on the desk. No mention of the race, but plenty about railroads going bankrupt and the financial woes of New York and Boston bankers. Before she could read the details, the agent returned.

"Sent off the message," he said. "It'll be a while 'fore I can expect a reply 'bout your race."

"Of course," Molly said. "I understand how these things are. Not everyone is as diligent in their business dealings as you are."

"Reckon so," he said skeptically. "You callin' me diligent?"

"That's a good thing," she assured him. "I saw your routes on the map. How soon will you begin shipping to Seattle and San Diego?"

"Don't have a date on them, but San Francisco is slated to open any time now."

"I'm sure you'll be ready to go then," she said. Molly started to leave, but the man called after her.

"I ought to get the message in a day or two, ma'am. Where can I get it to you?"

"I'll be back. Remember, don't tell anyone else," she said.

Molly walked a block down the street, then stopped a man and asked where the train station was. He gave her detailed instructions and she set off on foot, getting more anxious with every step she took. It hardly mattered what the colonel sent in way of directions for the race. If there was only one way west on the train, Molly would take that and go to San Francisco. No matter what the colonel planned at the finish of the race, it had to be in that city since he hadn't yet opened depots anywhere else.

She trooped up the steps to the railroad office and looked around, expecting to see her brother. It was foolish, but she kept expecting Harry to pop up unexpectedly.

"You waiting for someone, ma'am?"

"No," she said tartly. "One ticket to San Francisco."

"You got to wait a day, or you can go to Colorado Springs, take the narrow gauge over the hills, and then on to San Francisco."

"Will that route get me to San Francisco sooner than waiting a day?" If she hung around Denver, Harry might show up.

"Sure will. Narrow-gauge works better in the mountains and you'd get to the coast a couple days before the standard-gauge train."

"How much for the ticket to Colorado Springs and then on to San Francisco?"

The ticket clerk fussed a bit, came up with a number, and Molly paid, noting how little money she had left.

"You a bit hard up for cash?" the agent asked.

"My brother has our money."

"That him you were looking around for?"

"He has obviously preceded me and is expecting me in San Francisco," she said.

"Do tell. If you need some extra money, say a dollar, I know a way you can—"

Molly bit back her first response.

"I am one of Colonel Turner's racers," she said. "The colonel can be a very generous man—or a truly vindictive one. Or so the rumor goes. I doubt that he actually skinned a man alive and left him out in the sun to die."

The agent paled. "Train's coming now. You got luggage?"

"I travel light," she said. Molly wished she had been able to carry more with her, but she had what mattered. Reaching into her purse, she fingered the gold keys she carried. Harry had another one. If he didn't hurry, she would claim the gold for herself—provided one of her keys fit the strongbox with the gold. The way her luck had run lately, Harry would have the key needed to claim the prize, and he'd be stupid enough to get himself killed and lose the key before reaching wherever the colonel had stashed his prize.

The train wheezed up and slowed amid screeching wheels and hissing steam released in huge white clouds. She flinched when the whistle announced it was time to board. Molly hung back and watched the others board. She didn't recognize any of them as being in the race. From their small talk, they were mostly merchants from Colorado Springs who had come to Denver to arrange supplies. One man in particular rambled on and on about a hotel and mineral spa he ran in Manitou Springs and how people from all over the world came to take the waters.

She settled down where she could watch the station platform, hoping Harry would arrive at the last instant.

"Howdy, ma'am, this seat taken?"

Before she could reply, the man boasting of his hotel dropped beside her, and moved close enough to press his thigh against hers.

"They make these bench seats harder all the time—and shorter. You going to the Springs?"

"Beyond," she said.

"Then you got to come through my town."

"Manitou Springs," she said. His eyebrows rose and she added, "I overheard your tribulations getting decent supplies. Tell me about your resort."

"It's a mighty pricey place, but worth it," he said before launching into a sales pitch designed to entice her by appealing to her vanity and desire to hobnob with high society. "I'm worrying a mite about how the financial panic back East is going to affect my guests," he confided. "I get a fair number of the highest of high society from New England since my spa waters are excellent for curing arthritis and other joint ailments so common in that part of the country."

Molly's mind drifted as the man enthusiastically described his resort in every excruciating detail. She might be inclined to return and sample some of the sybaritic delights he so proudly boasted of, but San Francisco offered a more elegant society.

"Your husband in business?" the man asked.

"What? Oh, no. I am on my way to San Francisco to claim his—my—estate."

"A sizable one?"

"You are most impertinent, sir," she said sharply. Molly started to order him to move, then looked out the window and saw Sid Calhoun and the henchman with a stripe of white hair rushing to catch the train. She turned so they could not see her face. If it appeared she was with a man Calhoun didn't recognize, he might never give her a second glance.

"Didn't mean to be, ma'am," the hotel owner said. "I know how it is to be grieving. My own dear wife passed on only last year."

"Tell me about the waters. Are they restorative?"

He hurried on to tell her more than she cared to know about the sulfur springs. He faced her while she pretended to hang on his every word. As the train lurched forward, she chanced a look back. Calhoun and his partner had missed the train. That was good because it gave her a decided head start over him in reaching San Francisco and the $50,000 prize.

What wasn't so good was having to listen to the hotel man all the way to Colorado Springs. Somehow, even the lure of so much gold at the end of the trip wasn't enough to erase the tedium.

19

"Can't we ride faster, John?" Zoe Murchison rose in the stirrups and rubbed her hindquarters. "I'm not used to spending so much time in the saddle."

"I'm still worried about my mare's leg," he said.

"We have two other horses, and you're letting your horse walk along without a rider. Granted, the horses we took from . . . from the dead man aren't of the finest quality, but we can make better time if we pressed on."

"What's your hurry?"

Zoe glared at him before saying, "I have a story to telegraph to Mr. Zelnicoff. He will certainly fire me and strand me in the middle of nowhere if I don't continue to furnish fine copy for him."

"You going to relate how Harry Ibbotson tried to kill us and I shot him dead?"

Zoe opened her mouth, then snapped it closed. Slocum saw how conflicted she was on this point. There was no question she had participated in a killing and that, as a reporter, she shouldn't cover the death. Being part of the story made it imperative that another reporter who was more

175

objective write this story. As if the woman was an open book that he read easily, he knew she wasn't going to do that. She would send in her story with details blurred or even ignored so she would appear to be closely observing the colonel's race, with detailed interviews with the top participants.

Slocum snorted. He was not only a top contender, he might be the only one, other than Molly Ibbotson and the Calhoun gang. While those who had taken different routes might still be in the race, he had figured that the only way to the prize was through Denver. Molly wasn't anyone's fool, and was heading there directly on the stagecoach. Why Harry had tried to bushwhack them was open to dispute, but with the man dead, there would never be an answer.

Slocum touched the keys in his vest pocket. It might have been as simple as Harry wanting more of the keys to improve his chance of opening the colonel's treasure chest at the end of the race.

"San Francisco," Zoe said. Seeing his frown, she hurried on with her explanation. "We arrive in Denver and, no matter what the new instructions say, we go directly to San Francisco. There's nowhere else the colonel is likely to have the press coverage of the winner claiming his prize."

"If anyone claims the prize. Fifty keys, only one opening the box. How many have been lost?"

"How many men have died and given up their keys?"

"I know of at least one," Slocum said, jerking his thumb over his shoulder in the direction of the unmarked grave where he had buried Harry Ibbotson. "I'm sure there have been more."

"A lot more. That's part of my article," she said. "What will a man do to claim such a rich prize?"

"Murder's the least of it," Slocum said. "Harry might have been double-crossing his own sister."

"If she even was his sister," Zoe said archly. "They might have been more. I saw how they looked at one another."

Slocum shook his head. He had considered different relationships between the two, and had long ago decided Harry and Molly were siblings. She was the younger of the pair, but acted like his mother because of his impulsive behavior. Harry had never grown up—and Molly had grown too old for her years with her responsibility for him.

"What do you think we'll find in Dry Water?"

The sudden change of topic took Slocum by surprise.

"I doubt we'll find a whole lot," he said, "though there might be something new to occupy us. You came after me to say that Calhoun and his gang had ridden into Clarkesville and were on my trail. I haven't seen hide nor hair of anyone on this road."

"They might have taken a shortcut," Zoe said.

"Why head us off when they could ride up and shoot it out with us, if that's what was on Calhoun's mind?"

"They are dangerous men, especially the one with the white stripe through his hair. You can tell."

"I can tell," Slocum said. He had seen his share of men like Swain, and knew the only way to deal with them was to shoot first. What Zoe said about them riding ahead had put him on guard. Setting an ambush was the sort of trap Calhoun would fancy. The prairie was mighty flat through here, but ravines and the occasional low, rolling hill provided ample spots for a decent bushwhacking.

"Should we get off the road and cut across country?" Zoe asked.

"The road is as straight as an arrow from what I've seen and lets us make the best time. If Calhoun is ahead of us, tromping across the prairie will only slow us down and give him time to lay a better trap."

"Oh," she said. "So we *should* ride faster?"

Slocum had to laugh. The entire conversation had circled around to where it had started, with Zoe telling him to speed up. He dismounted, much to her chagrin, examined his mare's leg, and decided a faster pace wasn't going to hurt anything. As much as he hated to do it, when they reached Denver he would have to sell the mare and the other horses. Riding the train westward was quicker, and the notion of Calhoun or Molly or any of the others in the race getting to San Francisco first rankled him. He had shot at the others, and almost gotten shot himself, and gone through hell. Simply giving up on the chance of claiming so much gold wasn't in the cards.

Slocum wasn't a greedy man, but $50,000 would be reasonable payment for all that he had endured.

They trotted the horses, and only occasionally let them slow to a walk. Alternating the gait moved them to Dry Water faster than Slocum anticipated.

"Doesn't look like much," he said.

"It's so ordinary," Zoe said, "but there is a telegraph." She pointed to the pole alongside the road. "I've composed my article as we rode. It won't take more than a half hour to send it."

"You go on ahead and let me ask around."

"About further instructions on the race?"

"About Calhoun," he said. She tried to hide the momentary look of fear, then rode away without another word, leaving Slocum with his mare and the second horse they had claimed after Harry Ibbotson had died with a bullet through the heart.

Dry Water was such a small town that Slocum had no trouble learning that not only was there no Turner Haulage Company office, but that a trio of men had been asking the questions Slocum would have if he hadn't heard about the three owlhoots first.

The saloon gave him the obvious spot to begin his hunt for Calhoun and his two henchmen, but he didn't even have to go inside. Curly blundered out, roaring drunk.

"I'm the wildest, most dangerous-est cayuse in the whole damn West!" he bellowed. He drew his six-shooter and fired a couple shots in the air. Slocum waited to see who came. No marshal, no sheriff, nobody. It was as if a bubble had formed around Curly and he floated through an uninhabited town.

When the drunk began staggering down the middle of the street, Slocum followed cautiously. Curly had gone only a block before Slocum saw his chance and took it. He moved fast, came up behind the man, and wrapped his forearm around a turkey neck. Pulling back, he rocked Curly onto his heels and kept him entirely off balance. As the man tried to point his gun back and get off a shot at Slocum, his gun hand was momentarily vulnerable. Slocum grabbed the wrist and jerked hard enough to break bones. The six-gun dropped to the street from nerveless fingers.

"You hurt me, dammit!"

Slocum tightened his grip around Curly's neck until the man stopped struggling. Dragging the unconscious man down an alley, Slocum dropped him to the ground and then knelt, his knee in the middle of Curly's chest. The man gasped and began choking. Slocum let up just enough to let him breathe.

"Where's Calhoun?"

"He—don't know."

Slocum rocked forward and drove his knee down hard into Curly's belly. This doubled him up, and he started retching.

While he was incapacitated, Slocum rummaged through the owlhoot's pockets and found two gold keys. He added them to his collection.

"Where's Calhoun?" he repeated. "I won't ask again."

"Went on ahead. Him and Swain went on. I was left here to stop you."

"You certainly slowed us down," Slocum said. "It's taken a fair amount of time to get all that information out of you."

"Don't kill me. Please. That's what Calhoun was gonna

do. Or Skunk. Never saw a man who enjoyed killin' the way he does."

"What would happen if I let you go?"

"I'll head on back to St. Louis. Got cousins there."

"If I see your ugly face again, I'll blow it off," Slocum said in a level voice. Curly's eyes grew wide as he realized Slocum wasn't joshing him.

"You . . . you and Skunk Swain. You're like peas in a pod."

"Naw," Slocum said. "I'm worse." He let Curly get to his feet. The man staggered away, clutching his belly and trying not to fall over from all the liquor he'd imbibed. After he disappeared, Slocum returned to the main street and spotted Zoe waving to him.

"I've sent off my article," she said excitedly. "And I bought a newspaper. It's a little out of date, but I'm sure my first stories must be in it somewhere." She rustled through the pages, handing each to Slocum when she didn't see her name in print.

All he saw were reports on the spreading depression. The Panic of '73, some were calling it. Competing with such a financial crisis would be hard for any reporter, much less a cub reporter covering a race nobody outside St. Louis seemed to know squat about.

"I was sure there'd be mention somewhere," she said, disheartened.

"We're on our way to Denver. A big city'll have your stories in one of the papers."

He watched as she brightened. She stood on tiptoe and gave him a quick kiss, not caring that several citizens saw this unseemly behavior.

"Thank you, John. I keep forgetting this is the frontier."

He wondered if he ought to suggest they stay in Dry Water overnight so she could thank him more properly. Then he began worrying about the race.

"It's another couple days' hard ride to Denver. You up for it?"

"I was born ready," she said, grinning.

The days in the saddle were long and the nights filled with passion. Slocum wasn't sure he was grateful to see the Front Range with Denver and all its smaller camps settled at their base. Cherry Creek had been one of the first, born of a gold strike, but the town had become more than that. Commerce and the railroad had brought settlers and miners and men willing to gamble everything. Many failed. The ones who didn't prospered beyond even their dreams of avarice. Then there was Aurora and tiny Denver City, which had somehow spread and gobbled up the rest.

"Your horse isn't going to sell for much, John," Zoe said sorrowfully. "I'm sorry we had to rush so. Do you think the lameness will ever go away?"

"Doesn't matter," Slocum said. "From here, we have to get on the train and get over the mountains."

"Do you think Calhoun is already here?"

"That's what Curly said. I'm wondering if Molly Ibbotson has passed through already, too."

"We can find the office and get the instructions." She heaved a sigh and shook her head. "If we had only known the freight agent we could have bribed him to telegraph us the instructions."

"Being around so many crooks is making you like them. That's something I'd've expected Calhoun to think up."

"I'm trying to understand how a man like that thinks," she said. "For the article, of course."

"Not for the fifty thousand dollars," Slocum said, wondering if he ought to worry more about her honesty. Zoe was a delightful traveling companion, and the nights had been as tiring as the days, but in a more pleasurable way. The lure of money often outweighed any desire for fame.

"Of course not," she said, staring straight ahead so he couldn't see her face. "I'm a reporter. We cannot allow ourselves to become part of the story. That is unethical."

They rode farther into town, both lost in thought. After twenty minutes, they were surrounded by the crush of people, and Slocum began to get antsy. Zoe was about all the company he wanted right now. He found himself jumping at sudden noises and staring into shadows, wondering if Calhoun or another of the racers was drawing a bead on him.

"I'll find out where Turner's freight office is." It took longer than he thought since no one knew. He finally located another freight company that operated locally. The clerk directed Slocum to the Turner Haulage Company office.

A small crowd had gathered outside as they rode up. Slocum shook his head. A man was selling bars of soap for five dollars each.

"Why ever are they paying so much for soap?" Zoe asked. She frowned as she tried to figure it out. Before Slocum could tell her, a grizzled miner on the far side of the crowd held up an unwrapped bar of soap in one hand and a fifty-dollar bill in the other as he shouted, "I got me fifty dollars! I'm rich! Lookee!"

"He found such a large bill wrapped in the soap?"

"You don't want to get involved," Slocum said.

"But there's a story here. Whoever—"

"The man who's selling the soap has several confederates in the crowd." As Slocum spoke, it dawned on Zoe what was happening.

"They're working together. They're not actually finding fifty-dollar bills, are they?"

"The man doing the selling has the wrappers marked to give the right bar of soap to his partners."

"Why, that's dishonest! The others think they have a chance to unwrap a bar of soap and become rich."

"It's probably not even good soap," Slocum said. "Welcome to Denver."

"You can't allow them to be cheated. You have to tell them."

"Write a story about it," Slocum said, swinging his leg over and dropping to the ground. The impact of dirt under his boot soles jarred him. He had been on the trail too long, and his entire body ached from the ride from Dry Water.

"If you won't, I will."

Slocum went to Zoe's horse, reached up, grabbed the woman around the waist, and yanked, pulling her from the saddle. She kicked and fought a little, then stopped and glared at him.

"You're as bad as the men stealing from the others," she said. "You know it's all a confidence game, and you're doing nothing about it."

"If you bought a bar of soap for five dollars expecting to find a fifty wrapped around it, what'd you think?"

"That I was cheated!"

"Nope, you'd buy another bar, hoping to get the prize. Most of those in the crowd will end up with ten bars of very expensive soap. Some might end up with more, but it'll be a lesson they won't forget." Slocum said that only to pacify Zoe, because most of the men would never figure out they had been duped. Their need to get something for nothing was too strong. Greed was so powerful, they would spend a dozen times what they might hope to get just to win.

Slocum stopped at the door of the colonel's freight office, and wondered if his behavior was any different. He sought a king's ransom in gold and, at best, had only as many chances of winning as he had golden keys. A racer getting to San Francisco with a single key might win, and all of Slocum's efforts would then be worthless.

At least the citizens of Denver would receive soap as a reminder of their misadventure. Slocum had nothing but a trail of dead bodies to show for his efforts so far.

The clerk looked up, a sour look on his face.

"Git yer soap outside. From that one. Soapy Smith."

"We're more interested in directions for the race, Colonel J. Patterson Turner's Transcontinental Race." Slocum saw the sudden furtive look and wondered what was going on.

He drew his six-shooter and laid it on the counter, not quite aiming the muzzle in the clerk's direction.

"What are the instructions?" There was no way for the man not to realize what would happen if he didn't provide the requested directions.

"Look, I was paid to, uh, get the instructions. I didn't know nothing 'bout them until she—"

"She?" Zoe quickly described Molly Ibbotson. Slocum thought Zoe was a trifle harsh as she lingered on certain details, but he couldn't blame her too much. It looked as if the woman had abandoned her brother and cared nothing that he had been killed trying to commit murder.

"That's the one," said the clerk. "Real looker, she was. She told me not to show this to anybody." The clerk produced a yellow telegram and held it in a shaking hand. Slocum grabbed it.

"Salt Lake City," he said. "The next instructions are in Salt Lake City."

"The finish line is in San Francisco," Zoe said. "It has to be. There's no other conclusion. We should go directly there."

"San Francisco is a mighty big city," Slocum said. "What if the note in Salt Lake City tells us exactly where to go?"

"The train," Zoe said, slumping. "We need to go to Salt Lake City on the train."

Slocum stuck his six-shooter back into his holster by way of thanking the agent, and backed from the office. The crowd of avid soap buyers had dissipated, leaving the small salesman and three others to count and divvy the money.

"You were right, John. I'm sorry I doubted you."

"Let's hope you don't have call to doubt me again."

"Salt Lake City," she confirmed.

They rode to the train station, where Slocum spent fifteen minutes dickering with a man for the best possible price for his horses. He was sorry to sell the mare, game leg or not, but they needed the money, and the rest of the trip to San Francisco would be on a train.

"Yes, sir, you're a lucky stiff," the ticket agent said. "The train'll roll in anytime now. Won't be another one headin' direct fer Salt Lake City for another week."

"How about one making another stop?"

"Yesterday," the ticket agent said. "It left yesterday for the Springs and then over the mountains from there. On the far side of the mountains, the narrow-gauge goes on up through the middle of the territory, stops at Grand Junction, and from there you could catch a train to Salt Lake City."

Slocum let Zoe describe Molly again since she took such pleasure in it. He stepped out onto the platform and froze.

Sid Calhoun and Skunk Swain waited impatiently for the train to come to a halt so they could board.

20

"We've got a small problem," Slocum said to Zoe once they had boarded the train.

Zoe looked up, then frowned when she saw he was not making idle chatter. She gasped when he pointed to Calhoun and Swain shuffling their feet impatiently on the platform, waiting to board.

"We've got to get off! Right now!" she cried. Slocum grabbed her arm and pulled her back down to the hard bench seat. She struggled, but he clung to her hard enough to bruise her arm. When she realized he was not going to turn her loose, she subsided.

"What are we going to do if not leave the train? You can't shoot it out with them. Not with both of them and hope to get away. They're killers!"

Slocum considered doing just that, but discarded the notion for reasons completely different from what Zoe had conjured up. He could take both men because they were back-shooters, not men who faced others down with a drawn six-shooter. Not only was he a better shot than either of

187

them, but he had quicker reflexes, and knew he had the grit to do what was necessary without hesitation. What stopped him from swinging out of the train seat and gunning down the pair of owlhoots was the knowledge that the train would be halted and the Denver law would be summoned. Denver had a nasty police force, almost as corrupt and cruel as that in San Francisco. In that city, the remnants of the Australian gangs like the Sydney Ducks had pinned on badges and made their killings legal. Here in Denver, down-on-their-luck miners provided almost as deadly a brand of law en-forcement.

"Turn slightly and look at the rear door," he told her. His hand rested on the ebony handle of his six-gun. "If they come into this car, let me know." He took a deep breath to settle himself and prepared to spin around and blaze away. He and Zoe might escape through the front of the car and into the rail yard before anyone raised a hue and cry. Deal-ing with the railroad dicks was almost as difficult as dealing with the Denver police, but Slocum knew he had enough bullets to allow them to escape.

He just didn't want to leave behind a trail of bodies— and friends and relatives swearing eternal vengeance.

The train lurched, lurched again, and began to gather speed. The steam whistle let out its ear-splitting shriek, and then the cars rattled along more smoothly, leaving the sta-tion.

"They must be in the rear car," Zoe said. "They didn't come in."

Slocum relaxed a mite. His mind spun through all the different ways of dealing with Calhoun and Swain without simply walking up and murdering them. Nothing came to him right away, but it would. He leaned back, pulled his hat down over his eyes, and said, "I'm going to get some sleep. You keep a close watch for them and let me know if they come in."

"But, John, I—" Zoe saw that he was serious. Slocum's

last memory before he drifted to sleep was her cursing in a very unladylike way.

"We're getting into the mountains," Slocum said needlessly. They were forced into the backs of their seats by the steepness of the grade. Night had fallen, cloaking everything outside.

"My eyes are crossed from watching that door. I've done it ever since Denver, all the way out of Colorado Springs and into the mountains. I'm as nervous as a mouse in a cat factory."

Slocum looked at her a moment, then smiled. He pushed his hat all the way back on his head, made sure the six-gun rode easy, and then stood.

"Don't be scared, no matter what happens."

"John," she said, grabbing for his arm, "be careful."

He nodded and made his way back along the sloping car to the back door leading to the small metal platform. He slipped out and stepped across to the rear car, and peered through the filthy glass window in the door. Soot from the engine had completely shrouded the window, but he scraped away enough to peer in. The hissing, flickering gas lamps in the rear car cast shadows randomly, but he caught sight of Calhoun and Swain. The two men sat in aisle seats across from one another. He hadn't seen any other members of the gang enter, and knew Curly was probably still running like a scalded dog.

Slocum backed away, stepped across to the forward car, and then dropped to his belly to examine the linkage holding the cars together. A safety pin kept the coupling from opening. He yanked it free, but the coupling held. He got grease all over his hands as he worked diligently on the coupling, and was finally rewarded with a loud snapping sound. Slocum jerked back to keep his hand from being severed as the rear passenger car, with the caboose attached behind it, slipped backward into the night.

He watched as the cars gathered speed and ran back down the narrow-gauge track until the train huffed and puffed around a curve on the side of the mountain and the disconnected cars disappeared.

Going back into the car, he noticed that the train had sped up. It figured. Removing the weight of two cars had to give more speed to the remaining section of the train. He took time to wipe his hands off on a filthy rag he found near the hole in the floor that served as an outhouse, then worked forward to drop back by Zoe.

"Well, what happened? I didn't hear any gunshots."

"There weren't any," he said, pulling his hat back down. "I'm going to get some more sleep." He pushed the brim back and looked into her eyes when he added, "You can sleep, too. No need to watch the rear door. Calhoun and his crony won't be bothering us."

"What—?"

But he was already drifting off to sleep again. He had run too long on too little sleep and needed to catch up.

The train ground to a halt at the Salt Lake City depot two days after Slocum had sent Calhoun and the rest rattling backward down the east face of the Front Range.

"I'm anxious, John. I want to see a newspaper."

"For your article?"

"Of course, silly," Zoe said. "Mr. Zelnicoff must have syndicated my articles by now. I'm sure it will be on the front page of every paper."

"The *Deseret Bee* is the only paper I know of in town," Slocum said. It had been a few years since he had come through here, and he hadn't much liked his brief stay. There had been a bit of unpleasantness with the marshal and two of his deputies, and Slocum had chosen to hightail it out of town rather than argue the point. He still thought he was right, but they had the law on their side.

"Then that's the one I'll buy." Zoe pressed past him in her rush to leave the train. He followed, and found her fumbling for change to buy a newspaper from a sunny-haired, freckle-faced boy clutching a stack of papers.

"Is your article there?"

"I don't see it," she said. She stayed hopeful until she worked her way through the entire paper. Slocum took the front page from her, and saw more news about bank failures back East, along with two railroads declaring bankruptcy. He tried to remember the name of the railroad Colonel Turner was a director of, but couldn't. He wondered if it was one of the railroads mentioned in the paper.

"I am disappointed," Zoe said. Then she brightened. "Perhaps the stories ran in earlier editions. This is a daily newspaper. I can go to their morgue and look through the back issues."

"You do that," Slocum said, "while I go to the Turner Haulage Company and ask about the next instructions." He got the response he expected. She was conflicted. As much as she wanted to see her article in print, she wanted to keep covering the race. Letting him go ahead wasn't safe for her, not when he had already shown he was willing to leave her without so much as a fare-thee-well.

"Let's go to the freight office," she said firmly. "I can always find my work in print later."

"Maybe in San Francisco," he said, gauging her response. Again, he saw the conflicting emotions. Covering the story won out over the vanity of seeing old work in print.

They made their way through the crowded, bustling streets to the newly opened Turner Haulage Company office. Slocum knew it hadn't been open too long, because the paint was still drying on the sign on the plate-glass window. He peered inside, expecting to see the room deserted. To his mild surprise, two men sat at desks, working on stacks of paper.

"This is it," he said, holding the door for Zoe. She brushed past, giving Slocum a hint of why he hadn't simply kept riding when the opportunity had presented itself.

"We are racers," she said before he could speak. "We want the next set of instructions."

"How's that?" The old man at the nearer desk looked up and cupped his hand to his ear.

"The Colonel J. Patterson Turner Transcontinental Race," Zoe said loudly.

"No need to shout. I kin hear." He turned to his younger companion and said, "You got that stack of envelopes they sent up from the home office?"

"Surely do," the man said, fumbling in a pigeonhole on his rolltop desk. The envelopes went all over his messy desk, causing the clerk to frown and begin sorting through them.

"We can do that," Zoe said, looking over her shoulder at Slocum.

"No trouble," the man said, plucking one envelope from the stack and handing it to her.

"Where's mine?" Slocum asked. "I'm in this race, too."

"You got a key?" The clerk looked at him suspiciously. He shrugged and handed over another envelope when Slocum showed one of the gold keys he had accumulated. A tiny drop of blood clung to the serrated edge, but the clerk didn't notice.

"Well, John, what's yours say?"

Slocum looked back at the map behind the two clerks and worked his way through the trails drawn across the Wasatch Mountains.

"Looks like we might have been wrong that the trail led to San Francisco. There's a freight office in northern California, near Eureka."

"I noticed that, too," she said. "My letter says to ride for Reno."

Slocum nodded. His did, too. Reno had a rail line through it, but getting there would be easier on horseback.

They could cut miles off a difficult trip since they'd have to pick up the Virginia and Truckee Railroad at Virginia City otherwise, and that was out of their way.

"We might have to wait to see if others get different instructions," Slocum said, thinking how easy it would be to steal the letters from the old clerk and his assistant.

"We should push on immediately," she said. "I want to be at the finish line when the race is completed, to get the story."

"Not for the gold?"

Slocum saw the twitch at the corner of her lips as she thought about the lie. It surprised him when she said, "I want the gold. I know I've said this is all about becoming a newspaper reporter, but Mr. Zelnicoff didn't say anything about me joining in the race."

"That'd make you part of the story," he said as they left the office.

"Then I'll pioneer a new form of journalism where the reporter is integral to the story," Zoe said firmly. "I have to send another installment. We passed a telegraph office down the street. Where should we meet after I send it back to St. Louis?"

"The livery stable. We'll need horses and tack." He pointed to one farther along the street, probably the one supplying horses to the Turner Haulage Company for its wagons.

"Very well," she said. Zoe looked around, saw no one looking in her direction, and gave Slocum a quick kiss on the lips. She blushed just a bit, then hurried away, muttering to herself. Slocum heard some of it, and knew she was composing her article as she rushed away.

He ran his sleeve over his lips and wondered what he was getting himself into. His stride long and his resolve firm, he went not to the stable, but to the office of the *Deseret Bee*. A half dozen men toiled to print the current edition of the paper. The shop smelled of fresh ink and stale sweat.

"Howdy," said a man with cuff protectors on his sleeves. "What can I do for you?"

"Back issues. Where can I look through the past week or two?"

"Over yonder. That'll be a nickel to read 'em."

Slocum found a coin and spun it around and around on the counter. The man snared it between ink-stained fingers and made it vanish as if by magic.

Slocum went to a counter, perched on the edge of a stool, and began scanning the past few weeks of papers. There were plenty of stories about the Panic of '73, as the reporters called it, bringing down banks and wiping out fortunes, but nowhere did he even find mention of Colonel Turner's race.

"You looking for something in particular?" the counter man called.

"The Turner Haulage Company," Slocum said, spinning about on the chair. "What can you tell me about their business?"

"Business?" The man snorted. "No business to speak of lately 'cuz there's not much freight coming through from anywhere east of us. I had one of the boys ask if they wanted to run an advertisement to drum up some business, but they said they had to get approval from the home office. Never heard back on that," the man said, pursing his lips and making a notation on a scrap of paper using a stub of a pencil.

"You heard of a big race?"

"Well, now, I can answer that in the affirmative. It's not right to be gambling, I know, but seven of the largest horsemen in the area have races every Saturday night out along the shore of the Salt Lake."

"Big stakes? As much as fifty thousand dollars?"

The newspaperman laughed and shook his head.

"That's too rich for anybody's blood within hailing distance of the Great Salt Lake."

"That's what I needed to know," Slocum said. He rushed

back to the livery stable, knowing Zoe would be finished soon, even if she sent a long article to her newspaper.

As he came up to the stable, he slowed and then tried to remember where he had seen the man standing out front before. It finally occurred to him.

"Morrisey," he said. The man jerked around, eyes wide with surprise. Slocum saw how the man's right hand snaked toward the waistband of his fancy britches, then stopped. Since there wasn't a six-gun or a knife there, he had to have a derringer hidden away.

"You're Slocum, aren't you?"

"You were in Jubilee Junction."

"You got that right. You remembered my name, too. Morrisey. Ned Morrisey." The way he spoke the name made it sound as if he was trying to convince himself this really was his name. Slocum didn't much care what summer name he used. A man could have a variety of reasons for not boldly proclaiming his proper name. But he had left Ned Morrisey being beaten in the street by Calhoun and his men.

"Looks as if we're still rivals," Slocum said, studying Morrisey carefully. He began to doubt his memory since this gent and the one in Jubilee Junction looked to be one and the same.

"What do you mean? Oh, the race. I am not partaking of that. Not exactly."

Slocum saw the envelope sticking out of the man's pocket, and knew he had picked it up from the Turner Haulage Company. Why lie? And he had worn a splint, and claimed to be injured too badly to continue the race—before he died. Slocum knew a confidence man when he saw one, and Ned Morrisey fit the bill.

If Ned Morrisey was even his name.

"You looking to get a horse?" Morrisey asked.

"I am," Slocum said, seeing no reason to deny the obvious.

"Why don't we ride on together, you and I? Just for a while. For safety."

"How's that?"

Morrisey looked around when Zoe called out. She paid no attention to the small man as she came to Slocum and took his arm.

"All sent," she said proudly. "Do you have the horses?"

"You remember Ned Morrisey? From Jubilee Junction," he said.

Zoe's eyes widened and her mouth opened. Only a choked sound came forth.

"Mr. Morrisey wants to ride with us," Slocum said, gripping her arm until she winced. She stared at him and he read her lips mouthing, "But they were killing him!"

Zoe recovered and said in a voice passably calm, "Why, yes, I do remember him. I did not expect to see you on the trail, sir. You must have a fascinating story to tell."

"Why don't you get it while I barter for horses?" Slocum told her. He almost laughed at the differing reactions. Zoe pounced like a cat on a mouse, and Morrisey looked trapped. Whatever the man hid wasn't likely to be pried from him if Zoe asked questions only about the race. Slocum hoped she wouldn't come right out and ask how a dead man walked the streets of Salt Lake City right away, at least until he returned. He wanted to hear that story, too.

He went to the stable and looked over the horses for sale. Of the half dozen, two were good, but not the match for the mare he had to leave behind, gimpy leg or not.

"Help you, mister?"

"I'm here to pick up the horses for Turner," Slocum said.

"How's that?"

"The freight company. Colonel Turner? I'm supposed to pick up two saddle horses and gear for the colonel's niece."

"We supply horses for the freight company," he said, scratching his chin and confirming what Slocum had guessed, "but I don't know about any saddle horses."

Slocum scowled and finally said, "The colonel's niece is a bit flighty. She might decide to get horses somewhere else if I don't deliver them to her right away." The relief on the stable owner's face was quickly wiped away when Slocum continued. "And of course, the contract for the draft horses would go to wherever she said. The colonel dotes on her."

"Those two suit you?" The stable owner pointed. Slocum steered him toward the pair he had picked out, and within twenty minutes led the two horses, with gear and some provisions in the saddlebags, into the hot Salt Lake City sun.

"Mr. Morrisey rejoined the race after Jubilee Junction," Zoe said brightly. She gave Slocum a broad wink to show him she wasn't falling for any cock-and-bull story. "I have a wonderful tale to send along to Mr. Zelnicoff."

"Why not send it in Reno?" Slocum suggested. "We ought to get on the trail."

"Please, reconsider, Mr. Morrisey. Ride with us."

The man's furtive look warned Slocum that Zoe had been maneuvered into making the request so it appeared as if it were her own idea.

"I suppose all of us key holders ought to stick together—for a while," he said, chuckling. "Somewhere, it has to be every man—or woman—for himself—herself. The prize is far too great for any other sentiment."

"Suits me," Slocum said. He helped Zoe into the saddle. Standing close, he softly asked, "Did you tell him how many keys we have?"

"Why, John, I don't know how many you have, but I did allow as to how you have several. I've seen you toying with two."

Slocum mounted, got his bearings, and rode off, letting both Zoe and Morrisey catch up. He needed a few minutes without idle chatter to think through what was going on. Morrisey had been working a con game, possibly selling fake keys to the unsuspecting back in Jubilee Junction. Somehow, it had occurred to him how much money was at stake. He might have bilked some other racer out of his key, or taken it into his head that he was clever enough and quick enough to claim the prize for himself.

"Slocum, not that way," Morrisey shouted. "The other fork in the road."

Slocum drew rein and studied the signpost. He knew which way he ought to ride, and Morrisey was directing him straight north into the Wasatch Mountains rather than more westward. Telling the man they were parting company was Slocum's most obvious move, but Morrisey must have at least one of the golden keys—and an explanation.

"Your instructions call for you to go that way?" Slocum asked.

"Yours don't?"

"I got turned around," Slocum said. Zoe started to protest, but fell quiet when Slocum looked sharply at her.

They rode for the better part of the afternoon, until Morrisey insisted on breaking for the day and pitching camp. Slocum and Zoe worked to start a campfire as Morrisey shuffled about, not doing much of anything.

"I'll go see if I can bag something for supper," he said, drawing his rifle from the saddle sheath. He hesitated when Slocum turned slightly so his gun hand rested on the butt of his Colt Navy. If Morrisey tried to cut him down, he would have to deal with lightning-fast reflexes.

Slocum saw the calculation going on in the man's brain. Morrisey came to the right decision and turned to go hunting.

"Son of a bitch!" Morrisey cried.

"Freeze," Slocum said. "Don't move or we're all dead."

Coming from the tumble of rocks alongside the road were a half dozen Ute warriors, marked with war paint. Four had the three whites in their rifle sights, and the leader stood with a drawn bow, the arrow aimed directly at Slocum's chest.

21

Molly Ibbotson stretched tired legs and walked stiffly from the train as soon as it screeched to a halt at the Salt Lake City depot. She stepped off and took a deep breath, happy to let the salty tang replace the burned smell of coal in her nostrils. Traveling by train was far easier than stagecoach or on horseback, but the drawbacks were evident.

She looked around and wondered where the Turner Haulage Company office might be in the city. She'd followed her instincts to this point, and now had to find definite directions. The dearth of real messages from Colonel Turner might have been due to added difficulty in finding the gold, but she was beginning to doubt it. The economic woes sweeping over the country plagued the freight companies as well. Even venerable Wells Fargo was cutting back on its service. Colonel Turner's new venture had to compete not only with that company, but also with the sad fact that less cargo was being shipped anywhere due to business failures.

"Pardon me," she said, reaching out and tugging at a porter's sleeve. "I am looking for the Turner Company office. Can you tell me how to get there?"

The man frowned, pursed his lips, and stroked over a fairly clean-shaven chin. He shook his head, then turned and bellowed at the ticket agent.

"Jethro, you know anything about a Turner Company?"

"A freighter," Molly added.

"They ship things." The porter looked suspiciously at her. "You ain't workin' for the railroad, are you? They're lookin' to fire anyone not loyal one hundred percent."

"I assure you, I do not work for the railroad," she said earnestly. A bright smile eased the man's suspicions. "I am part of the . . . race."

"Race? What race might that be?"

She explained, and saw no comprehension on the porter's face.

"You figger out where this Turner Company is yet, Jethro?" The porter indicated that Molly should wait. She shuffled her feet and looked around nervously. She had gotten the jump on the others in the race by a day or more, but her luck could not hold. How far behind was Sid Calhoun? She had no desire to match wits with him again because he was inclined to kill anyone in his way to solve his problems. Molly wasn't above shooting him, given the chance, but she preferred staying ahead of him.

At the thought, she opened her purse and ran her fingers over the gold keys wrapped in a linen handkerchief. Her anger rose as she thought of her no-account brother. Harry had given her nothing but trouble all her life, and now he was off to who knows where with the key she had given him. If he had been lucky, he could have added to their store. With a dozen keys, she had a far better chance of opening the strongbox once she reached the finish line, but with the way her luck ran, the key that opened the box would be the one Harry held for her.

Molly worried that the train would pull out on its way to the coast before she found new instructions. The treasure had to be in San Francisco, but the colonel was wily enough to hide it anywhere along the coast. All he needed were a few reporters to cover the winner opening the box. It didn't matter where that might be, but Molly found it difficult to believe a man like J. Patterson Turner would not place the strongbox in the middle of the Palace Hotel lobby or perhaps on a pedestal in the center of Portsmouth Square. He wanted maximum exposure for his new company, with crowds murmuring about his largesse and how the racers had overcome great odds, as his freight wagons would, to reach civilized depots.

"There's a new place with that name. Turner Haulage Company, Jethro says. He keeps track of them in competition with the railroad," the porter said. "Ain't too far off, makin' us think they might ship by our train and then load into wagons to reach the nearby towns."

Molly got directions from the porter, then said, "I will be on the train for the coast. When is it due to leave?"

"Best guess," the porter said, fumbling out a pocket watch and peering at it, "is another hour. Might be less, though I doubt it. Got a powerful lot of repair work to do on the locomotive. Gettin' over them mountains is a chore for such a small engine as this." He turned and peered westward, as if he could see the Sierra Nevadas.

Molly hurried off, keeping her skirts lifted high enough to prevent the hem from dragging in the dirt. No matter where she went, the weather always worked against her. It rained too much in Jubilee Junction and not enough here. Mud, dust rising with every step, there was never anything in the middle for her. Her thoughts turned to damning Harry again, and before she finished a good round of cursing him, she found herself at the freight office.

She pushed in and saw the scrawny clerk working at the counter. He looked up, then down, and then back up again. She took a deep breath so her chest expanded a bit more than was comfortable. It captured the man's attention.

"I'm a racer. I need the next set of instructions. Do you

have to telegraph St. Louis or do you have them already?"

"Racer? Oh, yeah," he said, reluctant to take his eyes off her feminine charms. "I heard about that. The boss back East sent these along a while ago." He fumbled under the counter and pulled out a printed sheet, glanced at it, nodded solemnly, then handed it over. Impatiently, she snatched it from his hands.

A slow grin came to her perfect lips. She had figured out the course exactly. If she stayed on the train all the way to San Francisco, she would be ahead of all the rest. She tucked the paper into her purse, and once more made certain the keys rode safely within. If none of her keys opened the treasure chest and she was there first, she could make some sort of deal with those who came after her. One way or the other, she would cut herself into the golden treasure, even if she had to bushwhack the other contestants to get the $50,000.

Molly hurried back to the train station in time to see another train steaming up behind the train on which she had arrived. Her steps faltered when she saw it slow and finally stop. Two men jumped to the ground and ran forward. Her heart caught in her throat. She reached back into her purse, but did not draw her derringer. There were only two shots in it, and killing both Sid Calhoun and Skunk Swain with one bullet each wasn't an easy chore.

Unless she worked behind them and shot them both in the back of the head. One shot from each barrel. Otherwise, she had to find a six-shooter and use that.

Molly cursed constantly as she went to the depot platform, where she overheard Calhoun questioning the porter about the location of the Turner Haulage Company office. She considered using both barrels on the porter if he revealed that she had already inquired. But the way Calhoun interrogated the porter ensured that the man would clam up and say nothing, just point. Molly pressed herself flat against the wall as both Calhoun and Swain hurried down the steps in the direction of the freight office. She considered again her chances of taking both men out, each with a single shot.

She gave up on such a fanciful notion and let them rush off. It wouldn't be long before they returned. Whatever she did had to be done quickly.

"Porter," she called, lifting her skirts as she hurried up the steps to the platform. "How long before my train leaves for the coast?"

"We 'bout got the piston fixed. Wasn't anywhere near as bad as the engineer thought. Oiled it right up, he did."

"When?" she demanded.

"Few minutes," he said. He eyed her feminine charms, but her brusqueness caused her hypnotic spell over him to fade.

"Leave as quickly as possible," she said, unable to keep the sharpness from her words.

"Ma'am, that ain't up to me. The engineer and conductor, they're the ones who decide when to pull out, not me."

"I apologize. I am in such a hurry to reach San Francisco," she said. She looked around and feigned a touch of fright. "There are dangerous men chasing me."

"Men?"

Molly described Calhoun and Swain. When she was sure he had identified them as the men who had gotten off the second train, she rushed on with her breathless lies.

"My husband sent them to take me back. He beats me and I left him, but he is so rich and has hired gunmen to find me."

"Well, they was askin' 'bout the same place you was," the porter allowed.

"Oh, no!" Molly hardly had to feign being distraught.

"You get on board, and I'll do what I can. Might not be much, but there's not time enough to fetch the marshal and let him deal with them scoundrels," the porter said. Molly graced him with a quick kiss on his stubbled cheek. He blushed.

"You are a good man. Thank you!"

She swung on board, and considered where the best spot might be for her to sit. She heard the steam building as the fireman stoked the boiler and the engineer bellowed out orders to fill his tanks with water. If she stayed at the rear of the last passenger car, Calhoun and Swain might miss her. She would have a chance to remove them if they sat facing forward. But Molly saw no way that they could miss her, no matter where she sat in the passenger car.

Without hesitation, she opened the door into the mail car. The clerk toiled dragging heavy mailbags inside and barely slid the outer door closed when the train lurched and began moving from the station. She spun about and dropped to a stack of the heavy canvas bags and lay back, closed her eyes, and let the motion of the train soothe her. The time they had spent at the station was far less than the porter had thought, making it difficult if not impossible for Calhoun to return in time to board. Molly thought he would be destined to trail her all the way to San Francisco on another train.

She heaved herself to her feet, and cautiously went exploring back into the passenger cars. Molly got to the first car without finding either Calhoun or Swain. Sinking into a seat, she leaned back and heaved a sigh. Closing her eyes, she began imagining what she would do with the prize money.

Barely had she figured out how to spend the second thousand dollars than the train lurched—hard. She grabbed the seat in front of her and half stood.

"Derailment!" The conductor staggered back, shouting at the top of his lungs. "Hang on tight! We're goin' off the tracks!"

Molly let out a shriek of pure fright as the train slewed sideways and dragged along for a few yards. Her car began to tip precariously, causing her to cry out in fright again. Then the car stopped and canted at a forty-five-degree angle.

"No need to worry, folks," the conductor said. "This happens all the time. We'll be fine."

"What'll happen?" Molly asked.

"There's a train comin' along behind us in an hour or two that'll help us."

"Help us," Molly said weakly. The train would no doubt carry both Sid Calhoun and his henchman, and she was trapped here with no place to run.

22

"Shoot 'em!" Ned Morrisey shouted.

"Don't!" Slocum's warning fell on deaf ears. Morrisey was already lifting his rifle. He only got it halfway raised before a dozen arrows turned him into a pincushion. "Dammit," Slocum said. He stepped forward and thrust out his chin belligerently toward the chief. "You are a stupid son of a bitch, you know that?"

"John," Zoe said in a choked voice. "That Indian chief killed Morrisey and he'll kill you."

"Like hell he'll kill me," Slocum said, stopping so that the Indian leader's rifle poked into his chest. "He wouldn't do that, would you, Little Hand?"

"Not since you still owe me ten dollars," the Ute said.

"You cheated," Slocum said.

"John, what's going on? They killed Morrisey and you're—"

"Morrisey was an idiot and *he's* a card cheat."

Zoe stared open-mouthed as the Indian dropped the rifle and embraced Slocum. Slocum returned the grip and laughed.

"It's good to see you again, Little Hand. I'd heard the Arapaho had killed you."

"Them? Pah! They can never kill a Unitah Ute."

"Zoe Murchison, meet Little Hand."

"*Maiquas*," Little Hand said in greeting. He went to embrace the woman, but she stepped away and looked askance at him.

"She's a bit shy," Slocum said. "And your reputation rode on ahead of you. She knows you'd cop a feel if you got too close."

"Same old Slocum," Little Hand said. "And you were the one who cheated at cards."

"You were the one who came up with the five kings, not me," Slocum said. He turned to Zoe and said, "Little Hand and I scouted together for close to six months for the army."

"Most boring scout I ever rode with," Little Hand said. "If it hadn't been for Slocum and his crooked deck of cards, we would have deserted."

"You were in the army together?" Zoe swallowed hard and looked at Slocum and then Little Hand in disbelief.

"Civilians," Little Hand said. "Scouts. Not the same as being in the army." The Ute stepped over Morrisey's body without breaking stride and put his arm around Zoe's shoulders, guiding her away. "Slocum usually doesn't travel with ladies as lovely as you, Miss Zoe. There were always those rumors about him and the cross-eyed goat, but they were never proved."

"Always the liar," Slocum said, hurrying to join them. "Why are you out here all decked out in war paint?"

"Ouray doesn't approve but who cares? He's Southern Ute and would give the Shining Mountains to you white eyes for nothing more than a ride in a fancy carriage. My band decided to leave the reservation east of here, and the cavalry decided we shouldn't." Little Hand shrugged eloquently. "We'll return and be good red men one day."

"But not too soon?"

"Not so soon," the Ute answered. "Why are you traveling with a trigger-happy gent like him?" Little Hand glanced over his shoulder in Morrisey's direction. "He should have listened to you."

"Wait a second," Slocum said, spinning about and returning to search Morrisey's pockets, hunting for gold keys. He was nonplussed when he didn't find one. Morrisey had sold a key back at Jubilee Junction because he had a broken leg with a splint on it. Slocum began stripping off his pants, then looked at his leg.

"You need spare pants, Slocum? I can sell them to you," Little Hand said, watching.

"He's not injured." Slocum looked at Zoe.

"And he was killed," she said.

"Of course he's dead," Little Hand said. "My braves don't miss."

"He said back in Jubilee Junction he couldn't go on."

"So he lied," Zoe said. "But how could he fake his death?"

"This isn't the man we saw back in Jubilee Junction," Slocum said. "It might be his twin, or at least a brother. They must have been in cahoots since he knew my name."

"You mean this Ned Morrisey was already here, waiting for his brother?"

"He was waiting to get a telegram from his brother about who had keys so he could rob us." This was the only explanation that made sense to Slocum. Twins working together to steal keys and steal a march on anyone who chanced to be first at the finish line after running a legitimate race.

"What are these keys?" Little Hand asked.

Slocum explained. The more he went on, the more incredulous the Ute leader looked.

"You white eyes are crazy. Why do you kill each other for gold?" Little Hand shook his head sadly.

"But you played poker with Mr. Slocum," Zoe said. She frowned as she tried to figure out the discrepancy.

"I like to win. What do I care for your money or gold?" Little Hand made a dismissive gesture.

"We like to win, too. Think of this as a race where the winner gets great honor," Slocum said.

"Honor? Gold!"

"That, too," Slocum said, smiling. "We need to get through the mountains to reach this spot." He knelt and drew a rough map in the dirt. For a moment, he returned to riding scout with Little Hand years before. They had made quite a team, and nothing and no one had eluded them. Some of the scrapes they had gotten into had required them to depend completely on each other. There were men Slocum had known for years that he trusted less than he did Little Hand, even now.

"You want to get through Hidden Pass and reach the railroad station," Little Hand said, circling Slocum and the map to study it from all angles.

Slocum looked up sharply. There hadn't been mention of a railroad depot in their new race instructions.

"You didn't know?" Little Hand shook his head sadly. "This hunt for gold makes you stupid, Slocum. It is not like you to act stupid."

"It must be a new spur," Slocum said. He looked out of the corner of his eye at Zoe. If her confusion had been a fire, every forest in Utah would be ablaze. She understood nothing about their destination.

"You can ride straight to San Francisco from that point," Little Hand said. "You should join me, Slocum. We can ride and take scalps!"

Zoe recoiled at the suggestion.

"Bring your squaw if you want." Little Hand leered at her, then laughed at her reaction.

"I'm not his squaw!" The words exploded from Zoe's lips, and she glared at the Ute warrior.

"I'll buy her from you then, Slocum. Two horses. A stallion and a gelding."

"Newly stolen, I suppose?"

"From the army. Their troopers were mistreating them. Stealing the horses was a boon to everyone." Little Hand looked suddenly sly. "I will give you three horses, your choice. I won't even ask to see your squaw's teeth first."

"I'm not—"

"She's not for sale, Little Hand. We have horses."

"It's a dangerous trip over the mountains. Sudden snows, wild animals, many ways to die."

"You can have Morrisey's horse," Slocum said. He ignored Zoe's outrage. Slocum toyed with the notion of seeing how much Little Hand would pay for the woman, but he knew she would never speak to him again, even if he made the offer in jest. Somehow, that bothered him.

"I'd take it anyway," said Little Hand. "We killed him. Everything belonging to a dead enemy is taken by his killer."

"He was a great friend," Slocum lied. He bartered with Little Hand for more than an hour, each of them enjoying the dealing. Slocum eventually settled with the Ute when he saw that Zoe's patience had worn too thin. If he continued the pleasurable negotiation, she would say or do something that would jeopardize his bond with the Indian.

"Done," Little Hand said, sticking out his hand. Slocum took the stunted hand in his much larger one and shook to seal the deal.

They were on the trail within fifteen minutes, riding single file until Zoe urged her horse to a quicker gait to ride alongside Slocum.

"Do you trust him?"

"With my life," Slocum said. "He pulled my bacon out of the fire more than once, risking his own life to do it. The last time, they wanted to give me a medal when Little Hand was responsible for completing the mission. That's when I quit scouting and rode down into Mexico for a few months."

"He might have made up that railroad station. I never heard of it."

"Doesn't it make sense that the colonel would split the field again, force us to travel over a mountain range, and then put us back onto a train for San Francisco?"

"We could have stayed on the train," Zoe said. "If any of the others stayed on the train, they'll be ahead of us."

"Calhoun?" he asked, but he thought of Molly Ibbotson. The lovely woman had plenty to settle. Her brother was dead and she had lost the gold key he had carried. Slocum touched his vest pocket to be certain all the keys were still there. He jerked his hand away. Becoming obsessed with the $50,000—or even winning Colonel Turner's race—was not any way to live his life.

"There were so many others," said Zoe. "I needed to detail every racer, and I failed to do so. It's difficult to know who is most likely still in the race through pluck and grit."

"And a fast gun," Slocum said. This irritated her, and he didn't care. It took more than determination to win a treasure hunt like this. A quick six-gun or a willingness to shoot someone in the back trumped all else.

"You are going to fold your hand, aren't you?" she asked.

"What?" Zoe's comment took him by surprise. "Why do you say that?"

"I read people, John. You're fed up with all this," she said. Zoe looked at Little Hand's back as he rode ahead. "Perhaps it is something more. The Indian's invitation to ride with him interested you. Or maybe it enticed you with a siren's song of days long past."

"He's off the reservation and will be caught soon enough. Every cavalry post in the region is hunting him," Slocum said. "He knows his freedom is limited, but it doesn't matter."

"That's it," Zoe said in triumph. "You share that feeling of needing freedom, but you both know it is fleeting. You fear boundaries."

"I'm not afraid of anything," Slocum said, but the words

rang hollow in his ears. He knew she had reached out, grabbed his soul, and now squeezed. He wanted her to let him be, but she wouldn't.

"See this through, John. You're not a coward. No one could ever say that with any conviction. What you are is a romantic seeking a life that is always just a horizon away, always beyond your grasp."

"I'm content enough," he said.

"No, you're not. You're restless, and hunting for something that might not exist." She paused, thought on it a bit more, and added, "You might be running from something, but it's more likely you're running to something—and you don't know what it is."

Again, Slocum felt her silken touch tighten around him. The judge-killing charge lay in his past and sometimes bedeviled him, but he paid it little attention these days. Other things sometimes collided with him, but they meant nothing compared to his need to ride on.

Slocum listened to Zoe with half an ear, lost in his own thoughts. By the time they reached the pass Little Hand had proclaimed was the one leading to the railroad depot, Slocum had come to his conclusion.

He'd finish the race, with or without Zoe Murchison beside him.

23

Molly Ibbotson watched the conductor fifty yards down the track waggling the lantern back and forth to warn the approaching train of the derailment. She stood away from the train with her fingers curled around the derringer in her purse. Sid Calhoun had to be on the other train, and he wouldn't brook any competition.

Or would he? Her mind raced as she worked through various schemes. Her brother was likely dead or in prison because he was a fool. That meant she was on her own if she wanted to win the race. And she did, with every fiber of her being. The money was a lure unlike anything she had ever experienced in her life. Always before, success had been just beyond her grasp, and never as lucrative as this. She realized she had been a petty hustler before, but now had the chance to strike it rich—and big.

Creaking metal warned her to move farther from the passenger car. The crew levered the car back onto the rails. She looked from the men struggling to repair the tracks to the train now stopped down the line. She sucked in her breath when she saw a flash of sunlight off Skunk Swain's white stripe of hair. Sid Calhoun was nowhere to be seen, but he couldn't be far away. Molly slipped and slid down a cinder-covered incline away from the tracks and began walking downhill. It did her no good to hide. Without supplies and a heavy coat, she would die in the mountain pass before midnight.

She had to take the bull by the horns. She drew her derringer and began creeping back up the incline to the track bed behind the second train. Several passengers had climbed down to study how the other crew worked to get the car back onto the track. The loose rail that had caused the derailment had already been replaced, and when the passenger car sat on its wheels again, both trains could continue.

Molly ducked under the caboose and came out on the other side. Her hand turned sweaty, but was steady. When Swain appeared suddenly, Molly lifted her pistol and fired. The recoil startled her, but the spray of blood from the hole she put in Swain's skull caused her to flinch. A drop got into her eye and turned the world black, until she blinked the dead man's blood free.

When she saw clearly again, she whirled around to determine if her murder had been detected. The tiny *pop* from the derringer had gone unnoticed. She edged toward Swain and kicked him with the toe of her shoe. The surprised expression on his face didn't change. His unseeing eyes stared up at her in disbelief.

Molly dropped to her knees and began rifling the man's pockets. He had a few silver dollars in a vest pocket, but she left those and ripped the cloth, getting four gold keys free.

"You did me a favor," came the cold voice. "I was thinkin' on doin' the same thing to him that you just did. Swain was a back-shooter, pure and simple."

Molly pulled the keys closer to her chest and fingered the derringer. One round remained. She half turned and stared down the barrel of Calhoun's .44. It looked bigger than a railroad tunnel and darker.

"You won't shoot me," she said. "We need each other."

"Why's that? You stole the keys off Swain's corpse. I shoot you and steal them and whatever else you've got. I come out ahead all around."

"But why do it alone?"

This caused him to pause. Molly knew that every second she stayed alive and talking, the closer Calhoun came to letting her live.

"We can join forces, Sid, and more than double our chances to win."

"If I have all the keys, I win," Calhoun said. The six-shooter wavered just a mite.

"Maybe," Molly said. "Might be we get there and find someone else has beat us to the strongbox. Sometimes, how you get there is better than arriving."

"How's that?"

"And if we do lose out, I'll be there to console you—and you can console me."

"What are you going on about?" He sounded tough, but Molly knew he was weakening by the way the muzzle no longer pointed directly at her. She stood slowly, keeping the derringer hidden in the folds of her skirt.

"I like your looks, Sid. You're not namby-pamby like my brother. You're a man. A real man, and one I could get to like."

"Do tell?"

"We were meant to team up from the start, Sid, and it's taken me this long to realize I can't finish the race without you. And you need to think who you're teamed up with also. Swain wasn't right for you if you worried about him shooting you in the back."

"Curly wasn't so good either."

"Another weak link," she pressed. "Not like me."

"So I'd have to watch my back with you, too?"

"I didn't say that right. I'm not a weak link, but I am a soft, feminine one. And you've got a long and hard link," she finished. Her beauty was working on him if the growing bulge at his crotch was any indication. She licked her perfect lips, using only the tip of her tongue, and thrust out her chest just enough to be suggestive, but not so much that he thought she was leading him on.

"You thinkin' on teamin' up with me?" Calhoun asked.

"Why not? A woman always likes to go with the strongest man. That's you."

"You were the one who shot Swain."

"For you, Sid, for you." Molly moved closer. Her finger tightened on the derringer trigger, but her mind ran ahead, planning and figuring odds. She kissed him. For a moment it was awkward, the derringer in her hand and the six-shooter in his. They found a way to wrap arms around each other and make the kiss more satisfying.

"They about got the car on the other train ready to roll," Calhoun said.

"And I've about got you ready to roll," she said. Her free hand pressed against the man's hard belly and worked over his gun belt to rest on his crotch. She felt the pulsation there and, to her surprise, she felt something more. He excited her. She was willing to do whatever was necessary to win Colonel Turner's prize, but she hadn't expected Calhoun to make her heart race just a little faster.

"Let's get on your train," he said, "and find a spot where we can get some privacy."

"The mail car," she said, remembering how she had flopped down on the mailbags when she thought Calhoun and Swain were boarding back in Salt Lake City.

They hurried along and went up the metal steps between cars. Molly put her finger to her lips to keep Calhoun quiet as she opened the door and peered inside. The mail car clerk was nowhere to be seen. He had probably helped get the passenger car back onto the rails.

Calhoun crowded behind her and pushed her into the car. Molly swung about, grabbed him by the shoulders, and pulled him down on top of her as she flopped into the stack of canvas bags filled with mail. Calhoun fumbled, and got his hands under her skirt and lifted. She trembled as his calloused hands worked up against her tender inner thighs—and then went higher still. His thick finger entered her, and sent a tremor of stark desire throughout her body that shocked her.

"Do it, Sid. Hard, take me hard. I like it like that."

He didn't have to be asked twice. He scooted the rest of her skirt up around her waist as she parted her legs, eager for him. She felt all liquid inside, and then she felt his hardness driving inward. Molly gasped and closed her eyes, letting him have his way. As a lover, he was about what she'd expected. He stroked brutally, intent only on his own pleasure, but Molly needed that kind of power now.

She cried out as her muscles locked hard, and she clamped down around him. He grunted as he arched his back and tried to drive even deeper into her yielding core.

Calhoun heaved a sigh and twisted around to lie on his back beside her.

"Damn, lady, you're good."

"So are you, my prince, so are you," she said. He had needed what she offered, and she had gotten what she needed from him. It had been too long, but now that the animal hunger had been sated, it was time for her to think a bit harder about the gold and what she wanted from Sid Calhoun.

She stroked over his cheek until he snorted and turned away, going to sleep. The train whistle sounded, momentarily bringing him back awake, but Molly soothed him as she would a small child, as she had done so often for her brother, and Calhoun fell into a deeper sleep.

It wouldn't be long until the mail clerk returned. She disengaged her arm from under Calhoun's head and sat up to smooth her skirts. The train rattled along as it had before the derailment. The trouble had been minor, but it had set her back and let Calhoun overtake her. It was time to make this pay off.

She got to her feet and went to the small rolltop desk at the rear of the car. A bit of rifling located what she knew was there. A ring of keys rattled as she held them up. A few seconds of fumbling opened the ring and let the keys spill into her hand. She returned to where Calhoun snored loudly, sank down beside him, and began lightly touching every pocket until she located the gold keys he had stolen.

With the deft, sure fingers of a pickpocket, she pulled out the golden keys Calhoun had tucked away and replaced them with keys from the mail clerk's ring. The lurching train and the gentle roll to the car made the substitution tricky, but this was hardly the first time she had taken what she wanted from a sleeping man's pockets.

Only when she had a full dozen of the gold keys safely hidden away did Molly lie back and stare up at the roof of the mail car. Slivers of blue sky shone through followed by occasional glints of bright sunlight. The rays warmed her almost as much as the knowledge she was going to be $50,000 richer very soon.

24

"For another horse, I'll see you down into town," Little Hand said.

"But you're running from the law," Zoe protested. Then she saw both Slocum and Little Hand were laughing. "You two! Can't you ever be serious?"

"Life is too short for that," Little Hand said.

Slocum reached out and shook the Ute's hand. The Indian looked down and then shook back.

"So much for you having a healing touch. I still need to find the medicine man to cure it," he said. Little Hand made a mock salute, then wheeled about and trotted away without a backward look.

"He likes you," Slocum said. "I could have gotten a good price for you."

"You wouldn't!" Zoe settled down, her lips thinned to a line. "No more joshing, please, John."

"I don't kid around with many folks," Slocum said, "but Little Hand is one. He can joke about anything. Once we were trapped in a cave with Arapaho warriors coming in to scalp us and we found we'd hidden in a bear's den. The

221

bear came roaring at us, and Little Hand laughed the entire while."

"That doesn't make him sound too sane," Zoe said carefully.

"Maybe not, but he ran out of the cave with the bear charging after him. It let me get out and take a shot or two at the other Indians, but I didn't need to. Little Hand had led the bear straight through the middle of their war party. They scattered to the four winds, and some are probably still riding to get away. That was one angry bear."

"And one laughing Indian," Zoe said.

Slocum knew she didn't understand, and it hardly mattered. He and Little Hand had shared more than a few poker games and had grown as close as brothers. Slocum wished the Ute well and hoped he evaded the horse soldiers who hunted him. The reservation had to be a boring place for a man who could laugh in the face of death.

"Let's get a train to San Francisco," he said. He snapped the reins on his pony and made his way down the steep trail. Zoe followed, muttering to herself about crazy Indians and crazier cowboys. Slocum wondered if she was composing a story to send to her editor, or if she simply was trying to understand the man she rode with.

An hour after parting company with Little Hand and his braves, they rode into town. Slocum tried to make out the name on a painted sign, but weather had scoured the lettering off.

"They have a telegraph," Zoe said, eyes following the wires leading away along the spur line. "I can send in another story. I'm sure Mr. Zelnicoff is anxiously awaiting it."

"I'm sure," Slocum said, remembering his hunt through the Salt Lake City newspaper files and finding nothing had come out of St. Louis about the race, much less a story with Zoe's byline. He doubted that had changed, but he was willing to be wrong for the woman's sake. Becoming a full-fledged reporter meant as much to her as anything in the world.

Except possibly the lure of Colonel Turner's golden reward waiting in San Francisco.

"I can send the article," she said, "but I cannot pay for it. There's no money left. I need my editor to wire more if I am to continue."

"No need," Slocum said. "I'll sell the horses."

"We need them!"

"Not if we get on the train and ride on into San Francisco," he pointed out. "I'll see if we can get out of here or if we need to use a handcar to reach the main line."

"That would be a considerable amount of work. You'd do that to win the race?"

"I'd do that for you," Slocum said. The light that came to the woman's face was worth the compliment. "Go get your article sent. I'll do the dickering, after I find if there's a train out of town."

Zoe rode closer and bent over. If he had moved she would have kissed him, but he saw curious townspeople coming out to see who the strangers were. He shook his head slightly and looked in the direction of the citizens staring at them.

"Oh, John, you are such a prude," Zoe said. She stood in the stirrups and leaned over farther to give him an unsatisfactory peck on the cheek. "What do we care if they think I'm a loose woman? We're leaving soon, and I am a sophisticate from the big city. A St. Louis newspaper reporter!"

Slocum felt the hot eyes on him as she rode off. The townspeople blamed him for such a licentious display as much as they did Zoe. Getting out of town as fast as possible looked to be the only cure for the disapproval that welled up like floodwaters on the Mississippi.

He had felt such animosity before, and it didn't much bother him, but he didn't like the idea that Zoe was included in it. He dismounted and went into the train station. Two men played cards. The agent put down his cards and asked, "What can I do you for, mister?"

"We need to get back to the main line and then on into San Francisco. What's a pair of tickets cost?"

"Well, now, you're a ways toward getting there already, but you're out of luck catching a ride to the main line. This here spur's not been active for a couple months. No traffic on it since it ain't profitable enough now."

"Why does the railroad keep you on? Two agents?" Slocum looked at the other man, who might well act as porter or fill some other position easily enough.

"They ain't paid me so I moved in here. The roof's tight and the stove works after a fashion. Let 'em toss me off their property. First, they'd have to send somebody out from the main office, and they ain't about to do that. This here's my brother. Since he don't have a job either, he's moved in here with me. If you want to rent some space, I got a spare corner. You got to pay in cash. In advance." The man jerked his thumb in the direction of the far wall where a few blankets were piled.

"Just need to get to San Francisco," Slocum said.

Before the former station agent could respond, Zoe hurried into the station waving about a flimsy sheet of paper.

"I have it, John, I have it. The final instructions."

"For the race?"

"I sent a telegram to my editor and he sent me this. The colonel has announced details of the race to the press in St. Louis, including the location of the treasure box."

"Treasure?" The station agent perked up. "That why you're so all-fired eager to get to Frisco?"

Slocum leaned closer and said, "Pleasure. She wants some pleasure there."

"In her—oh," the agent said, smirking. "You're a sly one, ain't ya?"

"John, when can we leave here?"

"Doesn't look as if a train will be pulling out any time soon. Reckon we should ride along the tracks to get to the main line."

"You got that, mister. If you've a mind, the hotel in town's not much but it might do you. Ain't no reason to set out on the trail this time of day, since you wouldn't get far at all 'fore nightfall."

"Thanks," Slocum said. He took Zoe by the arm. She had missed most of the byplay with the agent, and for that Slocum was glad. She would be furious at what the two men thought.

"John, look at this," she said eagerly when they got outside the train station. "Mr. Zelnicoff sent it. For some reason, they printed the final instructions in the newspaper in St. Louis. If we can get to San Francisco, we can find the strongbox and open it. I know we can!"

Slocum touched the keys in his vest pocket, then damned himself for bothering to check. There was no way he could have lost the keys since the last time he made sure they rode easy in his pocket.

"Even if we find the strongbox, there's not much chance one of our keys will open the lock."

"We're going to win the prize. I know we are!"

"What's the final set of directions tell us?" He took the page she thrust out, and quickly read the terse message. "This doesn't tell us too much. 'The box rolls like Turner Freight.' That doesn't tell us anything at all."

"It's in San Francisco so it must be at the freight office there. What else could it mean? We get to the terminus and we'll be rich!"

"What would your boss say about a reporter taking a cut of the money? You think he'd make you reimburse your newspaper for your expenses?"

"I've filed stories aplenty," she said angrily. "I'm earning my keep. Anything extra I make, why, that's fodder for a special edition! An extra with our pictures on the front page!"

Slocum wasn't so sure. He had known his share of hard-nosed editors, and the one thing they had in common was pinching a nickel so hard that the buffalo squealed. If Zoe's editor wasn't like that, he was a rare breed indeed.

"The station agent is right about it getting dark soon." Slocum watched the western ridges look as if they had been dipped in fire as the sun vanished behind them. "A small town like this isn't likely to have a big hotel, but then we seem to be the only visitors, so they should have a room."

"Do we have the money for two rooms?" The way she asked the question made Slocum smile.

"Don't think we have enough for two, but we do for one."

"With a big enough bed?" Her eyes twinkled.

"Not too big," Slocum said.

Together, they went in search of the hotel, and found the one-story building smack in the center of town. Slocum put their horses into the stable behind and tended them, then went into the lobby where Zoe argued with a frightened clerk. He wondered what the woman had said to make the mousy man look around for a way to escape.

"Cain't put the two of you in the *same* room," the clerk protested. "That wouldn't be right since you said you ain't married and all."

"Then give her the room," Slocum said. "I'll sleep in the stable."

"John, no!"

"Any problem with that?"

"Nope, don't think so," the clerk said, still uneasy. His eyes darted about like a rabbit hunting for a hole to escape a hungry coyote.

"Will you carry in the lady's bags?"

"She ain't got any," the clerk said, frowning now. He leaned forward over the counter and looked for Zoe's non-existent bags.

"Then I'll carry them in for her. You can't object to that, can you?" Slocum stared the man down.

"Go on, but I don't see no bags."

Slocum let Zoe take his arm, and they went down the hallway to the room at the far end. She worked at getting the lock to open. Slocum finally added his strength and forced the rusty lock to yield. The door swung inward on unoiled hinges.

"You were right about there not being many visitors to the town," she said. Zoe sat on the edge of the bed and bounced. A tiny dust cloud rose from the blanket. She sneezed and made fanning motions to clear the air in front of her face. "This must have been last cleaned when Hector was a pup."

Slocum forced the door shut and tossed the key onto the dresser, where it fell onto a thick layer of dust. The mirror on the dresser was obscured with cobwebs, but he doubted they would have much use for the mirror.

"John." She said his name so low, it was almost a whisper. He turned and caught his breath. Zoe had shed her jacket and blouse and sat on the bed naked to the waist. He didn't know where to look. Her breasts were snowy marvels capped with coppery disks, but somehow he found himself staring into her eyes.

"See anything you want?" She leaned back, supported herself on her elbows, and lifted her feet to the edge of the bed so her skirt slid away, exposing herself to him.

Slocum walked slowly to the bed, shedding his gun belt as he went. He pulled off his coat and vest, then found her eager hands working to free him from his jeans. She leaned forward and pressed her cheek into his thigh. He ran his hand over her hair. Although they had been on the trail, her hair was silky and lustrous. Feeling it made him just a bit harder than he had been—which was mighty hard indeed.

He gasped when she finally freed him from his jeans, but he had no time to worry about the cold air surrounding his manhood. Her eager lips closed on the plum-colored tip as Zoe slowly took him entirely into her mouth. The heat and wetness and the way she used her tongue against the sensitive underside of the mouth-filling shaft turned him weak in the knees.

He sank down, and she let him slip free. Zoe leaned back on the bed, and once more hiked her feet up and spread her knees wide. His face was only inches from her nether lips. Then no distance at all separated them. He buried his face between her legs, and licked and lapped and brought forth tiny trapped animal sounds from the woman while using only his tongue.

He gave as good as he had gotten. She reached down and put her hands on either side of his head to make sure he didn't abandon her. He had no intention of doing so. His tongue explored her hot center, and then worked over her nether lips until a tiny shudder passed through her.

"M-more, John, I want more. You know what to do. Please."

He kissed a bit higher onto her belly, and then repositioned himself on the bed so he supported himself on his stiffened arms and looked down into her lust-glazed eyes. His hips levered forward, he missed, and then he found the right spot. He slid easily into her. They both froze once he had buried himself fully, and simply relished the sensations. Slocum felt himself begin to twitch, and knew Zoe's beauty and willingness had pushed him too far. He began moving slowly, trying to keep a steady rhythm that would excite them both. This didn't last long. He sped up, and then his movements turned jerky as shudders of delight ripped through him. She shrieked in joy, and he followed seconds later.

"This bed ought to be used more often," he said.

"Only if it's used like we just did," she said. "Maybe we can do it again and—"

Slocum jerked upright, then jumped off the bed. He was buttoning himself up as he went. It took only a second to retrieve his Colt Navy from where he had carelessly discarded it.

"What is it, John?"

He pressed his ear against the door panel and clearly heard the clerk say, "They must be in that there back room fornicatin', Marshal. He went back there with her and they ain't come out yet."

"I got word what a lewd show they put on out in the main street for God 'n everyone to see."

"Arrest 'em, Marshal," urged the clerk. "I knowed they was evil people first time I set eyes on 'em."

"Joshua, you go tell Deputy Farnham to get on over here. The man had the look of a gunfighter. If lead gets to flyin', I want somebody I can trust behind me with a scattergun."

"John, what's wrong?"

"Get dressed. Right now," Slocum said urgently. He grabbed the edge of the dresser and pulled it to block the doorway. Getting the door open on its rusty hinges would be a chore, but he wanted to make it harder for the marshal to get in.

"Tell me what's going on."

"They have laws in this town against what we just did. It's time to let them enforce the laws the way they see fit—and we ought to be miles from here when they try."

Zoe worked to get into her blouse. Slocum had just finished slipping into his coat when he heard the footsteps in the hallway.

"You back me up, Farnham," the marshal said. "They might resist arrest."

"Should I shoot 'em then, Marshal?"

"Damned straight."

Zoe teased the window open far enough to slip out and into the night. Slocum wasted no time following her. The marshal failed to open the door, and applied his shoulder. Bits of plaster exploded off the wall as the frame collapsed under the lawman's assault. Slocum wiggled through and hit the ground, got his feet under him, and ran after Zoe toward the stable where he had left their horses.

As he sprinted through the night, Slocum laughed with joy. He felt more alive than he had in years—and $50,000 in gold waited for him in San Francisco. What more could a man want?

25

"We ought to go straight on to the freight office," Sid Calhoun said. "As much as I like layin' 'round with you in this fancy hotel room, there's gold waitin' to be claimed—by us."

Molly lounged back in the soft bed and stretched like a cat. She was still sore from the train ride into town and other, more enjoyable activities she and Calhoun had engaged in after she insisted they rest before going to the Turner Haulage Company. It had flattered Calhoun, making him think he was more important than the gold, but Molly intended it that way. He was still in a position to shoot her down and take her keys.

He didn't need a reason other than he was lower than a rattlesnake's belly, but he would have plenty of one when he found she had stolen the gold keys and substituted the mail car clerk's. She had to figure a way of getting rid of him that wouldn't land her in jail. Spending some time between the sheets eased her tensions, and relaxed her mind enough to come up with a plan.

"You're such a good lover, Sid," she cooed. "I couldn't wait to do it right."

231

"What do you mean?" He turned and stared at her.

"I wanted you in a bed, not on a pile of mailbags."

"You got it, babe. Now let's hie on over to Turner's and collect . . . our gold." He began dressing. Molly caught her breath when he clutched at the pocket holding the fake keys, but he didn't take them out and examine them as she feared. Then she relaxed. He intended to double-cross her, and wasn't about to give her a look at the keys since that might give her the wrong idea.

Molly was sure she had all the right ideas now, especially after the way Calhoun had almost said "collect my gold," but had caught himself in time.

"Why don't you help me get dressed? It's only fair since you helped me get out of my clothes," she said. It worried her the way he gripped his vest where the keys had been stashed. She sat up and swung her shoulders from side to side enough to make her breasts jiggle. This made Calhoun forget all about the keys and come over.

It took longer for them to get dressed, because she stripped off Calhoun's pants and they made love again. Afterward, he sank back and snored gently.

Molly hastily dressed and slipped from the room. She hurried down to the room clerk and said, "My companion will pay for the room."

"You checking out?"

"Yes, we are. But he is sometimes forgetful. When he comes down, be sure to remind him, will you?"

"Can't let you go without paying, now can I?" The room clerk smiled brightly at her. Molly adjusted her neckline just enough to give him a small glimpse of snowy flesh as a reward.

"You are too good an employee for that," she said. As she left, she waggled her butt to give a final reminder. He wouldn't forget to stop Calhoun and demand he pay for the room. She turned from the hotel just off Portsmouth

Square and headed west. As Molly rounded the building, she ran smack into a man and rebounded.

"Excuse me," she said automatically. Then she looked up into Calhoun's grinning face.

"You thinkin' on leavin' me behind?"

"How'd you—?"

"I went out a window. I've had a bit of experience doin' that," he said. "It occurred to me I didn't have any money, and you don't strike me as the sort to pay a gentleman's bill for him." He leered at her, forcing Molly to unconsciously put her hand to her neckline and pull up the blouse.

"I was only stepping out for a breath of fresh air."

"Fresh air," he said sarcastically. Calhoun took a deep breath, then coughed. "Nothing but smoke in the air. And dead fish stink blowin' in from the docks. Reminds me of St. Louis."

"You would have left me behind," she said.

"Reckon we understand each other. Let's go on over to Turner's and get this done with." He rested his hand on the butt of his pistol, which was thrust into a linen sash.

Molly wished she had her derringer in hand, but she hadn't been able to do anything more than verify that she still carried it since she had shot Swain. At least, on a public street with traffic passing by all around, Calhoun wasn't as likely to shoot her like a dog.

"Very well," she said, taking Calhoun's arm as if he escorted her. "I'm ready to become fabulously wealthy." As they walked off, Molly felt how tense Calhoun was. Her mind raced trying to find a new way of cutting Calhoun out so she would be sole winner of Colonel Turner's race.

"We're ahead of everyone else," Calhoun said. "We got here first."

"Do you know that for certain?"

"Look at the newspapers. Any of the racers that went south after Jubilee Junction are stranded out there. More

than one railroad went belly up right after the race started."
Calhoun stopped and pointed to an article in the *Alta California* being sold by a street urchin. Calhoun pushed the
boy away when he demanded a nickel for the paper.

"So you think only the northern train route was good?"

"I know it. And we were ahead of all the others."

"You killed some of them, too," Molly said.

Calhoun laughed, and it wasn't a pleasant sound. He
walked faster, forcing her to almost run to keep up.

"There's the office," Calhoun said as they entered Union
Square.

"It doesn't look too active. I expected reporters to cover
the first of the racers." Molly pursed her lips as she thought
of other freight offices along the way and how they had
been undermanned or even still waiting to open. The colonel was no one's fool. He would have offices at the start and
finish of his race booming with business so the reporters
would be sure his company was already successful.

Calhoun muttered under his breath as he pushed ahead
of Molly to get into the office. She hung back to open her
purse and take out the derringer, just to be safe.

"We're here to claim the prize money," Calhoun said
gruffly.

The clerk looked up with a disgusted look on his face.

"You and 'bout everyone else," he said.

"What's that?" Molly cried out in surprise. "We're not
the first?"

"Who got here before us?" Calhoun reached over the
counter and grabbed the clerk's shirt and pulled him closer.
"What son of a bitch beat us here?"

"N-nobody in the race," the clerk said.

Molly moved to the side, and saw that the clerk had
been rifling the desks and had a pile of the most valuable
items.

"You don't work here," she accused. "You're a sneak

thief!" Molly knew instantly she was right from the way the blood drained from the man's face.

"They all left an hour back. Nobody works here anymore. I . . . I'm an accountant next door, and I figured I could take what I needed. Th-they owed me money and never paid up!"

"What'd they owe you for?" Calhoun shook the man and twisted his grip to tighten the shirt on the captive man's throat, choking him until he went from white to bright red.

"Accounting. I'm an accountant," the man gasped out. "If they owe you money, take something. Th-that's what I'm doing!"

"You lying sack of shit," Calhoun said. "Where's the gold?"

"Gold? There's no gold. Nobody's been paid in a week. That's why they upped and left." The rest of the man's babbling answer died in a gurgle as Calhoun squeezed even more on the scrawny throat.

"Sid, no," Molly said. "He's telling the truth. Look at him. Would he lie to a real man like you?"

"Hell, no. He doesn't have the balls."

"Not like you," Molly said to soothe him more. If she wanted the prize money, she had to keep Calhoun from killing the only source of information they had. "Why don't you look around to be certain? There's a back room where they must have a vault."

"Yeah, I see it." Calhoun dropped the accountant, kicked through a low gate dividing the public space from the office, and marched into the back room.

"Thanks, lady. You saved my—" The accountant went pale again when he found himself staring down the barrel of her derringer.

"I'll ask once. Answer me truthfully and you can go. Lie and you'll wish my intemperate companion was still strangling you. Was there gold here?"

"I don't know. Honest!"

"You don't know anything about a cross-country race to publicize the new company?"

"No!" He cowered away from her. "I'm not lying. On my mother's grave, I'm not!"

"One last question. Who was the office manager and where can I find him?"

"Will Cassidy's his name. He . . . he—I don't know where you can find him!"

Molly cocked the derringer. The accountant closed his eyes as he waited to die with the .44 bullet in his skull. She decided not to waste a bullet when she heard Calhoun roaring like a gored bull in the back room about the vault being looted. She backed away and left the office. A quick look around Union Square was all it took for her to find her next destination. Molly ran, holding up her skirt to keep from tripping. She had to get out of sight as quickly as possible if she wanted to lose Calhoun. He was no longer useful to her.

She rounded the corner and followed the signs to the livery stable. Hardly slowing, she slipped between the partly open doors, and into the barn to see a man rummaging through a tool bin. He looked up. The guilty expression on his face told Molly he didn't belong there. He was as much a thief as the accountant back at the Turner Haulage Company office.

"You work for the freight company, don't you?" She saw the man was more likely to be a clerk than a stable hand, so it wasn't much of a leap in logic.

"Who are you?" he asked.

"I wanted to send some freight back East, to St. Louis," she said. "The office was closed. Are you out of business?"

"Damned right we are, lady. The colonel hadn't paid us all month so we took—so we took off." He held a crowbar in his hand.

"We?"

"All the people working at the freight company. He had

the nerve to come here personally and tell us to keep on working and that he'd pay us after the race."

"After the race," she said. "Colonel Turner is in San Francisco? Did he take the fifty-thousand-dollar prize?"

"He tried, but we beat him to it." The clerk turned and held the crowbar like a club now. "You're one of them in the race, aren't you? You think you're going to get rich. You're not. The gold's all gone."

"Is it now?" She came closer, ignoring the way he threatened her with the metal bar. "Let me think this through. You took the gold—the prize—as your pay, but something is keeping you from getting it? What might that be?"

"It's in a vault. It'll take a lot of work to pry off the lock to get into the gold."

"You and the rest in the office stole the gold?"

"Not the rest," the man said, his eyes dropping to Molly's cleavage. "Just me. I drove off with it."

"Drove off?"

"The vault's in the back of the biggest freight wagon the colonel has. Must weigh two tons, and it's all steel."

Molly moved closer still, and rested her fingers on the man's cheek and stroked slowly, letting a single finger touch his chin before her hand moved to his chest and worked down to his heaving belly. She turned slightly and ran her hand lower yet, and felt him standing at attention.

"We can be a team, you and I."

"Why?"

"I can offer you things beyond your wildest dreams."

"That much gold can buy me all that," the clerk said.

"Why buy what you can get for free—when you can get it all willingly?" She kissed him lightly on the lips as she squeezed the bulge at his crotch. "Maybe you'd like me to do it the other way around?"

"What do you mean?"

Molly slipped her hand from his crotch, thrust a finger into his mouth, and pulled it out slowly as she dropped to her knees. She unfastened his fly and began kissing what rushed out. It took only a few minutes before the clerk was babbling about where he had hidden the wagon with the steel vault in it.

"Show me," she said, standing and wiping her lips. "I can do ever so much more for you."

"More?"

"I can open the lock on the vault without you having to exert yourself."

"I should save my strength for more, huh?"

"Definitely," she said, licking her lips. It took all her restraint to keep from laughing at how easily she had seduced the man and gotten him to accept her as a partner in his theft.

"Out back. Come on."

Molly slid her derringer free as she followed the man. She wasn't too surprised when she spotted two bodies hastily dumped behind the woodpile. The clerk wouldn't share with his coworkers and had killed them to get the gold.

"There it is."

Molly stared at the wagon. She had expected a strongbox. She had not expected a bank on wheels. Even knowing the vault weighed a couple tons didn't prepare her for the size of the huge box.

"It's got foot-thick walls. The key unlocks the door, but the lock itself is buried behind steel plates. I was going to pry off the front and yank out the mechanism, but if you've got the key, there won't be any need to go to that trouble."

She looked around, her eyes passing quickly over the evidence of the clerk's murderous ways.

"Not here," she said. "Where can we drive this and open it in private?"

"I know a place down the peninsula," he said. "I'll get the team."

As he went for the sturdy draft horses, Molly studied the

lock. She wanted to begin trying the keys in her purse to see if any opened the lock. She had a dozen, but that meant any of the thirty-eight gold keys that she didn't have might be the true way in. Until she had a chance to find out if she carried the right key—and there was only a one chance in four that she did—she needed the clerk to provide the muscle to force open the vault.

Still, the urge was almost overwhelming to try just one key.

"Ready. Come on. I'm anxious to get rich and . . ." His voice trailed off.

Molly joined him on the hard driver's seat and smiled winningly.

"I'm anxious to get rich, too. And to feel your strong body alongside mine in a bed. What's the most luxurious hotel in San Francisco? Never mind," she said before he could name one. Let him fantasize. "We'll try them all."

"With champagne?"

"Only the best. Gran Monopole?"

"I suppose that'll do," he said. From the way he answered, Molly knew he had no idea. "I'll drink it out of your belly button while you're layin' back naked on the bed. How'd you like that?"

Molly giggled like a schoolgirl and snuggled close to the clerk, glad she had her derringer close at hand. They rattled and clanked through the San Francisco streets heading south. Within an hour, they reached sparsely populated farmland. The clerk took a rutted road toward the ocean, and finally yanked back hard on the reins, bringing the rig to a halt. The gunmetal gray Pacific Ocean crashed against rocks twenty feet below, and a stiff breeze caused Molly to work constantly to keep her hair from her eyes.

"You ready to be rich?" the clerk asked.

Molly was. She let him help her down, and then forced herself not to hurry as she walked to the rear of the wagon.

Reaching into her purse, she felt the outline of the keys—and her pistol. She pulled out a handkerchief she had used to wrap the keys.

"Here," she said, handing the keys to the clerk. "You deserve the honor of trying."

"And if one doesn't open the lock, I get to rip off the door," he said.

"Go on," she urged. "The suspense is killing me."

She stepped to one side to watch as he tried one after another of the dozen keys.

"Damn, that doesn't work. Doesn't even fit into the lock." The clerk threw the key away and tried the second. As he worked, Molly grew more apprehensive. Then he cried out in triumph. "It fits! The other wouldn't even go into the lock, but this one fits!"

Molly drew her derringer and fired. The bullet entered the back of the man's head and drove him forward into the vault door. The sick crunch as bone hit metal was smoothed by a gust of wind and the pounding surf below. He recoiled, sat down, and then bonelessly slid from the back of the wagon.

Molly stepped over the body and climbed into the wagon bed. She took a deep breath and tried to quiet her racing heart.

"I've done it. I'm rich!"

She put her fingers on the key, trying to turn it, but it wouldn't budge. It would go in the lock but not turn. The next thing she knew a bullet smashed into the back of her head just as the key dropped from the lock. She died as quickly and surely as the clerk had.

26

"We're too late. I know we're too late," Zoe said over and over, until Slocum wanted to gag her with his bedraggled bandanna. "We took too long getting to the railhead, and now they've beat us."

"Aren't you interested in writing their story?" Slocum asked. He stepped out into the brisk San Francisco morning and shivered from the cold wind blowing off the Bay. The sky was clear, which he counted as a blessing. Too many times he had been in this town and never seen anything but gray fog clinging tenaciously to the streets. Having a cloudless blue sky above made him believe all would be well.

"Of course I am," she said hotly. "But it's the principle of the matter that grates on my sensibilities. You should win the prize, not someone else. Look at all we've been through!"

Slocum noted how she changed back and forth between mentioning him as the one who should win and then including herself.

"We're not far from the freight office. Not more than a fifteen-minute walk," he said. "If we go there straightaway, we can find if we're first or if someone else has won." He

241

touched the keys in his pocket, not damning himself this time for such a display. He traced over the jagged edges that would turn tumblers and open the strongbox. Even if others had reached the office first, that didn't mean they had opened the box.

He frowned as he remembered the last bit of doggerel in the instructions. "The box rolls like Turner Freight." That didn't make any sense, but they would find out when they reached the freight office.

Zoe chattered like a magpie the entire distance, and paid scant attention to what Slocum saw right away from a block off. The Turner Haulage Company office was deserted. When he reached the door, he prodded it open with the toe of his boot, his hand on the butt of his six-gun. The office was dimly lit and papers had been strewn all about. The only sound that he heard from within was the soft scurrying of a rat moving from one room to the next.

"We're too late," he said.

"I don't understand," Zoe said, going in and looking around. "What happened?"

"If you don't leave, I'll call the police," came a tremulous voice from behind him. Slocum glanced over his shoulder and saw a frightened little man wearing a green eyeshade like a bank teller, with cuff protectors spotted with ink.

"You work here?" Slocum asked. "The lady'd like to know what happened to everyone."

"Gone, all gone. The owner of the business told them he had gone bankrupt, and they wouldn't be paid. They turned ugly and . . . and did this."

"Really?" Slocum saw the man knew more than he was letting on. Some of the pilfering had probably been done by his ink-stained fingers.

Seeing Slocum's intense gaze, the man averted his eyes and muttered, "They owed me for my work. They weren't going to pay. The colonel himself said as much to me, and they owed me for a month's accounting."

"Colonel Turner was here in person?" Zoe pulled her notebook out and wet the tip of her pencil to make better marks. "When?"

"Yesterday."

"What about the race?" Slocum asked, cutting through the likely questions Zoe would ask. The man was on the brink of bolting. Slocum had seen the same look in the eyes of a deer before it leaped into the woods to take refuge from a hunter.

"The race, the race. Is that all any of you people are interested in?"

"What others have asked?" Zoe elbowed Slocum out of the way, and he let her. Her questions might soothe the accountant since it had become increasingly obvious that Slocum might just shoot him in the leg to get what he wanted to know.

"Not two hours ago. Another man and a woman." The man swallowed hard.

"She was beautiful, wasn't she?" Slocum asked.

"Never seen a woman purtier, and I been over at the Bella Union a great deal and seen women from France."

"Yes, of course," Zoe said, her lips pursed in distaste. "What did Miss Ibbotson say?"

"That her name? The owlhoot with her tried to strangle me."

Both Slocum and Zoe knew this had to be Sid Calhoun. Slocum wondered how long the unholy alliance between Molly and Calhoun would last. Not long, if they located the gold.

Zoe continued to inquire about the business, and asked personal questions to get the man to feel less anxious. The story slowly unfolded about as Slocum had expected. The Turner Haulage Company was out of business and the unpaid, fired employees had made off with the wagon holding the $50,000.

"The box rolls like Turner Freight," Zoe said, her eyes

widening. "The strongbox is in a freight wagon! It could be anywhere!"

"Not likely the employees would drive it too far before trying to bust it open," Slocum said.

He left Zoe with the accountant and saw the signs to the livery stable. The horses and loading dock couldn't be far from the office, and they weren't. He stuck his head into the stable and saw a half dozen horses standing contentedly. He went to the tack room and found gear there, and saddled a pair of horses that looked to be broke for riding. Only then did Slocum hunt for the stable hand. The man had curled up behind the livery in a pile of hay. From the empty whiskey bottles around him, he had gone on quite a bender.

Slocum led the horses back around to the front of the office, and lashed them to a nearby hitching ring. Inside, Zoe still interrogated the accountant, but Slocum broke the spell she had the man under. He hastily left without another word.

"Something I said?" Slocum looked after him.

"You remind him too much of Sid Calhoun," she said solemnly. Slocum looked at her, and then she broke out laughing. "Just my little joke. The interview was over, and he was trying to determine what our status was." Slocum said nothing. Zoe went on. "Between you and me, since we're obviously not related or married."

"He could tell that?"

"No wedding ring," Zoe said, holding her left hand up for him to see.

"You'll be able to get all the rings you want without getting married when we get the prize."

"I don't think we have much chance of that, John. Colonel Turner's disgruntled employees took the wagon with what sounds like a formidable vault in it as their due. Whatever chance we had disappeared when the colonel went out of business."

"Companies are going bankrupt all over the country. The colonel started his freight business at the wrong time."

"He should have lived up to the letter of his rules, though," she said. "I'm going to send a very nasty article to Mr. Zelnicoff about this. If the colonel hadn't gone out of business first, this would certainly damage him financially when the world reads what a crook he is!"

"I saw a telegraph office not far from here. You want to send your article while I nose about?"

She saw the horses in the street.

"Very well, John. You *will* wait for me?" His nod satisfied her. Slocum watched as she bustled off, mumbling to herself as she composed her scathing attack on devious business practices.

Slocum walked around, speaking to people for close to twenty minutes before Zoe came out of the telegraph office. Her shoulders were slumped, and she might as well have worn lead shoes for all the spring in her step. Slocum had never seen her byline in any of the papers as they'd made their way across country. He thought he knew what she was going to tell him. But he was wrong.

"The newspaper is bankrupt, John. They aren't going to pay me. They never printed a single one of my stories!"

He had anticipated the lack of ink on the page, but not the newspaper going under in the economic tidal wave swamping the country. It was high time for him to get back into the mountains where he could live off the land for a year or however long it took for the financial woes to abate.

"I know the direction Molly went with the wagon," he said. "She and the chief clerk at Turner's office left an hour or so before we got here. Nobody else has come by to claim the prize."

"She drove off with the clerk? In the money wagon?" Slocum nodded, and found himself being hugged and kissed by an excited woman. "This is wonderful! We can track them down and get the gold for ourselves. One of our keys has to fit. It has to. There's no way any of those cheats could possibly win!"

"Even if none of Molly's keys fit, do you think that would stop her from getting the gold? She's thrown in with the clerk." He sucked on his teeth a moment, then asked, "Where'd Calhoun get off to?"

"She dropped him like a hot potato."

"Calhoun had Swain with him. I don't see either of those owlhoots ever giving up if they caught the scent of gold."

"Let's ride. You said you knew where they went. Where?"

"Figured out the direction, but not much else. We can ask along the way. Molly's beauty is going to attract attention, even if a wagon with a bank vault in the bed doesn't."

"Do you think she's pretty, John?"

"I do," he said. Before Zoe could pout, he added, "And she's as treacherous as she is beautiful. I wouldn't be in the clerk's boots for anything right now."

This smoothed Zoe's ruffled feathers, and she smiled almost shyly, then looked down to the back of her horse's neck. Her smile broadened until Slocum couldn't see it anymore as she galloped ahead.

The road was deeply rutted from traffic, but Slocum thought he'd found one set of wheel marks leading from San Francisco that were considerably deeper. While the tracks might have been left by any wagon conducting commerce farther south, Slocum had nothing better to go on. When the tracks cut sharply to the west and the ocean, he hesitated. This was the all-or-nothing gamble.

"I can hear the surf," Zoe said. For some reason, this convinced Slocum he was on the right track.

"Let's head that direction."

"We're getting close, aren't we? I feel it in my bones."

"We're riding faster than a weighed-down wagon can roll," Slocum agreed, but he had no similar sense of being closer to Calhoun and Molly. Another twenty minutes brought them to a butte overlooking the ocean. Slocum saw the body before Zoe did.

He dismounted and handed the reins to her.

"Stay here." He slid his six-shooter from its holster.

"John," she said in a choked voice. "There's a body."

"I know." Slocum moved closer and rolled the man over using the toe of his boot. The front of his face was a bloody mess. The hole in the back of his head was small. but the exit wound was in the middle of his forehead and almost as big as a fist.

"Another one? Oh, my."

Slocum looked up sharply, and saw that Zoe just noticed the clerk's body. He swung around as a gust of wind caused a billow of skirt not ten yards away. Approaching carefully, he saw that Molly Ibbotson had come to the end of her trail. For a few seconds, he worked through the way two bodies had ended up on a butte overlooking the gray waters of the Pacific.

"She shot the clerk, then somebody shot her. Since she was shot in the back of her head, I've got to peg Sid Calhoun for the murder."

"I see tracks going southward," Zoe said from her perch mounted on her horse. "The ground is softer here."

"Sea spray," Slocum said. He scouted the area and found gold keys strewn about. A grim smile came to his lips. "Calhoun didn't get into the strongbox. He stole the wagon and is looking for a way to open it without a key."

"There's a town not too far off, John. I see smoke rising from dozens of chimneys." Zoe pointed. Slocum walked to the edge of the butte and down to the sandy beach. Then he looked to where she had pointed.

He mounted and they rode for the small coastal town using the deep ruts left by Turner's prize wagon as a guide. Slocum hoped Calhoun would get mired down, but his luck didn't run that way.

"What are we going to do?"

"Molly tried all her keys and probably Calhoun's, too. He double-crossed her and left her up there for the seagulls. The only way he'd try to open a strongbox or a bank vault is dynamite."

"He'd blow it up? Wouldn't that destroy everything inside?"

"Depends on the size of the vault. From the depth of the wheel ruts, that's one damned heavy vault. Calhoun will do what he's most comfortable doing."

"Blowing it up," Zoe said with distaste. "Has he robbed banks like that?"

Slocum didn't reply. All he knew of Calhoun was what he had seen since they boarded the train in St. Louis. The outlaw was a coward and thought nothing of shooting a woman in the back. The rest of his gang had likely met a similar fate so Calhoun could accumulate more gold keys. Since Molly had traveled with Calhoun, she had probably seduced him and stolen his keys, but she would have ended up dead even if she hadn't crossed him. Calhoun wasn't the sort to share such wealth.

Slocum smiled ruefully. Molly Ibbotson hadn't been either.

"Would a town this small have a store selling dynamite?"

"They have to build roads," Slocum said. "Stumps need to be removed. There's a call for it." His attention fixed on a store selling mining equipment. There wasn't much call for such tools, not since the Gold Rush of '49, but somehow the store had stayed in business. Slocum went to it like a homing pigeon to its roost.

It took less than five minutes to get the information he wanted.

"Well, John? He bought explosives, didn't he?"

"He did. Why he needed a full crate is a poser, but that vault must be bigger than I thought. The owner didn't see the wagon because Calhoun walked in. I doubt anyone in town saw the wagon either. It's not something Calhoun wants to advertise."

"Where is he?"

"Down by the ocean," he decided. "If he finds a cove with high walls, the sound of the explosion will be muffled. The surf will hide the sound that isn't swallowed up by the rock, and he can rifle through the contents without worrying somebody will come to investigate the blast."

"He won't be able to drive such a heavily laden wagon on the beach," Zoe said dubiously.

"That's why we look for a cove with a road leading down into it."

Just when Slocum began to despair, he saw a turnoff from the road leading toward the ocean. The roar of the surf, even a half mile away, was almost deafening. Calhoun could blow the safe here and never be heard, but Slocum knew the outlaw wouldn't do that. He'd play it close to the vest.

"I wish I had a gun," Zoe said. "I'm getting goose bumps thinking of what'll happen when we find him."

"If you've never fired a six-gun before, you're better off without one."

"I wouldn't shoot you by accident," Zoe said indignantly.

"I'd be more worried about you shooting yourself."

Before she could protest, Slocum held up his hand to quiet her. He pointed to a steep section of the road. From the look of the tracks, the wagon had run out of control. Slocum leaned out and looked down off the brink of the road and saw a dead horse.

"The wagon brake didn't work, or Calhoun didn't apply it hard enough, and he ran over one of his own horses."

"He won't be using that team to pull the wagon back up the road," Zoe said.

"He'll use the remaining horse to ride out and leave everything else behind."

"A corn husk. He'll take the corn and leave the husk."

Slocum motioned for her to remain on the road where she'd be out of range when the shooting started—and he knew it would. Calhoun wasn't going to peaceably turn over the wagon and its contents. After what the outlaw had done, Slocum was going to kill him even if he tried to dicker. Molly Ibbotson might have been as crooked as a dog's hind leg, but she was a woman and Calhoun had shot her in the back of her head. She had deserved better.

Slocum snorted. She deserved a knotted rope for the way she had killed the freight clerk, but she shouldn't have been gunned down the way Calhoun did it.

Slocum rode to the base of the cliff, and looked back to be sure Zoe wasn't coming to see the fight. She remained hidden around a curve in the precipitous road. Dismounting, Slocum drew his six-shooter and went the final dozen yards to see an inlet lined with trees, a finger of ocean reaching inland. The wagon was parked nearby, canted to one side because of a broken wheel. Even if Calhoun hadn't killed a horse on the way down, this wagon had reached the end of the line without considerable repairs.

Slocum usually depended on his sense of hearing for hints that trouble brewed, but the very reason Calhoun had driven down here robbed Slocum of that. The roar of the ocean reverberated along the steep cliff walls, and the trees sucked up any small sounds that might alert him to danger. Slocum pressed his back against one cold, wet stone wall, and advanced until he reached a spot where he had a better view of the wagon.

Calhoun was nowhere to be seen, but the dynamite crate had been broken open and a few sticks removed. Try as he might, Slocum couldn't find a bag holding fuses or blasting caps. That more than anything else made him wary. He craned his neck around and looked up toward the front of the cliff.

He stepped out, aimed, and fired three quick shots. Sid Calhoun had crouched on a shelf ten feet above him with a bundle of dynamite and a cigar already lit. The outlaw had put the coal to the fuse, which now sizzled and popped as it made its way down to the blasting cap.

Slocum dug in his toes and ran as hard as he could. He barely escaped the worst of the blast as the rock face twenty feet above Calhoun shattered from the explosion and sent out shards of stone sharper than any knife blade. Slocum staggered, took another step, and then fell headlong onto the ground as debris showered down on him. Dazed, he shook off the confusion that addled his brain, and felt hands fumbling at his arms.

He tried to swing his six-gun around and shoot, but he had dropped it. His face was a bloody mess from a dozen scratches, and dirt blinded him.

He fought the best he could. Fists swinging awkwardly, he tried to connect. Then small hands pushed against his chest hard, and he sat down hard. Through the roar in his ears, he heard Zoe's distant voice ordering him to calm down.

"Zoe?"

"I'm here, you big idiot. He could have killed you!"

"I shot him." As his vision cleared and he saw the woman kneeling in front of him, Slocum pieced it all together. Gunning down Calhoun hadn't been a great idea since the man had lighted dynamite on a ledge above him, but there hadn't been any other choice.

"You might have only caused him to drop the dynamite and then he blew himself up," she said.

"I killed him." Slocum groped about and found his six-gun. It felt right in his hand, as right as the bullet he had sent into Calhoun's belly. Being a sniper during the war had allowed him to get a feel for where his lead went. Sometimes, he knew he had missed clean. Other times, it was only a nick he'd inflicted. This time he had the unshakable faith in his marksmanship. He had hit Calhoun smack dab in the belly and probably killed him outright.

He had killed Calhoun, not a dropped stick of dynamite. All the gold in the wagon wouldn't equal the satisfaction he got from killing Sid Calhoun.

"Come on, get to your feet," Zoe urged. "We've got to open the wagon. Where are the keys?"

Slocum stumbled along, and regained his balance by the time he joined her at the rear of the wagon. He let out a long, low whistle. All the way to San Francisco he had thought Colonel Turner had put the gold in a strongbox. This was a rolling bank vault.

"Your keys, John, try your keys."

He reached for the vest pocket where he had the keys, and felt a sinking sensation when he discovered the vest had ripped away, spilling the keys. They had to be around somewhere, but finding them would take a while.

"They're gone," he said. "I lost them. All except this one." He pulled out his watch and tapped the key he had put onto the watch chain. "I won this in a poker game back in St. Louis." The key gleamed in the sunlight filtering through the trees.

"One key out of fifty?" Zoe sighed. "I'll start looking for the others you lost."

Slocum stepped up and thrust the key into the lock. It fit. He heard Zoe catch her breath as he turned it in the lock. A click louder than the surf and the rustling leaves above sounded. Slocum grabbed the handle on the vault door and pulled.

"John, John, we're rich!" Zoe cried. Her excitement died when she got a better look into the vault.

It was empty.

27

"I'm still so mad I could chew nails and spit tacks," Zoe said. She had ridden the entire way back to San Francisco muttering curses and sitting so stiffly that Slocum thought she might topple from the saddle. Her anger kept her going.

He had been surprised to find the rolling vault empty, but unlike Zoe, he wasn't expecting to get rich. The ride back let her curse, and let him think on the matter, until he was sure he knew how to find where the gold had gone.

"It was never in the vault," Zoe said. "He was a crook trying to dupe everyone. Why, how dare Colonel Turner try to *lie* to a news reporter!"

Slocum had fought to keep from laughing that she'd said such a thing. As far as he could tell, not much of what was told to a reporter was the truth, and even less of what they printed counted as being in the same county as the truth.

"We need to do some searching through the stacks of newspapers," he told her.

"The morgue. That's what they call it. And if I find Colonel Turner, he'll end up in a real morgue. How dare he!"

253

"Think this paper's been around long enough to build a morgue?" Slocum drew rein in front of the *San Francisco Times*, a hole-in-the-wall publication. Peering through the tiny window on the street allowed him to see three men struggling with a press in the rear of a single long, narrow room.

"Why not? What is it you want to find out?"

As they entered, Slocum said in a low voice, "You look for any coverage of the race and get the names of any reporters assigned to cover it. I'll check for other stories."

"Very well." Zoe bustled in, spoke at length with one of the men who had been struggling with the printing press, and finally shook hands with him. She didn't seem to mind that his hands were drenched with printer's ink. After all, this was the profession she had chosen to follow. Slocum hung back until she led him to a smaller room stacked floor to ceiling with newspapers.

"Y'all just go on and do your readin'," said the man. "Don't worry none about keepin' the papers in order. We don't."

Slocum inwardly groaned. If they didn't keep the newspapers stored in chronological order, he might be weeks shifting through the piles to find the ones he wanted.

"Ain't nobody come back here to look for anything, so you got the room to yourselves." The printer wiped his grimy hands on his apron and cast an admiring eye at Zoe. "If you need a job, we got one for a reporter. Don't pay squat, but in this town, there're ways of makin' a few extra dollars as a reporter."

"I beg your pardon?" Zoe cast a gimlet eye at him, as if she intended to impale him like a bug with a pin.

"What I'm sayin' is that favorable mention of a store or restaurant might get you a free meal or merchandise. If you find the right politician and the jam they're in is bad enough, they might pay you to ignore a story. Ain't what you were taught 'bout reportin', I know, but this is San Francisco and we make our own rules as we go. You folks need anything, just holler." With that, he went back to his work.

"I declare," Zoe said. "That's downright unethical what he was saying."

Slocum paid her scant attention. "The piles are in order. They dump new copies on top of old until the stack threatens to topple. Then they start a new one. These two are likely the only piles we need to go through."

There was only one stool in the room. Slocum let Zoe use that while he sat on the floor and began searching through the papers for economic news. Even knowing the *Times* wasn't likely to report bad news about local companies, he found plenty to set him thinking.

"I don't understand this, John. There's nary a word about the race. It's as if Colonel J. Patterson Turner's Transcontinental Race never existed. That doesn't make any sense, not with the huge coverage in St. Louis at the start. You'd think he would want even more at the end. After all, that was the idea behind the race."

"I think the Turner Haulage Company was about bankrupt when the race started. The railroads going under, along with so many Eastern banks, did the colonel in financially."

"Then the race was a hoax. He never had fifty thousand dollars in that mobile bank vault of his. It was all a fraud."

"Go ask the gent working the press if the colonel had approached him for a reporter to cover something special. I've got a few more papers to leaf through." As Zoe went to inquire, Slocum found the proper society page, and finally located the story he'd expected to find.

"The *Times* was supposed to send a man when the colonel asked, but he never did," said Zoe, coming back in.

"The colonel arrived on a train just two days ago."

"So he stole his own gold?"

Slocum nodded slowly. "There's another story that is mighty interesting, too. The colonel is leaving for Boston on a sailing ship with the evening tide." Slocum stretched his legs out on the floor and said, "What are the odds he has fifty thousand dollars in gold with him?"

"Our money! Your key would have opened the vault door, and we were there first. He's stealing our money."

Slocum didn't bother correcting her about whose gold it was. He had won the key fair and square and had managed to hang on to it—and his life—across the country to fulfill the rules of the race. Nothing said a racer's companion had to be given any of the prize. And Zoe Murchison had begun the race as a reporter. It was her bad luck her paper had gone bankrupt with so many other businesses in what Slocum had read was being universally called the Panic of '73.

"So? What are we going to do about it, John?"

"If I'm right, I know where he'll be just before the evening tide. Until then, there's nothing to do but wait."

"Wait? Never. I'd go crazy thinking about that crook Turner. How dare he?"

"I'm going to rest up. You want to join me?" Slocum had made his invitation clear, but Zoe ranted on about Turner and how the reporters in San Francisco were all corrupt.

"I need to find out more about the situation here, John. I'll meet you later. When and where should we get together?"

"The Embarcadero, Pier Three," Slocum said. "You can ask when the tide is and be there an hour before. That should give plenty of time to settle accounts with Colonel Turner."

"Very well." Distracted, she gave him a small kiss on the cheek and left the room. In seconds, she was arguing with the printer. Slocum didn't much know or care what had her so riled about corrupt reporters in the town. He doubted they were any worse here than in St. Louis, especially since her editor had taken her stories and had never printed them. He might have sent her on what he thought was a wild-goose chase to get her out of his hair.

If Zelnicoff was any kind of newspaperman, he might have realized Turner's race was a hoax. For all Slocum knew, Zelnicoff might have been paid off to provide spectacular coverage for the Turner Haulage Company although he knew the colonel was bankrupt or close to it. The best way to do this without revealing the fraud would be to send an inexperienced reporter like Zoe to cover it.

Slocum found himself not caring about any of the details. The one thing he kept burning bright in his mind was what $50,000 in gold looked like. He had some bartering to do.

Finding Turner proved easier than Slocum thought. The colonel had a mountain of luggage stacked on the pier ready to be loaded aboard the *Vermont Queen*, leaving for Boston with the tide. Wandering around, Slocum spotted a short man dressed in an impeccable white suit arguing with a dockworker. He walked closer until he could eavesdrop on them.

"I tell you, Colonel, this is a problem."

"There's no problem, my good man," Colonel Turner said. "You can deal with it. You know how."

Slocum considered going to the colonel and shoving a gun in his belly and demanding the gold, but he stopped when he heard the rest of the argument.

"You want to know where we took her?" asked the dockworker.

"No, and I don't care, I tell you. You sell women into prostitution all the time. I don't want to know the details, but she must not continue nosing about. Her newspaper is bankrupt, but the local papers are doing well and would love a story about me that is . . . totally untrue."

"You can sail with clean hands," the roughneck said, "if not clean conscience." The dockhand ducked away, leaving Slocum with his hand on his six-gun. What had been said chilled him. The colonel had to be talking about Zoe—and he had told the dockhand to deal with her on his own. The colonel didn't know or care what would happen to her.

Slocum came to a quick decision. The ship wouldn't sail for a while, and Zoe had dug herself a grave. Slocum pushed past the colonel, who grunted and said something about rudeness. Turner was quickly left behind as Slocum ran to catch up with the dockhand. In the crush of the Embarcadero, it was difficult to single out one man he had seen only in profile. Slocum grew desperate when he couldn't locate the man.

Then he saw him. The dockhand spoke with two ruffians. Money changed hands and the dockhand returned to his work. Slocum thought about the chain of events and followed the two. The dockhand had only passed along the colonel's orders, and probably knew nothing about where Zoe was being held.

Slocum stayed close to them, hoping they kept together. If they parted, he had to grab one and make him talk fast. From the scars and missing body parts, neither would give in to threats, and there wasn't time to convince them that he meant business. They worked their way through the edge of Chinatown and north to the Barbary Coast section of town. If the docks had been a rough area, this was a battlefield. Crime ran rampant. Even in broad daylight, Slocum saw several robberies being committed on drunks.

The streets began to wind about and turn narrow, making Slocum increasingly wary. He was an intruder here and stuck out like a cross-eyed carpenter's thumb. He slowed and waited when the two men he followed opened a door and cast furtive looks around. Neither saw him as they went inside and closed the door behind them.

Slocum drew his six-shooter and went to the door. He opened it a fraction of an inch to peer inside. Pungent smoke billowed out. His nostrils flared as he recognized opium mixed in with tobacco smoke. Hesitation now meant death— or worse—for Zoe Murchison. As sinuous as a snake, he slipped around the partially opened door and tried to make out what he faced inside. A half dozen men were stretched out on bunks in various degrees of intoxication. All had opium pipes nearby, showing they had been successful chasing the dragon.

"Go on, smoke it. You'll feel better," came the strident command.

Slocum didn't hear the response, but recognized Zoe's voice. Four quick, long strides took him across the room to another doorway. A few feet down a hallway, he saw three men. Two he had followed here, and the third was trying to force an opium pipe between Zoe's lips. She had been tied to a chair and had fought, from the look of her disheveled clothing. Tossing her head from side to side did not keep the man from thrusting the pipe between her lips. He took a handful of hair and pulled her head back.

As her head rocked back, she saw Slocum. Her eyes went wide. Something about the change in the way she fought alerted the trio.

Slocum lifted his six-shooter and fired four times. Three bullets struck one man in the chest. He gasped and dropped to his knees. The fourth shot was a lucky one in the dimness and hit the second man in the head, killing him instantly. The one holding Zoe whipped out a wicked knife and held it to her throat.

"You drop that gun now or she'll be smilin' out of a second mouth." He pressed the sharp edge against her throat and drew a thin red line of blood.

"You got me wrong," Slocum said. "I want to buy her from you. The colonel took a fancy to her and changed his mind."

"I can get a hunnerd dollars sellin' her to a madam. She's a looker. She'll do twenty men a day. More till she wears out."

"That's why the colonel wants her for his own."

The man with the knife hesitated and Slocum acted. He

fired his last two rounds. The first broke the man's wrist. The second went into his chest, and sent him stumbling back to crash into the wall. He slid down, clutching his wrist and trying to stanch the blood flowing from the hole in his chest.

"John!"

Slocum picked up the fallen knife and slit the heavy hemp ropes binding her. She collapsed forward. He awkwardly caught her, then sat her up in the chair.

"The cut's not too bad on your throat, but you need to keep pressure on it." He ripped off a part of her dress that looked cleaner than the rest and put it against the wound. Her hand shook as she tried to slow the bleeding.

"Am I going to die?"

"Not today, but you ought to for being so stupid," he said.

"I shouldn't have confronted him. He wasn't hiding. He was waiting on the dock to board the ship. All I wanted was a story."

"Let's get out of here," Slocum said. He helped her to her feet, then took the time to reload.

The one he had shot in the head was definitely dead. The other two were still alive.

"You might not think so, but this is your lucky day. I'm letting you live."

"I'll have ever' man jack in the quarter after you in a thrice," shouted the man who had wielded the knife. "You won't see sundown."

"And it won't matter to you at all." This time Slocum had plenty of time to aim and finish the job.

"The other one, John. Kill him, too."

"You want to do it?" He handed Zoe his six-shooter. It told him a lot about her when she took it and clumsily pointed it at the third man. Her finger was turning white on the trigger when Slocum grabbed the pistol away from her. "Never mind him. He won't set the hounds on us, will you?"

The man shook his head. The fear in his eyes told Slocum there wasn't any need to kill this one also.

"Where's the way out?" Slocum nodded his thanks to the man when he pointed to a battered door at the far end of the hallway. Backing away just to be safe, Slocum watched as the man slumped onto his side and lay still. Shooting him would have been a waste of lead, but Slocum was glad to know Zoe wasn't some hothouse flower and could defend herself when she wasn't doing something stupid.

The air was far from clean and fresh out in the street, but Slocum had never smelled anything sweeter.

"Come on," he said, half dragging Zoe. Her dress was soaked in blood, but she had applied enough pressure to stop the shallow wound from bleeding further. They attracted some attention, but many pointedly looked away when they saw the six-gun clutched in Slocum's hand. More illegal activities went on in this part of San Francisco than legal ones, and no one became too curious unless they wanted to die.

A half hour later, they were in a better part of town. Slocum found a doctor's office and insisted that Zoe be treated.

"It's not serious, John. I can still talk. I can certainly still write!"

"Why did you accuse Turner of being a crook when you knew he could do something like this to you? He sold you to a pimp."

"He's an evil man. And I'm a reporter." She slumped. "I'm trying to be a reporter."

"That doesn't give you a shield against men like him."

"I figured it all out. His freight company went under when the railroad he was a director for went bankrupt. He had already sent the prize money for the race to San Francisco, and needed it to start over. He has some kind of messenger service in Boston he can use the money to finance."

"So the race started as a legitimate advertising scheme?"

"It seems so," Zoe said.

"The doctor's going to treat you now," Slocum said, seeing the man motioning from his surgery. "I'll be back in an hour or so. You get patched up, then we'll deal with Turner."

"We?"

"We," he assured her. She gave him a kiss, and Slocum tasted her blood from her lips.

Slocum left the doctor's office and looked around. He knew what he had to do, but getting it done in time might be difficult. He made sure his six-shooter was fully loaded before he set out to get a drink on Meigg's Pier.

"It feels like a noose around my neck," Zoe complained. She touched the bandage the doctor had applied.

"You have no idea what a noose feels like," Slocum said.

"And you do?"

He didn't respond to that. He knew. Escaping being hanged rivaled not having your throat cut, but he wasn't going to argue the point with her.

"How can we stop Turner?" she asked when Slocum didn't answer her question. "I want him arrested. I want him to spend years in jail. I've heard the Yuma Territorial Prison is a terrible place. I want him sent there."

"Convicting him of anything isn't too likely," Slocum said. "He's responsible for too many people getting killed. If he hadn't started the race, using those rules that had to bring out the killer in everyone, a whole passel of folks would be a lot happier."

"You're right. I have the story ready to sell. I think the *Alta California* might buy it, but there's not much interest in San Francisco about the colonel."

"Maybe you'd do better with it in St. Louis."

"Possibly, though I have been thinking about Clarkesville."

"Why?" Even as he asked, Slocum knew the answer. Zoe had gotten on well with the owner of the newspaper there.

More than that, she and his son had been drawn to each other in the brief time she'd been there. Slocum sighed. Riding on with Zoe, at least for a while, would have been good, but he understood her need to be a reporter. The small town was a decent start and, depending on how it went, perhaps her destiny. Being married to the newspaper owner's son wasn't so bad for a woman like her.

She deserved more than almost getting her throat slit.

"There, John, there he is! He's getting away."

"You sure of that?" Slocum walked to the edge of the dock and saw three men helping Colonel Turner into a skiff. The tide would be right for sailing within the hour, and a half dozen ships in the harbor prepared for their long ocean journeys. All around, dockhands worked to get last minute cargo aboard and, for most ships, only the passengers needed to be loaded before setting sail.

"Of course I'm sure. That's him. That's the man I talked to earlier, the one who . . . who tried to sell me into a brothel."

Slocum didn't bother telling Zoe she would have been lucky to end up in a whorehouse. More likely, the men buying her would have used her on the street corner.

"I'll get a policeman," she said. "He can stop the colonel."

Slocum grabbed her arm and spun her around so he could look into her eyes, maybe for the last time.

"Do you trust me?"

"Why, yes, John, of course! You're about the only one I can believe in."

"Trust me now. The colonel is going to pay for what he's done."

She looked out into the Bay as two sailors rowed and the third held Colonel Turner upright. She frowned as she watched, then looked in a different direction, and finally back to the small boat bearing Turner to a China clipper.

"That's not the *Vermont Queen*. That boat's sailing for

the Orient. Why is he getting on it when his business is in Boston?"

"I had him shanghaied," Slocum said. "The men who hang out at Meigg's Pier, a particularly nasty place, drunk or sober, are known for their connections with shanghaiers." He fumbled in his pocket. "I got a hundred dollars for him. Here, take it. You can buy your train ticket to Clarkesville with it."

"You *sold* him?"

"He'll be a sailor on the *Orient Dynasty* for the next two years. The captain, I've heard, isn't a gracious man."

"They're kidnapping him? But he's not putting up a fight."

"Drugged. One of them probably offered Turner a shot of whiskey as a final memory of San Francisco. It'll be that." Slocum smiled as he watched the distant ship rocking at its anchor and the three sailors hoisting Colonel J. Patterson Turner aboard. He was in for a long and arduous trip that might pay back the debt he ran up organizing the bogus race.

They stood for another twenty minutes until the *Orient Dynasty* unfurled its sails and caught the breeze needed to carry it through the Golden Gate.

"Good riddance," Zoe said. "I hope he falls overboard and drowns."

"I hope he doesn't. There's worse punishment than dying."

They stood pressed close to one another, and finally Zoe said, "It's been quite an adventure, John. I'll miss you so much."

He knew better than to ask her to come with him.

"You'll make a fine reporter in Clarkesville or St. Louis or wherever you go." He kissed her. With some reluctance, he let her slip from the circle of his arms and hurry away. He stood staring after her for a while, until the cold wind off the ocean forced him to go.

Slocum mounted his horse, rode slowly to the dock where the pack mule was, and smiled. The last of the cargo bound for Boston on the *Vermont Queen* had been loaded on the ship—all save two crates.

"Get those onto the pack mule," Slocum called to the dockhands. "Here's the rest of your money." He paid the dockhands the other half of the money he had gotten by selling Turner to the shanghaiers. It only seemed fair to give Zoe half for her trouble and use the other half, which he had not mentioned to her, to drive the final nail into Colonel Turner's coffin.

"Damn, mister, these are heavy," complained a dockhand as he held one of the crates in place while the other worker lashed the crate to the mule's back. "What do you have in them? Gold?"

"Yeah, gold," Slocum said, laughing. "You didn't ruffle any feathers not loading those crates onto the ship, did you?" Slocum cared nothing for the trouble the dockhands might be in for failing to load the colonel's gold into the ship, but he wanted to be sure he could ride away without having to look over his shoulder for police sent to retrieve it.

"We loaded boxes of rocks in place of these. Shoulda loaded lead to equal the weight."

"Spend your money well, gents," Slocum said. "I hear the Cobweb Saloon is a good place to drink."

They laughed, and the two dockhands began arguing over what saloon should get their newfound wealth. Slocum tugged on the mule's rope, and got the animal moving with its load of $50,000 in gold.

He made his way south out of town, intending to cut back east when he reached the tip of San Francisco Bay. In spite of what he had been told, Slocum watched his back trail with a wary eye. Men had died—and women, too—for the gold he now carried. If any of the other racers successfully reached the Turner Haulage Company office, they'd find nothing but memories there. They had no reason to think he had the money—or that anyone did.

By midday, he was ready to take a rest. That was when he heard a galloping horse coming hard down the road behind him. He touched the butt of his Colt Navy, then relaxed.

"What brings you out on a day like this, Zoe?" he called.

"You, John. I decided to ride with you for a spell."

"Not going to be a reporter?"

"I sold the story on Colonel Turner to the *Alta* for two dollars," she said. "I got to thinking about Clarkesville, and decided working for such small pay wasn't for me. Besides, there's the last part of the story left to be written. I wanted to do the follow-up on what happened to the gold."

"What happened to it?"

"It hasn't been spent yet."

"You're right, it hasn't." Slocum grinned. "How do you think we should start doing just that?"

They found a way.

DON'T MISS A YEAR OF

Slocum Giant
by
Jake Logan

Slocum Giant 2004:
Slocum in the Secret Service

Slocum Giant 2005:
Slocum and the Larcenous Lady

Slocum Giant 2006:
Slocum and the Hanging Horse

Slocum Giant 2007:
Slocum and the Celestial Bones

Slocum Giant 2008:
Slocum and the Town Killers

Slocum Giant 2009:
Slocum's Great Race

penguin.com/actionwesterns

M457AS0409

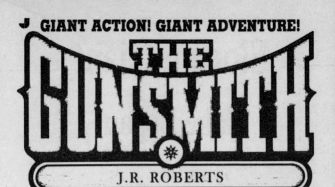